GOOD GIRLS DIE LAST

NATALI SIMMONDS

HEADLINE

First published in Great Britain in 2023 by
HEADLINE PUBLISHING GROUP

First published in paperback in 2023 by
HEADLINE PUBLISHING GROUP

1

Cataloguing in Publication Data is available from the British Library

ISBN 978 1 0354 0014 0

Typeset in Sabon by CC Book Production

Printed and bound in Great Britain by Clays Ltd, Elcograf S.p.A.

Headline's policy is to use papers that are natural, renewable and
recyclable products and made from wood grown in well-managed forests
and other controlled sources. The logging and manufacturing processes
are expected to conform to the environmental regulations
of the country of origin.

HEADLINE PUBLISHING GROUP
An Hachette UK Company
Carmelite House
50 Victoria Embankment
London EC4Y 0DZ

www.headline.co.uk
www.hachette.co.uk

To all the women who have ever been scared . . .
but lived their lives anyway

BBC Breaking News • @BBCBreaking
London reaches boiling point as highs of 41°C are
expected today. 'This heatwave is only going to get
worse,' UK **@metofficenews** confirms.

I've woken up in Matt's bed.

Stifling a yawn, I glance over at him. He has his bare
back to me; messy hair, long limbs and pale white legs.
He couldn't be any further away, curled up on the edge of
the mattress like a mountain climber clinging to a rocky
precipice. His skin is so translucent I'm able to count each
knobbly vertebra jutting out of his spine.

The bed creaks as I roll on to my back. I'm sticky, a thin
film of sweat coating every inch of me. I go to wipe myself
on Matt's sheet, but it's on the floor, where we kicked it off
last night. He's pretending to sleep so I play along, careful
not to make a sound as I gather my clothes up from the
floor and tiptoe out of his bedroom and back to my own.

I'm being generous calling it a bedroom. My room isn't
even a room. It's a windowless cupboard with a bed. From
the threshold I can touch every item in here. A single bed,

a clothes rack that fits seven hangers, and a bedside table that's actually an unpacked crate with an old scarf draped over it. A teetering column of boxes containing winter clothes and books are stacked behind the door. Yet as soon as I saw Matt's ad on the flat-share website three months ago, I snapped it up, even though the rent is more than I can comfortably afford.

The tiny apartment is on the top floor of a large white Georgian building on Suffolk Street. Before I found this place, I didn't even know real people lived in the centre of London. I thought it was all embassies and office blocks. Matt told me, more than once, that his father bought the place for him when he went to university nine years ago. He talks about how rich his dad is a lot. I've no idea why he bothers to rent out my room. Maybe Daddy's hand-outs aren't enough to live on.

'It's just a foothold on the property ladder,' Matt says about this ornate apartment, with its high ceilings and filigreed cornices moulded in plaster. And I always nod and mumble a 'That's nice.' Because it must be.

He normally gets up at 7 a.m. and there's only one bathroom, so I don't have long to get ready. Turning the shower to the coldest setting, I don't even shiver as I step into it, rubbing my eyes and letting the cool water run over my face. My mascara-coated lashes are rough and spiky beneath my fingers. I should probably be using some fancy eye-makeup remover – taking off my mascara this way is only making my face dirtier – but I keep rubbing anyway.

I turn thirty in two days. Sunday. I was meant to have my

life in order by now, but I guess I can move my deadline to thirty-five. I'm on the right track, I'm sure I am. Moving to central London and renting a room walking distance from the office was because of the job I started three months ago. The job that's going to change my life.

All I need to do is get through today's meeting, then everything will be fine.

I massage the shampoo into my hair, digging my fingers into my scalp as hard as I can, my nails scraping my skin. It hurts, but it distracts me from what I did with Matt last night. I don't want to think about anything any more. Not about work, or who's waiting for me there, or that this time tomorrow I'll be back home in Spain, getting ready to walk my baby sister down the aisle. I rub the shampoo suds all over my face. It's making my eyes sting, but I'm thankful for a pain I can control. As I rinse the water off my shoulders my finger catches in the necklace around my neck. A single diamond on a fine gold chain. I never take it off, just like my mother never did before she gave it to me. Tomorrow will be the first time I've seen her since my father died.

There's no bathmat. I leave tiny puddles of water on the wooden floor as I pad to my room, a soapy trail no one will follow. The electric fan does nothing to cool my boxroom, so I stand naked before it, eyes shut and long hair dripping water down my back. There's a soft thud of footsteps in the hallway. Matt. I keep my eyes closed and my arms spread wide.

My meeting with HR to discuss my future at Swan &

Swallow is at ten today. Three more hours and I'll finally be able to say I'm a full-time graphic designer at one of the top PR and marketing agencies in the country. I'll finally be who my sister and mother believe I've been for the last three years. I'll finally be able to stop lying – more or less.

Staring at what passes for a wardrobe, I pick out my new pencil skirt, a bright green-and-pink sleeveless blouse and wedge shoes. My forehead is already beading with sweat. Adding face cream feels like a crime, but makeup is a mask, and today I need that extra layer.

My phone buzzes. I have three likes on Twitter and one new follower, thanks to this morning's post. I hit two hundred followers last week. A lot of people must like my vague one-line tweets. I type another one and accompany it with a selfie of me in my smart outfit, but with my face cut off, as usual. I try a few different poses, choosing the one that makes my tits look best.

> **Words will never hurt me** • @Em_Dash_93
> It's called making love, so why is it so easy to fuck the ones we hate?
>> **Alan Botterwell** • @AlanBot69
>> Replying to @Em_Dash_93
>> I'd fuck you

The photo on my Twitter bio is not of me but of a white rose dripping with blood – I read once that there was no point writing anything unless you were making a statement. That's all I use Twitter for: my wry, overly dramatic one-line observations. The bio simply says, 'I've come a long way to get nowhere.' Deep.

I've posted pictures of my body a few times, a body without a face, but only when I'm drunk. Those weak moments when I've felt too old, too fat, too invisible. Like I didn't matter. The comments are predictably thirsty, and sometimes they sting, but it's what I asked for. To be looked at, to be judged, to be told my worth.

I have fifteen minutes to eat before I have to leave. There are only three rooms in this flat (four, if you count my cupboard). Matt is at the breakfast bar in our open-plan lounge, watching the London news. A hosepipe ban, a drowned girl found at Westminster Pier and two streets in Streatham with no water.

Matt ignores me as I turn into the kitchenette and stick a slice of bread into the toaster. He's eating Rice Krispies out of a Captain America bowl, slurping the puffed grains off his spoon, milk coating his lower lip. I think about last night. Matt's face buried between my legs, the way he murmured with gratitude, his chin glistening. Perhaps I'd tugged a little too hard as I'd threaded my fingers through his damp hair and pushed him deeper, the light breeze from the window making the hairs on my arm stand on end. When he kissed me, I'd tasted myself and thought of Nikki.

I butter my toast and drop the knife into the sink with a clatter. Matt finally looks up, wiping the milk from his chin with the back of his hand.

'What time's your flight?' he asks, nodding at the purple suitcase by the door.

'Nine fifteen tonight. I'm leaving straight from work.'

He nods. 'Becca will be here at six.'

'I know.'

That's the arrangement, and why (as he likes to remind me) my rent isn't as high as it could be for a central London flat-share. His long-term girlfriend, Rebecca, is a teacher in Manchester. Matt doesn't want to live up north, and she doesn't want to move to London, so she stays at his flat every Friday to Sunday and I make myself scarce. Basically, I don't live here for two nights a week. Not much of a bargain, really.

I've never met Rebecca, but I found her on Twitter. She likes *Friends* and middle-grade novels, she wears her hair in plaits on Fridays, and when she goes out she drinks Prosecco. She has a pet rabbit called Sniffles and she hates spicy food, even though she loves a good curry. She wants to get a fringe but she's too worried it will make her face look fat. It will. Her favourite colour is mint. Not turquoise. Mint. She hates being called Becca.

Most weekends I stay with my friend Kate in Stratford. When she's busy, I spend Friday and Saturday nights wandering around London like I'm somehow different to any other woman alone, in the dark, in a big city.

This time I'm going home for one week and two weekends. Matt couldn't be happier.

'About last night . . .' he says.

I take a bite out of my toast, but it doesn't taste of anything. I chew and nearly gag at the silkiness of the butter on my tongue.

6

'Emmy.'

My name isn't Emmy, but that's what Matt's called me since I told him my name and he declared it was too hard to pronounce. I didn't fill in any forms to rent this place, no proof of ID or referrals needed, just a quick visit – a look up and down – and a name that has never been mine.

'Emmy.'

I look up. He has pretty eyes. Brown, with thick lashes. Like a cow.

'It can't happen again,' he says. 'I love Becca.'

I keep chewing.

He loves Becca so much that as soon as I came home from work last night he waved a bottle of wine at me and raised one eyebrow. He loves Becca so much that when I went to open the bottle he pressed himself against my back in the kitchen and I could feel how hard he already was. He loves Becca so much he didn't even bother to remove my underwear before we were fucking against the kitchen counter, my face pressed against the marble, his fingers leaving bruises on my hips.

Yeah, he loves her so much.

'This isn't fair,' he says, adding his bowl to my knife in the sink.

'What isn't?'

'I didn't ask for this, you know.'

True. He didn't. He took and I gave.

I place my plate on top of his bowl.

'When you applied to be my flatmate you said you'd split up with your *girlfriend*.' Matt's voice is usually low

7

and slow, his plummy drawl betraying his roots. Now his voice is whiny, like the mosquitoes London has suddenly acquired with the heat. 'When I told Becca about you, she said she was cool about a gay moving in. She said a woman like you would keep the place tidy but wouldn't fancy me. The perfect combo.'

I don't know where to start with that.

He lets out a sharp sigh, squeezing the bridge of his nose and closing his eyes. 'I thought you were a *lesbian*, Emmy!'

He shouts the word 'lesbian' like it's a butch full stop, hairy and unwavering.

'I'm bisexual.'

He knows this. I mentioned it in my first week. I remember because his eyes grew wider as the edges of his lips flickered upwards – the face of a teenage boy who's just been handed his first porn magazine. He'd asked if I'd had a threesome (yes), if I was into open relationships (no), and if I would let him watch me with another woman ('It's a joke, Emmy. Can't you take a joke?').

'What we have . . .' he says.

We don't have anything. It's just sex. Not even good sex. The first time I was sad and drunk, the second time curious about whether it would actually be good the second time, but since then it's become a distraction. Because when Matt's busy fucking me, I'm there, right there, rooted in the moment. My mind can't go anywhere else. And that's a good thing.

'What we have,' he continues, 'it's . . . I don't know. Like animal attraction. You're hard to resist.'

Matt gestures at me, like I'm a painting in the Gallery of Women. A painting entitled 'It's her fault because she looks like that'. He stares down at his bare feet then slowly looks up at me, his big brown eyes covering more of my flesh than his hands ever do. I want to slap him. I want to sit on his face.

'You warm-blooded Mediterranean types,' he says. 'All that passion, eh? You can't control yourselves.'

Ah yes, the Spanish thing. He talks about that a lot. My long, thick hair, the way I use my hands when I talk, my olive skin, how red my lips are, how striking my eyes are, how round my breasts are. What do English girls look like in bed then? Maybe they just lie there, silent, pale and still. I doubt it. Maybe that's just Rebecca. I doubt that too.

'We do have fantastic sex, though,' he adds, stepping towards me. His pupils are expanding, his gaze settling on my cleavage. Is my shirt too low for an HR meeting? It's pinching under my arms. Maybe I should have bought a larger size.

I do up my top button and step back.

'I'll see you in ten days, Matt.'

He snaps out of his trance and wipes his hands on his trousers.

'Maybe you shouldn't live here any more,' he mutters.

'I'll see you in ten days.'

2

The sun is violently bright today, even with sunglasses on, and my hair is already sticking to the back of my neck before I've shut the front door. I fish about inside my handbag for my headphones then realise they're already packed away in my suitcase.

Continuing to rummage inside my sack-like handbag, I take out my phone, my thumbs swiping in tandem as I doom-scroll. Reading and walking isn't an issue in central London at this time in the morning. No dog mess and no tourists.

The Sun • @TheSun
Woman found dead in the Thames by Westminster Pier. Suspected drowning after late-night swim.

> **Daisy Espenalla • @DaisyChain99**
> 'Suspected' drowning? Don't they know for certain?

> **Linda M • @LindaCraftMagic**
> How many women go late-night swimming in the Thames? I don't even go for late-night walks in London! Sounds suspicious.

Dan Livingstone • @DanBLivingstone
Replying to @LindaCraftMagic
You not noticed how hot it is lately? Loads will be
pissed up and swimming!!!
V. Kennedy • @VSA_Kennedy
Thoughts and prayers
Linda M • @LindaCraftMagic
Wasn't a young woman found dead in St James's
Square on Monday? Looks suspicious to me.
Keep Britain Great • @KeepGBGreat
Replying to @LindaCraftMagic
So? People die in London all the time. Disgusting
place. Went there once, not one English person.

Matt's flat is only a ten-minute walk away from the Strand, where the office is. I told myself what I pay in extra rent would have been spent on the commute anyway. I've got good at lying, especially to myself.

I've lived in London for over three years, but I'll never get used to walking through Trafalgar Square to work like it's my local high street. It's quiet. Not the kind of quiet you get here on a Sunday morning before the tourists descend but the kind only severe heat can bring. A stillness that smothers everything, like the pause before the crack of thunder. There's less traffic than normal. Fewer people on the pavement. Even the handful of pigeons that remained have disappeared.

I keep scrolling through my phone, my eyes flickering at the words and pictures, nothing registering. I find myself feeling just as indifferent about a stranger's disappointing dinner than I do about a dead girl. I keep scrolling. Cats. Someone's angry about something I don't understand. A team lost. Dogs. A politician got caught. Someone is angry about something they can't change. More news about the dead girl in St James's Square.

I read something on Twitter yesterday about how reading the news is bad for you. Apparently, humans weren't made to take in so much information at once; we were made to live in a village and know up to one hundred and fifty people. Our brains haven't developed quickly enough to process this much input, this much news, this much interaction with strangers.

I guess there's only so much we can care about before we shut down and stop caring altogether.

I step out of Pret clutching a paper bag, ignoring the mutterings of a man accusing me of taking the last bottle of water. How is it the last bottle when the shop only opened two hours ago? They'll restock.

I normally make my own sandwich, but I couldn't stand to be in the kitchen with Matt any longer than I had to this morning. Maybe the newspapers are right. Maybe if I stop buying my cheese baguettes I'll be able to afford a house of my own.

My suitcase makes a whirring sound against the pavement as I cross the road again and step into Trafalgar Square. The handle is loose, so I have to hold it at an angle to stop it jamming. I don't have to go this way, but I can't pass the lions without saying hello.

'Hey,' I say, reaching up and patting the giant iron paw of one of the four statues. Always the same one. Nikki's king. Every morning I stop here for a moment, in the exact spot where she told me the story about the lion and her father. The first time she made me cry.

Sometimes, on a weekend when I'm keeping away from the flat, I bring my Kindle to the square. You're not meant to climb on the lions, but you can do what you want in the dark. The beasts never sleep, and neither does this city. On weekends, I don't either.

There's no water in the fountains. It hasn't rained for over a month. I lean against the base of Nelson's column and take a sip of water from one of the bottles I just bought, placing it against my brow then the inside of my wrist. I've spent most of my life in Spain so I thought this heatwave would be nothing, but London heat is something else. It's a grimy, thick blanket that smells of dusty metal and soaks your clothes in minutes.

Crossing the empty road, I head along the Strand, slowing down as I pass Charing Cross station. Like everywhere else, it's deserted except for one person. Pressed up against the wall, sheltering in a streak of shade, is a young lad.

'All right?' he says, shielding his eyes from the sun as I approach.

'Hey, Moby.'

That's not his real name. I don't know his real name, but he sometimes uses a tattered copy of *Moby Dick* to balance his McDonald's paper cup on so I call him Moby. His cup is empty this morning.

'Here.'

I hand him three cold bottles of water, along with a cheese sandwich and a blue cap sporting the Maldives logo. Moby gives me a lopsided smile, licking at a sore on the corner of his mouth.

'You're always so nice.'

I roll my eyes. 'It's hot today. Stay in the shade.'

He nods and puts the cap on. It looks good on him. Matt won't miss it.

'Off to work?' he asks, like he does every morning.

I nod.

He rips the packaging off the sandwich and takes a bite, pointing at my suitcase. 'Going on holiday?'

I shrug and screw up my nose. 'Family.'

His smile's so wide I can see the masticated mush in his mouth. 'My father's a cunt. Never knew my mum.' His accent is northern, maybe Leeds or Sheffield. Unlike most Londoners, I can't tell a person's postcode by the way they say the word 'bath' or how they describe a bread roll.

'Yeah,' I reply. For a fleeting moment I want to say a lot more. I want to sit beside him and tell him everything; what happened at work, and how my family hates me, and why I fuck up every relationship I've ever had.

Instead, I put a couple of quid in his cup. He gives me a grin, the creases of his smile like dirty streaks on his face. He's young, younger than I was when I came to London. I take a sip of my water and swallow down the acrid taste building in the back of my throat. I know just how hard that pavement is after a few hours.

'Stay hydrated, Moby.'

He laughs. I know he gets my joke.

I'm less than a minute away from work when I feel my phone vibrate in my pocket. It's a voicemail on WhatsApp from my mother. As usual, it's nearly five minutes long. She hates talking on the phone. Maybe she thinks if she doesn't call me I'll visit more often.

'*Hija.*'

She always calls me 'daughter' – and she says it with a pained expression, as if it contains five syllables. My younger sister, Marianna, gets to keep her name. She doesn't need to be reminded of what she's meant to be.

'I'm just checking you're definitely coming tonight. I know you keep saying you are, but you're a busy woman with an important job and London is a busy place.'

My mother has never been to England. In her mind London looks like it does in the movies and you can't go unless you have a fancy job or the King himself invites you. She once asked me whether it was true that men wore bowler hats to work.

She pauses and I double the message speed so I can listen faster. 'Marianna is worried you're cutting it so fine. Her wedding wouldn't be the first important thing you've not made it over for.' A pause. 'You missed your own father's funeral.'

That didn't take long. And I didn't miss it, I *chose* not to go.

'Walking your sister down the aisle is a big honour,' she continues.

What she doesn't say is that I was the only option after a dead father and a mother who can barely walk any more. As I listen, I play with her necklace around my neck, moving the diamond pendant back and forth along its chain.

'Now, are you sure Nick can't make it? *Ai, hija*. All these years – I can't believe we haven't met him yet.'

For one blissful second, I forget who she's talking about. Then my stomach contracts with a painful twist. She's talking about Nikki. My ex. 'Ex' is such a tiny word for such a huge thing. I imagine the scar on my heart shaped like a giant X, belonging only to her. As soon as I think of her, I can feel her, smell her. It's like she's standing right next to me. The woman I was going to marry. The woman I told my family was a man.

'But we all understand how busy Nick is. I'm sure his accountancy firm can't spare him at such short notice.' She sighs, a happy sigh, accompanied by a hum. 'I thought you and Juan would be together for ever,' she says. Juan. The boy from home who I met at eighteen and tried to fully love for so many years, until he became nothing more than a friend who never really knew me. Lovely Juan. I really messed him up. 'But this Nick? Ah, he's a good man, *hija*. You hold on to him!'

My mother worships my fake fiancé based solely on one photo I showed her of me and some random guy I got chatting to in a pub once, drunken arms around each other, gurning at the camera. Nikki – *my* Nikki, the real one – is a florist who will only have her photo taken if she's the one pressing the button.

In my fake life my accountant fiancé and I have a big house in Hampstead. In my fake life we both earn lots of money and are house-hunting for a place in the country. I would have broken up with Fake Nick a long time ago if he didn't make my mother so happy.

I wait for the next line. My mother shoots arrows to the heart like she's ticking things off a shopping list.

'It won't be long until *you're* married and have babies of your own. Don't wait *too* long, *hija*. You're thirty on Sunday.'

And there it is. All the reasons why my younger sister is better at being a woman than I am. The only thing my mother has ever prayed for is that her daughters marry a nice man and have babies – the father, the son, and the holy matrimony. Guaranteed safety, in her eyes.

I often wonder if marriage and children was her dream at my age. She says it was, says we were all she ever wanted, but I've seen the way she flicks through fashion magazines. The way she used to stroke the fabric of the dresses she made Marianna and me when we were younger. My mother was in her first year of fashion college when she met my father and got married five months later. Does she ever wonder who she could have been, if she'd followed her own path and not his?

'*Ai, mi niña*,' she moans. Three words carrying so much pain, so much suffering. It's a Catholic thing and a Spanish thing, and I'm immune to it by now. Where I'm from, no mother truly cares about her children if she doesn't show how much they're hurting her. 'I can't believe I haven't seen you since . . .'

Since my father died. Since I left for London. Since I told myself I'd have a better life than my parents ever did, then failed. I push my sweaty hair off my face and check my screen. Ten seconds left of her message. Her voice goes thick. 'Come home.'

I don't know if she says anything after that because I swipe off WhatsApp and throw my phone into my handbag. Moby is waving at me in the distance, bottle of water in hand, his cap shining brightly in the shadows. I wave back.

You don't need water to drown.

The entrance to Swan & Swallow is a black door with a number 2 on it, their logo — two intertwined S's shaped like wings — engraved on a copper plaque on the wall. Subtle, sleek, professional. No one would guess that behind this door lies the UK's most prestigious PR and marketing agency, made famous by their award-winning campaigns full of big brand collaborations with celebrities. Their offices span the entire top floor of the building, above a sandwich bar, an HSBC, a Boots and a Pizza Express.

It's been three months, but my chest still aches with hope and excitement as I step inside, the aircon snapping at my bare skin as soon as the door shuts behind me. I stop for a moment, pulling my shirt away from my damp chest and releasing my hair from its ponytail.

My suitcase handle wobbles in my hand as I wheel it over to the lift which takes me to the main offices. Reception is in two parts, the front desk, where Kate is currently sitting, and the waiting area. With a perpetual smile plastered to her face, Kate's frantically taking notes and agreeing with whatever someone on the other end of the phone is saying. Her job is to look friendly, answer calls and accept the dozens of free gifts we receive from brands desperate to work with us.

Next to her is the mini library. It's not officially a library, but I think of it that way. It fills the entire corner of reception, a whole wall full of bright magazines shining over even brighter armchairs.

I still have five minutes until I have to be at my desk, so I have time to compose myself after my sweaty walk. I sit in one of the chairs, soaking up the colour from every magazine cover, and check my balance on the bank app on my phone: £108. I scroll down, wondering where the rest of my money has gone, until I remember my flights to Spain and all the new outfits I had to buy for this job. I get paid in a week. That will cover rent, but not much more.

My left hand is aching. I didn't realise I was still gripping the handle of my suitcase.

Having cooled off a little, I get to my feet, wondering how I'm going to get my suitcase to my desk without banging into everyone's chairs. It's only hand luggage, but it's heavy and bulky. My desk is on the other side of the floor, in a corner beside the fake palm and the water cooler. There's no way I can push past everyone without knocking a pile of books over or getting wedged by the filing cabinet.

'Hey! You look nice.' Kate looks up from her screen and gives me one of her all-teeth smiles. Her glasses have slipped down her nose and wild curls are escaping from her messy bun.

She points at my suitcase. 'Oh yeah, the wedding!'

Kate was the first person to talk to me on my first day here. Everyone loves her. She's like a human Labrador in Birkenstocks. Her wireless headphones are still balanced on her head as she walks around her desk and gives me a quick hug.

'How's your mum doing?'

I stiffen and pat her shoulder, but I don't answer. Her hugs are always at least three seconds too long.

'Why don't you pop your luggage behind my desk? Good morning. Swan & Swallow, how can I help you?' she chirrups into her cordless headset, still smiling at me.

Caroline, the head of HR, marches past us and grabs my case before I have a chance to say anything.

'I'll keep it in my office,' she says, without breaking her stride.

She tuts as the handle gives way in her hand and she has to push it back in. I give Kate a tight smile and follow Caroline.

'Meeting at ten?' I call out to the back of her head. Her blonde hair sways in time to her fleshy hips.

'Ten o'clock.'

3

The Guardian • @guardian

PM suggests 'women wear shorts, not skirts' after
current spate of sexual attacks in the capital. 'Crime of
this nature always rises along with the temperature,'
@metpoliceUK say. 'Women must take precautions.'

I have a lot of work to get through before my meeting, so
I resist the urge to check how well my last Twitter post
did. This job is only a three-month maternity placement,
but they still have me working on big accounts. Swan &
Swallow are famous for their hard-hitting campaigns, so
I've taken on as much work as I can because this is what
dream portfolios are made from.

Kate is convinced they'll offer me a full-time role. It's
probably what Caroline wants to talk to me about.

Twenty-eight minutes left.

Dante, as always, is sitting opposite me, chewing gum.
He's one of our web guys. We're not in the same team,
but we're often lumped together because we're the token
different ones. When the topic of diversity comes up in a
meeting, everyone glances at us. Dante's Black, and I'm just

about queer enough *and* I have a bit of a foreign accent. That will do. Three boxes ticked.

Dante cocks his head to one side. 'You all right, Em?'

I give him a flicker of a smile and nod.

On my first day at the agency Caroline introduced me to everyone as Em. It felt rude to correct her, so I didn't, and it stuck. I've noticed people like to shorten your name, make you theirs. Nikki never did that. Nikki always introduced me to people by my full name, always checking that she was pronouncing it properly.

'Saw you talking to Karen earlier,' Dante says quietly. That's what he calls Caroline. 'That pole up her arse gets bigger every day.'

I bite back a smile.

Dante has the darkest eyes I've ever seen. Kate says that when they shine, like they are right now, they look like two wet pebbles in a stream. Kate says a lot of soppy shit about Dante. She keeps denying that she likes him, but like any eager Labrador, she's hardly subtle. Dante's cool. I like talking to him. I don't know if it's the low hum of his voice or the way he listens with an unnerving stillness, but being near him is like having a cat on your lap. It's not often a guy makes me feel calm. Kate should go for it.

'I have an HR meeting soon,' I say. He makes a face, and I smile properly this time. 'It's all good.'

'Don't let her fuck you over, Em.'

I don't answer, keeping my gaze trained on my screen.

'Sandwich in the park?' he adds.

I nod. It's our Friday thing. Most days, I take my Kindle

to Trafalgar Square and eat with the lions, and Kate works shifts so I don't always see her, unless I hang out with her on the weekend. But on Fridays Dante and I sit in Victoria Embankment Gardens by the river with our sandwiches and watch the tourists. I don't know what we'll do in the winter. Maybe we'll take a flask.

There's ten minutes until my meeting, so I use the time to go to the bathroom and splash cold water on my wrists. I really want to add some powder to my shiny face and put more lipstick on, but my makeup is in my suitcase, which is in Caroline's office. I shake my head, adding volume to my hair, which has gone a bit limp on top, and keep an eye on the bathroom door. I don't like this room. Nowhere feels safe in this place any more.

As I head back to my desk, planning to refill my bottle at the water cooler, I stop. Paul Wilkes is there. I try to swallow, but I can't. My mouth is too dry, my throat closing up. Breathe. Breathe. *Fucking breathe.* His thick mane of hair is slicked back, the sleeves of his light linen jacket pushed up his tanned arms. I'm guessing the *Guardian* recently ran a fashion article on how to dress like someone in *Miami Vice* while simultaneously saving the planet.

Paul turns and sees me staring at him. He raises his hand in greeting and I catch a glimpse of the wording on his pale yellow T-shirt. FAMINIST. He's told me about this slogan before. 'Feminism starts with the family, Em.'

I return his greeting because it's the right thing to do while, inside, I'm screaming.

* * *

23

I've been in Caroline's office for less than five minutes, but she's already said everything she needed to say. No niceties, no comment on the weather or how pretty my hair looks, no time to waste. Now her voice is muffled, like she's holding me under water.

'Is there anything you would like to add?' she asks.

I blink three times, but I can't speak.

Her blonde bob falls forward and a strand of hair sticks to her sweaty forehead. She wipes it away. 'I need to know you understand what this means, Em.'

I nod. It means I'm unemployed. It means all my hard work was for nothing. This job isn't going to change my life after all.

Caroline clears her throat and shuffles the papers on her desk like a newsreader. She's waiting for me to say something, but all I can think about is the size of the damp marks under my arms. I should have chosen a different top. I hook my finger beneath the tight fabric and pull it away from my skin.

'This is not a reflection of your abilities,' she continues. 'We love the work you have done with the company, and we will be using a number of your designs on our biggest campaigns next season. It's simply a matter of . . .' She searches for the right word. 'Budget. We will ensure you get a good reference, of course.'

Oh good. A reference. That will pay the rent.

She hands me a limp piece of paper. 'Your P45.' Her fingers are thick, her nails bitten down to the quick.

I glance at the document in my hand. It says 'Emily'. I'm

not Emily. And she's only used one of my two surnames. The contract I signed was one of those online forms. Maybe my phone autocorrected my name; it does that all the time. Maybe my details on their system have never been correct and I never realised because they all call me Em. Is a P45 valid if it has the wrong name on it?

'Any questions?' Caroline asks, rubbing her thumbnail along her teeth.

I shake my head.

'Jolly good. And one more thing.'

She clears her throat again, although this time she looks down at her desk, where three pencils are neatly lined up, side by side. She straightens them.

'Paul.'

My mouth goes dry. Caroline has a jug of water on her desk. She sees me looking at it but continues talking.

'As you know, Paul is one of the finest creative directors in the business.'

I know. Paul is up there with the big boys. An office full of women called Emily and a board of white, middle-aged men.

'He came to me a few weeks ago and . . .' She leans forward, a pained expression on her face. 'Em, he really tried to help you, you know. This was a great opportunity for someone like you. What a shame you couldn't see that.' She leans back again with a long sigh. 'I must say, considering the circumstances, Paul has been very kind to let you continue until the end of your placement.'

Kind? What has he told her?

'He's worried about you, about this conversation we're having, and that you may react . . .'

While she chooses her next word carefully, I use the back of my wrist to dab at the sweat collecting on my top lip.

'. . . poorly, to the news that we can't keep you. So, as I said, he has been very kind, and you will receive an extra £439 in your salary at the end of the month.'

'I'm being paid off?' I croak.

She purses her lips and raises her eyebrows, glancing at the clock on the wall behind me. I've been listening to it ticking the entire time I've been sitting here.

'Let's call it a bonus. Although after what he told me I'm surprised I haven't been asked to speak to you sooner. I get it – Paul is handsome and friendly, and he really did champion you when you started. I can see how easy it may have been to get swept away.' She sighs again. 'Office liaisons are ill advised for this very reason – they always end in tears. Please be more careful in your next place of work'

Liaisons?

'Caroline, I need to explain . . .'

'I'm afraid, as of today, you're no longer employed here, so there's nothing further to discuss.' She smooths down her blouse. 'Don't make a fuss, Em. No one likes a woman who brings attention to herself. Paul is a happily married man, he has three beautiful children, and he doesn't need any unnecessary drama. I suggest you use this opportunity to start afresh and think carefully about the next person you choose to . . . admire.'

Caroline's smiling. She's proud of her carefully worded judgement. Proud that she's nothing like me.

'Where is he?' I ask.

'Paul? I don't think you should—'

'I'd like to thank him for his generosity,' I mumble. I need to see his face. See if he feels an ounce of guilt or culpability.

Her smile is tight now, making the red of her lipstick bleed further into the cracks around her thin lips.

'No. You've done more than enough.'

I haven't. But I nod and stand, pulling at my skirt, which is now sticking to my damp thighs like clingfilm. I've left two glistening patches on the plastic chair.

'Thanks,' I say, reaching for the suitcase beside her desk. The handle jams again and I wiggle it back and forth until it slots back into place.

'Oh, I forgot you're going on holiday today!' Caroline exclaims.

She hadn't forgotten; she knew I was going away because she had to sign it off.

'How lovely!' Her fake voice is like a primary-school teacher trying to get kids excited about their times tables. Her shoulders have already visibly lowered now the hard part is over, now there's nothing unsavoury left to deal with. 'Off to a wedding, aren't you? Where you going? Back to where you came from?'

I nod, remembering how pleasantly surprised she was when she interviewed me and discovered I was Spanish, exclaiming, 'How funny. Your English is ever so good.' She glances at something on her desk. A birthday card, with three messages scrawled in it. One is Kate's, the other Dante's; I can't read the third one. She pushes it beneath a pile of paper.

'And it's your thirtieth on Sunday. How nice you get to celebrate it with family. Who's getting married?'

'My sister. Same day as my birthday.'

'Oh.'

'My mother's ill,' I say, grasping the handle of the suitcase tighter. 'So the wedding was moved forward.'

Caroline opens her mouth like she's about to say something, then closes it again. 'Well, at least now you get the whole day to relax before your flight.'

Yes. I feel very relaxed.

It's not like the movies. I don't have a big cardboard box to fill with files and a pot plant to take with me. I just grab my handbag off my desk and wheel my suitcase past reception. Kate's talking into her headset and mouths, '*What the fuck?*' as I wait for the lift with my luggage. I give a small shrug as she ums and ahs into the phone, widening her eyes at me and holding her hand up to stop me getting into the lift.

'Hey,' she hisses, whipping her headset off and running around the side of the reception desk. Her Birkenstocks flap against the tiled floor, her arms tight at her side like a penguin. 'Where are you going?'

I don't answer. I just keep blinking.

'No way,' she says, pulling me into a big hug. I stiffen, as usual, but she doesn't seem to notice, or maybe she doesn't care. I hold my breath. She smells like an airport Duty Free.

'Bastards,' she sighs into my hair.

'It's fine. It was only a temporary freelance job. It's not a big deal.'

'I bet Paul's behind this. You shouldn't have kept quiet.'

I bite at the dry skin on my lip, but I don't answer. The office phone is ringing. Kate ignores it.

'What will you do now?' She looks at the suitcase in my hand. 'Oh sweetheart, your poor mum . . . and your sister! Listen, just get to Spain and, when you're free, call me. I can help. I've got friends at other agencies. God, I feel like this is all my fault.'

It's not her fault. None of this is.

'You know . . .' She waves her hand up and down, her eyes glassy. 'I was there, at the pub, and I could have gone to Caroline with you and backed you up, but—'

The lift announces its arrival with a *bing* and the doors slide open slowly. I take a step towards it, but Kate throws her arms around me again. The phone keeps ringing. The lift doors shut again.

I turn my head to the side and gulp down some air. I need to get out of here.

'It's not a big deal,' I say again.

It's heavy, though, what I'm feeling. The painful lump growing in my chest. It's hard like rock, gnarly and sharp. I pull my hair back into a ponytail and straighten my skirt. My thighs are already stinging from the chafe of this morning's walk.

'Let Dante know I've gone,' I say to Kate. 'He wasn't at his desk when I grabbed my things.'

I search inside my bag and pull out the BLT baguette I bought at Pret. 'Tell him he can have my sandwich when he goes to the park.'

Kate is about to say something, but I'm already at the stairwell, heading down.

4

Kelly May • @KellyTMay

Can't believe what I just saw. Two blokes having a
punch-up in my local Co-op over the last bottle of
water. The fizzy drink shelves were also empty and
there's no ice left. There's nothing left but milk.

All the flowers are dead.

The garden at Victoria Embankment runs parallel to the
Thames, although you can't see it from the Strand. It's
beautiful and kind of posh, with its statues and flowerbeds
and benches all in a row. Depending on the season, there
are roses, tulips and pansies. But not any more. Now it's
just mosquitoes and the stench of still, hot water emanating from the river. This is where Dante and I always
sit. *Sat.* Coats spread out over the grass, eating our limp
sandwiches. He always makes a big deal about us taking
our full lunch hour.

'Your wages ain't a gift, Em,' he says. 'You swap your
time and skills for their money. But your lunch hour's for
you. Don't give it to them.'

Maybe Swan & Swallow would have kept me on if I'd

stayed at my desk to eat my sandwiches like Caroline does. No, of course they wouldn't have. Hard work has nothing to do with success when the world is run by people like Paul.

Standing beside a long-dry fountain, I run my finger along the petals of one of the paling flowers. It crumbles in my hands. One rose remains, white and wilting, velvet petals tinged with rust. I smell it, but it has no scent. Everything is just dust. I push my sweaty hair away from my eyes and sit on a bench, the wooden slats dry and hot against my legs, which are itching like I'm going to get splinters. A mosquito buzzes in my ear and I swat at it blindly.

Most of the park is empty and no one is sitting on the ground as usual; the grass is yellow and spiky, like every lawn in England right now. One month without rain and two weeks of hosepipe bans and already people are panicking. A couple of streets in Streatham are without water and now the whole country thinks they're next, emptying the shops of bottled water like it's another pandemic.

I stare at the fountain surrounded by its tangle of thorny dried twigs and its one wilting rose and I think of my ex. My X. The scar on my heart. I can't look at a flower without thinking of Nikki. Even the dead ones.

The first time I met Nikki was at her shop. It was the day after I arrived in London. I was renting an Airbnb room in Enfield and I'd gone to look around the town. It was all cheap shoe shops and discount stores and the same unimaginative clothing chains you get on every high street. And then there was her shop – a bright barrage of colours, as if its interior had once been full of pots of paint that had exploded. Nikki had even trained ivy to grow around the door. I was inside before I knew what I was doing.

And there she was.

The thing about Nikki is that she doesn't look like any other woman I've ever seen. Some women look like a million other women, whereas she looks like a million different people all at once. Even now, if the police were to ask me to create a profile picture of her, I couldn't. I guess even unforgettable people can be hard to describe. I sometimes wonder if I ever really knew the real Nikki – or if she ever has either.

'Can I help you?' she said. They were her first words to me. 'Can I help you?'

She did. But at the same time, she couldn't really. No one could.

'I'm looking for some flowers.'

She gave me a wry smile that made me want to run out of her shop as fast as I could. My first words to her, and that's what I said. She could have been a dick and replied with something like 'You're in the right place, then.' But she didn't.

'Anything in particular?'

I shrugged. 'Funeral. It's tomorrow.'

'What's the address?'

I wrote it down and she gave a light laugh. Then apologised.

'I only do local funerals. I can't send flowers that far, they'll get ruined, plus it will cost you a fortune.' I turned to walk away, but she grabbed hold of my arm. That's Nikki for you, the kind of woman who touches a stranger.

'Don't waste your money on flowers,' she said.

What kind of florist tells you not to spend money on flowers?

'Not for funerals,' she continued. 'Some florists, especially this time of year, will use the flowers they've brought back from an event or wedding the day before, flowers that have already been displayed and paid for, and they'll use them on the wreaths. After all, it doesn't matter if those flowers are dead in two days. No one goes back to the grave to check. And the dead certainly don't give a fuck. Give your money to a charity instead.'

I'd only said seven words to her and she was already sharing secrets. I couldn't stop staring at this woman – her unusual hair, the jewellery, the dimple on her right cheek. I wanted to know if her hair smelled as sweet as the roses in her shop. I wanted to count the light scratches on her hands.

'Bye,' I said. And left.

It took me nearly four weeks to find the courage to return to her shop. She recognised me right away, because Nikki never forgets a face, and asked me the same thing again.

'Can I help you?'

'I'm looking for some flowers.'

'For anyone special?'

Three seconds passed before I answered. 'No. Just myself.'

'Then you're wrong.'

I frowned.

'You said "no one special" – but *you* are special. We all are. Buying ourselves flowers is an act of self-love.'

I stepped closer to the counter as she leaned forward. That smile. That dimple.

'You said not to waste money on flowers.'

'I said don't buy flowers for *dead* people. The dead don't appreciate a nice arrangement as much as the living. Oh. Snap!'

I looked at what she was looking at, my hands on the counter beside hers. The nails on her first and middle finger were shorter than the others, just like mine.

'Our tattoos,' she said.

Right. The semicolons on the inside of our wrists. Mine was still pink and fresh from the day before, the light sting a reminder of just how close I'd got to stopping and not carrying on. I wondered what her story was.

'I'll make you up a colourful bouquet,' she said. 'Anything you don't like?'

I shook my head as she walked about the shop grabbing handfuls of flowers that I still don't know the names of. I didn't have spare cash to spend on anything that lavish, I'd have to go light on the food shopping that week, but it was worth it just to watch her in her natural habitat. She reminded me of a bee, bouncing from flower to flower.

'How much?' I asked, hoping she wouldn't hear the uncertainty in my voice.

'One Hennessy on the rocks. Maybe a double.'

I'm perfectly bilingual, it's rare for English words to elude me, but I didn't understand what she was saying. Was she teasing me?

'Take me for a drink,' she said. 'I'll give you these flowers, as a gift, and you get the first round in.'

I can't remember what I said in reply, but she shut the shop early and we went to the pub opposite. Those flowers never made it to my room in the Airbnb because our date lasted three days, and within two weeks I was living with her.

That was before I fucked everything up.

Words will never hurt me • @Em_Dash_93
I miss you. I miss you, I miss you, I miss you

I don't know how long I've been sitting on this bench, but my backside is numb and I have a headache. I've been mindlessly scrolling through my phone, reading old messages from Nikki, silly things like 'Don't forget to buy more milk' or 'Do you know where my blue shiny earrings are?' I didn't know WhatsApp threads remained even after you delete the number.

I scroll up, past messages from Kate and people whose numbers I haven't even saved on my phone, until I reach all the messages my sister has sent. It's been a while since we've been in touch directly and not through our mother.

There aren't that many exchanges between us. When Marianna first got engaged, she shared photos of table centres and wedding dresses with me. I found the messages boring. Then, after Nikki and I separated, I found them upsetting. Now I feel bad that most of the time I replied with a thumbs-up emoji or just one word, like 'nice' or 'pretty'. I know Marianna needed more than that.

'Wish you'd been with me to choose my dress,' she'd written in one of the messages, and my guilty heart had mustered up nothing more than a GIF from *Bridesmaids*.

I scroll up further, not dwelling on the photos she sent when our mother was first in hospital, up up up, until I get to the very first message from her. The first time she sent anything to my UK number.

'Dad's funeral went well,' she wrote. 'The priest said that Mama should get up and say a few words. She couldn't do it – she could hardly say hello to all the well-wishers without bursting into tears. So I did it.'

This was three years ago. Marianna was eighteen. A child.

'I was so scared. I kept looking for you in the congregation, like I used to when I was in school plays and you'd sit in the front and wave. Back then I used to pretend it was just you I was putting on a show for, like all the plays I did at home for you and Mama. Remember them? You were so patient with me, haha. But you weren't at the church today, so I had to focus on everyone else's faces instead. Mama's was the hardest. Looking at her was worse than seeing Dad in his coffin. I don't understand why you didn't come back. If not for him, then why not for us?'

I didn't reply to that one. I remember reading it as I was getting ready for bed. I hadn't been on my date with Nikki yet; I was still new to London. I'd looked at it, got dressed again and gone to the nearest bar to get drunk. I think I even got laid that night. I can't remember.

My phone is getting hot in my hand so I put it back in my bag.

Why the hell am I still sitting here, depressing myself and sweating?

I need to get back to the flat, have a shower, take off these tight shoes and get myself together before my flight. But I can't move. Now I've stopped distracting myself with my phone, the enormity of what just happened at work keeps hitting me like one wave after another, knocking me over, pushing me under, waiting for me to feel OK then reminding me once more that I can't relax.

I don't have the luxury of feeling guilty about the past or worrying if I'm making enough fuss over my sister's wedding. I don't have a job any more. No money. No career. Everything I've been working towards for months has gone.

Every time I close my eyes I see Paul in his stupid linen suit waving at me this morning, smiling, the whole time knowing that today was going to be my last day. I bet he's relieved now I've gone, making sure everyone in the office knows how the new girl had boundary issues.

'It's hard, in my position, not to attract that kind of attention,' I imagine him saying to the rest of the directors. All men just like him. All nodding along, because it's so hard to be where they are. 'You try and be a role model for these young people and they always take it too far.'

I take a deep breath. It's fine. It's going to be OK. I have all day to get changed and do some job-hunting before my flight, to update my LinkedIn and my CV, maybe even call my old temp agency, and . . .

My head is spinning and I reach out for the bench to steady myself.

Lunch. I need to eat something, and drink something, then I'll be able to think straight. I pull up the handle of my purple suitcase and swear under my breath as it nearly comes away in my hand again. Maybe there are some tools at home that will fix it, or Matt will lend me one of his bags.

My suitcase snags on the paving slabs as I traipse up the short hill towards Charing Cross. The streets up there are a bit busier, and the road is full of back-to-back red buses. A haze emanates off the pavement and combined with the car fumes my head begins to pound again. I strain my eyes looking for Moby and his bright blue cap, but I can't see him. As I near his usual corner I see that his blanket and bag of belongings are there, along with his empty cup. But the boy's gone.

My suitcase and I are in the way of the station entrance, and I'm jostled out of the way by three guys, all shirtless and wearing shorts tucked beneath their bellies. They shove their way on to the pavement, then slow down as they reach Moby's cup. I should walk away, whatever they're about to do it's not going to be good, but instead I just stand there.

'What's that homeless bloke doing with a bottle of water when Boots says they ran out hours ago?' one of them says.

He moves Moby's blanket with the tip of his trainers, revealing two more bottles beneath it.

'Cheeky bastard,' he cries, reaching down.

'Don't touch it, Steve. It's probably full of piss.'

'Yeah, or meth.'

Steve isn't listening. He's picked up one of the bottles I gave Moby and is peering at the seal around the cap.

'It's not open. None of them are.'

I watch the other men pick up Moby's water, but I stay silent. In my head I'm telling them to stop, I'm snatching it out of their hands, I'm smacking the bottles against their bulldog meatheads. But in reality, I say nothing. All I can do is grip the handle of my broken suitcase tighter.

'Enjoying the show?'

Steve's noticed me watching and is walking towards me.

'Like what you see?' he says, rubbing his nipple and wiggling his tongue at me.

People walk past; they're seeing this too, but no one says anything. Steve laughs and cracks open the bottle, pouring it into his mouth from a great height, letting it wash over his mouth and bare torso.

'Don't worry your pretty little head about it, love. He's probably dead,' one of his friends says to me. 'You know, the tramp. He's probably gone to shoot up somewhere. He don't give a shit if we take his water. I bet he got it free off some charity or something.'

I turn my head away and they finally leave, Steve saying something about stuck-up bitches with too much time on their hands. I stay there for another minute, maybe three, staring at Moby's ratty blanket and empty cup.

Children are taught to speak up when they see bad things happening, do something, but that's not reality. That's not what I learned as a child. In reality, when something bad is happening and you make a sound, that bad stuff happens to you next. Silence is safety. My own father taught me that.

'Back again already?'

I look up. Moby has returned, clutching a fistful of napkins printed with a Cornish Pasty logo.

'I was getting a bit sweaty,' he says, holding up his hand. 'So I grabbed these from the stand over there.'

'Those guys took your water,' I say. 'I'm sorry.'

He looks over at his stuff, then at the backs of the three men on the pavement drinking his water and laughing.

'I wanted to stop them. I saw them do it and I wanted to say something, but . . .'

'Hey,' Moby says. 'It's fine. I have an empty bottle. I'll fill it from the station loo, like I always do.'

Right.

'How come you're not at work?' he asks.

I blow out a long breath. I can't take his pity when everyone has already taken everything else from him.

'Headache. Boss said I could go home early. It's not been the best day.'

Moby smiles, displaying one cracked tooth and making the sore on his mouth glisten with blood.

'Yeah, I get it,' he says. 'It's never the big things.'

'What?'

He nods at the men walking away, their voices still carrying through the thick, heavy air.

'It's not the big things that send you over the edge. People think it is; not having a house, losing all your money, all that. But it's not. It's the little things that kill you. The stuff that sneaks up on you while you're busy holding on tight to the big things.'

I think about Nikki and my job and Matt saying I should move out and I know Moby's wrong. Big things matter.

'I'm sorry about your water,' I say again.

He shrugs. 'Look after yourself, yeah?'

I scoop out the last of the coins from my purse and drop them into his paper cup.

5

Trafalgar Square is almost empty. No tourist wants to be
traipsing around a city looking at historical sites in this
weather. I bet everyone goes to Brighton this weekend, or
Southend, or anywhere by the sea.

I wonder if anyone will turn up tomorrow night. I don't
know why they're bothering with this mournful gathering.
Hanna Nilsson wasn't the only woman to be found dead in
the UK this month, or even this week, but she *was* a rich
Swedish student and the daughter of an ambassador. The
newspapers announced her death using a photo of her in
a bikini, a pretty brunette smiling into the camera, with a
caption about how she was top of her class at UCL. They
went on to say how she'd been strangled, a stripy blue tie
stuffed in her mouth, but she wasn't raped. Nice of them
to highlight that part. Lucky Hanna. I wonder how many

women they're going to save tomorrow night by holding candles in an empty square. Everyone patting themselves on the back for 'doing something' . . . until the next woman dies.

This is the kind of shit I used to argue with Nikki about. She would go to all the marches, all the gatherings, all the sit-ins. Her Instagram is full of black squares and raised fists. I called it performative once and she didn't speak to me all day. She said she was doing something about the things she felt passionate about. I said she was fooling herself, that no one listens, that all she was doing was centring herself in someone else's pain and directing the same hate back on to herself. She asked me how far my own silence had got me.

'Hey,' I say, patting the lion statue's paw as I walk past him for the second time this morning. Mufasa. Nikki's king. Her protector.

It was late November and I'd been living with Nikki for a couple of months when I told her I still hadn't ventured into the centre of London.

'Are you kidding?' she'd exclaimed. 'You're telling me in all this time, all you've seen of London is Enfield and that shitty Wood Green pub you work at?'

I worked most evenings, she worked six days a week; I hadn't got around to doing the tourist thing yet.

'I'm taking you to Covent Garden,' she'd said. 'Tomorrow. You're not working, I'll shut the shop and you're going to see what Christmas in London really looks like. The full *Last Christmas* movie experience.'

The next day, I was grinning from ear to ear when I saw

the centre of London in its winter-wonderland glory. Nikki had been right: it was exactly like the film. Every shop window was decorated, and every inch of Covent Garden was covered in foliage and twinkly lights. We clutched our boozy hot chocolates and laughed as the tips of our cold noses got covered in whipped cream. My hometown of Ronda was beautiful all year around, but winter was never this magical. Christmas really did belong in the cold and the dark.

Everything Nikki showed me was exactly as I'd imagined, until we arrived at Trafalgar Square.

'Where are the pigeons?' I'd cried out over the howling wind, giddy from the rum in our hot chocolate. It wasn't quite snowing and it wasn't quite raining either. Nikki called it sleet, which I'd never heard of. The giant Christmas tree hadn't been put up yet, but it was so cold the water in the fountains had turned to ice.

'We got rid of those dirty winged rats years ago. Forget them – these are the only animals you should care about,' she said, leading me right here. To her lions.

She rubbed the iron statue's paw. 'This is Mufasa.'

'Like from *The Lion King*?'

She smiled, but it wasn't a happy smile. 'OK, get comfortable,' she'd said. 'And I'll tell you about my king.' And she began her tale.

'My father died when I was seven. It was sudden – pancreatic cancer – three weeks from diagnosis to his last day. He knew he didn't have long and, according to my mum, he wanted to tell me himself. He wanted a day together, just us,

45

so he took me to the big Leicester Square cinema to watch *The Lion King*. I cried when Mufasa died, and I cried even harder when my dad told me that he would be going soon too. As you can imagine, I was inconsolable, the finality of death is hard enough for an adult to understand, let alone a child, so he brought me here and he lied. He said this was a statue of Mufasa and Simba and the rest of the pride.'

I ran my hand over the giant iron paw of the statue up on the plinth. The sleet had turned to rain, but I hadn't wanted to move. I wanted to know more about this little girl with a father as brave as a lion. I kissed Nikki's cold cheek, tasting the salt from an errant tear.

'He carried me all the way from the cinema to right here, holding me so tight I thought it was because he was worried about dropping me. Now I realise it was because he didn't know how many more hugs he was going to get. He showed me this exact lion and said that although people leave us, their memories don't. No one really dies for ever.'

She sniffed, and I'd thought of my own father and everything he'd left behind.

'He placed me up on to the plinth and I clambered on to the lion, hugging his mane, imagining it tickling my nose and covering me like a blanket. During the days that followed I pictured this huge, invisible lion walking beside me.'

These statues are bigger than real lions. Every time I pass them, I see a tiny girl walking through hospital corridors with the giant shadow of a great beast keeping her safe.

'Mufasa never left my side, not once, until the day my father died and neither of them came back,' she said.

46

'I'd lost them both. I searched for my lion everywhere, convinced that if I found him, maybe my dad would return too. Every night for a year I stared out of my bedroom window, expecting my king to leap out of the bushes or for my father's face to appear in the night sky. Neither of them came, and eventually that gaping hole was filled with other things, other memories and other people. When I turned seventeen, I got this.' She pulled up her sleeve to reveal the lion tattoo I'd kissed a million times. 'And when I'm sad I come here. I climb on to Mufasa's back and I hug my king. Every girl deserves at least one good man in her life, and I'll never forget mine.'

We'd both shed a tear that day, both of us thinking of our fathers. Her tears were for a man who'd loved her fiercely, whereas my tears were for me, for what I'd done and the monster he'd turned me into.

I shield my eyes from the sun, squinting into the distance. London looks beautiful in sunlight. Everything looks almost clean. How different the city is in the summer compared to its frosty winter sheen.

I trudge on past the National Gallery and the Canadian Embassy until I reach my front door, where I crouch beneath the shade of a spindly bay tree. My suitcase topples over and I sit on it, pulling my handbag off my shoulder. I'm panting, and I don't know if it's from the heat or the weight of the bags I've been lugging about all morning. I need water. I wish I hadn't given all the bottles to Moby – it's not like he even got to enjoy them.

My handbag is like a sack. Every day I tell myself I'll get

a smaller one, one with pockets or compartments, and every day I carry this thing around. A bag big enough for two Pret sandwiches and copious bottles of water but impossible to find my sunglasses and chewing gum in. I root about. I can't hear the jingle of my keys, neither can I feel the sharp edges of the giant metal keyring shaped like the female sign. Nikki bought it for me so I could find my keys in my bag more easily at night, even though it means I can't ever fit them anywhere smaller than this stupid bag. I shake it, I take out my purse, phone, passport, Kindle, phone charger, my crumpled P45, four pens, two bookmarks and an empty bottle of water. Where the fuck are my keys?

I turn my bag upside down. Nothing. Then I pat my pockets, knowing full well my tight pencil skirt has no pockets. This can't be happening.

My eyes are stinging from my mascara, which is melting from the heat. I run my finger under each eye and blow my hair out of my face, adjusting my mother's necklace as it sticks to my collarbone. A fly keeps hovering over my face, trying to land on my mouth. I bat it away and try to think. Did I leave my keys inside the house?

Most of the buildings on this street are large, cream and Georgian. Like something out of *My Fair Lady*. Most are embassies or owned by millionaires; they have all the floors to their building, complete with little blue round plaques and perfectly round shrubs in pots. Matt's building is split into three apartments and . . . where the fuck *is* Matt?

I buzz the intercom, leaning heavily on the button. I then press the other two buttons. I've never met our neighbours;

most people don't live here full time. The apartments are rented out to businessmen, the kind who come to London for meetings or need a place to fuck their high-class escorts while the wife stays in the farmhouse in Cornwall. No one answers or lets me in.

Snatching up my stupid handbag, I stuff everything back in except my phone. I jab at Matt's contact details. It rings, but he doesn't pick up so I send him a WhatsApp: *Call me. Emergency.*

Two blue ticks appear right away, but no answer. I wipe my clammy forehead with the back of my hand and call him again. Nothing. I'm not going to stop.

Matt finally answers on my seventh attempt.

'What the fuck, Emmy?'

'Are you home?'

'No. Why?'

'I'm locked out. When are you back?'

'I'm on a train.'

His voice is muffled, like he's got his hand over the mouthpiece.

'When are you back?'

'Becca is going to be there at six.'

I know Becca is going to be here at six. Becca is here at six every Friday. That wasn't my question, Matt. My question wasn't about Becca. I need to get into the flat.

I push my hair off my face again. Even in the shade, it's getting unbearably hot. I pull the elastic out, twist my hair into a bun and pull the elastic over it. It snaps in two, leaving me with even more hair in my face.

'I need to get inside!' I shout.

'You're being shrill. Calm down.' He makes the last word have four syllables. 'Why aren't you at work, anyway? Don't you have a flight to catch tonight?'

'Yes. I do. So you're not back until late?'

I pull my shirt away from under my armpit. There's already a red mark from where it's been rubbing.

'I'm in Canterbury for a business thing.'

What business thing? Matt doesn't do business things. The most work I've ever seen him do is trade cryptocurrency with his daddy's money, sitting on the couch all day in his pants.

'I'm meeting Becca at Euston station when I get back, then we're coming home together,' he continues. 'It's not my fault you left your keys at home.'

Did he see them? Did he know I'd locked myself out and leave without telling me?

'I have to go, Emmy. Stop calling.'

'Wait!' I lift my hair away from my neck. 'Who has a spare key?'

Matt sighs. 'My father.'

His parents are divorced, he mentioned that once, and his father lives in Kensington. OK, that's not that far. I have enough time until my flight to collect the keys and get ready. 'Is he home?'

Matt scoffs. 'It's July, Emmy.'

What does that mean, Matt? What are you talking about?

'My father's on his boat in Capri. You know that, Emmy. *Think!* I mentioned it just the other day.'

Of course, the fucking yacht Matt's always talking about. He never mentions his mother, though. I guess she doesn't have a boat. I shift on my suitcase, my skirt like a bandage around my legs.

'Bye, Emmy. See you in ten days,' Matt says, then hangs up.

Every inch of me is wilting. This isn't the nice kind of holiday sun, the soft kiss of rays on your shoulders, it's the relentless press of heat where your hairline stings to the touch and your throat dries out with each inhalation.

Think, Emmy. Think.

My phone says it's nearly 1 p.m. My flight's at nine fifteen. I have over eight hours until my flight, six hours until I need to be at City Airport – but it only takes forty minutes on the Tube. What am I going to do in all that time?

I lean back against the wall of my building, weighing up my options. Which doesn't take long, because I don't have that many. Airports have showers, don't they? And aircon and places to eat, bookshops, lots of quiet seating areas. Nothing's stopping me from heading to the airport now and hanging out there. I have a suitcase full of clothes. At least at the airport I can get changed and out of this heat.

I pull up Google Maps on my phone, calculating the quickest way east. Piccadilly Circus Tube station is just up the road, but that means getting the Piccadilly Line to Green Park, then the Jubilee line, then the DLR. Three Tubes in this weather? No. I rub my temples. I'll go straight to Green Park. Walking anywhere with luggage right now is going to be hell, but it's still better than being crammed forty metres underground, squashed into a Tube carriage with my face pressed against someone's sweaty armpit. If I cut through the side streets, I can go to Tesco Express and buy some water too. Hopefully they won't have run out.

I grab my wobbly suitcase, straighten my skirt and start walking.

The cool water leaves an icy trail from my mouth to the pit of my stomach as I gulp it down. Well, they call it water, but it's actually carbonated water with a hint of lemon. It was all the shop had left.

I'm heading down Jermyn Street, with its high-end men's fashion brands and fancy tailors, following the map on my phone. I think this is the way to Green Park, but I'm not totally sure. It doesn't matter how long you live in London; you will never not get lost.

'You can't come down here.'

I look up from my screen and into the face of a police officer.

'What?'

He nods at the bright yellow tape behind him. There are three police cars, a police van and even one of those little white tent things. We're on the corner of Duke of York Street, the one that leads to . . . Oh no.

'Is this about Hanna Nilsson?' I ask.

'Who?' But the policeman isn't looking at me, he's peering over my shoulder at a delivery guy on a bike trying to navigate the barricade.

'The woman who was murdered,' I say.

'Yeah. That's right. Crime scene. Move along.'

My gaze follows a bead of sweat travelling from below his cap and down his cheek, disappearing at his not-so-white collar.

'Come on. Move along.'

I haven't allowed myself to read about Hanna Nilsson, yet even when you try and avoid a story online it still manages to find you. She was murdered four days ago, five minutes from where I live, strangled at ten o'clock at night as she waited for her dad in St James's Square. Her father was a Swedish ambassador, he'd taken her to dinner at the East India Club, they'd finished, and she'd said she felt dizzy and needed fresh air. She was sitting on the bench in the park, in front of the horse statue, while her dad settled the bill and went to the toilet. He hadn't been able to find her at first, but when he called her phone and followed the sound of it ringing, he'd found her body half hidden among the dry flowerbeds. She'd been strangled, a blue stripy tie stuffed in her mouth.

Her father was the first suspect, of course. But there were enough witnesses at the restaurant to confirm she'd been outside alone for at least fifteen minutes. More than enough time to end a life.

'Where are you heading?' the policeman asks as I carefully pull the handle of my luggage up and manoeuvre my suitcase around.

'Spain.'

He frowns, and I shake my head.

'Sorry, I mean City Airport. I need to get on the Tube.'

'Piccadilly Circus is rammed,' he says. 'You want to avoid it.'

I nod, turn back the way I came and for the third time today head for Charing Cross station.

As my suitcase wheels whirr and catch against the paving slabs, I wonder whether Hanna walked down these same streets the day she died. I wonder what she looked at, what she was thinking, whether she liked her life before she lost it.

We live our days – preoccupied, futile, mundane – not knowing what's around the corner. Not knowing that a bronze horse and dying flowers will be the last thing we ever see. Would we live them differently if we knew how long we had?

6

Metro Newspaper UK • @MetroUKNews

Union strike: London Underground is deemed 'unfit
for humans'. Tube workers demand better working
conditions on one of the hottest days in British history.

I know something's wrong before I've even reached the
Strand. A line of black cabs has gathered outside the train
station and groups of people are milling around, many of
them with luggage, just like me.

I comb through the sea of faces and bare limbs, every
one of them clammy and irate, trying to pick out a blue
cap. Moby isn't there this time, and neither is his stuff. I'm
not sure if I'm relieved or concerned.

'What's happening?' I ask a woman beside me. She has
a baby in a carrier, rivers of sweat coating her chest where
the baby's damp head is resting. His head isn't much bigger
than my fist, his sun hat like something a doll would wear.

'Tube strike,' she says.

What? I take my phone out of my bag and scroll through
Twitter. It's everywhere. Conditions on the Underground
are getting inhumane, apparently. Drivers are refusing to

work. One woman fainted from the heat, hit her head on the platform floor and is now in a coma. I keep scrolling until I reach a *Metro* article.

'Temperatures inside some Tube carriages have reached nearly 50°C. According to EU regulations, even cattle cannot be transported in temperatures of over 30°C. We may no longer be part of the EU, but we're not animals,' Keith Andrews, leader of the Transport and General Workers' Union, said. 'It's not safe for our members to be working under these conditions, or for the general public to be travelling in them. All London Transport workers, including bus drivers, will not be returning to work until ventilation measures are put in place, or this heat subsides.

Bus drivers too? How am I meant to get to the airport?

I look up from my phone. People are getting out of stationary buses on the Strand and just standing on the pavement, hands on hips, looking around as if someone is going to rescue them. There's a short clip of Piccadilly Circus on my phone, people shouting at a man in a hi-vis vest ushering them out of the station, and aerial footage of abandoned double-decker buses blocking various roads. The news team are interviewing passengers: some are saying they couldn't breathe on the Tube; others that transport workers should suck it up and keep working.

I wheel my bag over to the shade and sit down. My phone's on 32 per cent. I take a deep breath, but it's like swallowing hot water.

Chris T Rennolds · @CTR_85

London's a mess. Murders and transport issues. What's @mayor doing about it?

> **Beth Samson · @BethanyBoo**
>
> My dad's in hospital and I can't get to him. You can't shut down London just because it's hot.
>
> **Proud to be British · @gregsmith007**
>
> Why is everyone complaining? Get in a car, ffs
>
> **Chris T Rennolds · @CTR_85**
>
> Replying to @gregsmith007
>
> Are you stupid? Most Londoners don't even own cars because IT'S IMPOSSIBLE TO DRIVE AROUND LONDON. Plus people are stranded far from home.

Home. I don't even know what that means any more.

A line has formed for black cabs. I'm not in a rush; I have hours to spare. I join the queue in the full glare of the sun.

Fifteen minutes later, and my blouse is soaked with sweat, red welts beginning to appear beneath my arms where the tight fabric is chafing.

'Where are you going?' a man behind me asks.

I saw him earlier as everyone raced to the queue, noticed the way he practically ran. He's wearing the kind of wrap-around sunglasses better suited for skiing, a camel-coloured suit jacket and a blue tie. I think of Hanna. I try not to think of Hanna. How can he wear a knot around his neck in this heat?

I pretend not to have heard him, even though he's so close

I can feel his hot breath skimming the top of my head. He taps me on the shoulder, his fingernail jabbing my sore skin.

'Hey, I just asked you where you're going.'

I turn to face him and gesture at my suitcase. 'The airport.'

'Me too. We can share a ride. Wait. What airport?'

'City.'

He makes a face, his eyes rolling up to the bright blue sky. 'I need to get to Gatwick. Why are you getting a taxi to go up the road when some of us have to actually cross some distance?'

Up the road?

My phone is still in my hand. I look at the time – 1.47 p.m. Google Maps is on the screen, the blue line still showing the best Tube route to the airport.

'Nine miles is hardly up the road,' I mutter, dropping the phone into my bag.

A black cab pulls up in front of me and I go to open the door, but the man covers my hand with his as we both reach for the door handle.

'Come on,' he says. 'I have to be on a flight in two hours. It's important.'

His fingers are slick against mine, his chest pressing against my shoulder.

'So do I,' I lie. Except I don't; I have more than enough time. The man is tall and broad and looming over me.

I try to open the door, but he presses closer.

'Please,' he says, pulling at the door with my hand still trapped beneath his. 'Be nice.'

I yank my hand away and he shoves me out of the way. I drop my suitcase, and while I stoop to pick it up he bundles into the back of the cab, dragging his Samsonite case behind him. I go to say something, but he slams the door in my face and the cab pulls off.

'I'm in a rush too,' a man behind me in the queue says.

I'm about to tell him I'm going to the airport, that it's important, but I'm distracted by my phone pinging. I glance at it – three consecutive texts from my mum. All voice messages.

Another cab approaches, and the man's wife and children avoid my eye as they follow his lead and edge closer to the front of the queue, all four of them pushing past me and clambering into the vehicle as I try to listen to my mother's first message. It's three seconds long. Silence. It moves to the next message, but the people talking behind me are too loud and I can't make out what she's saying. I try not to think of all the 4G I've already used up this morning.

'Ai, *hija*,' she says. Then it breaks off again.

I imagine her calling from a hospital bed, wires attached to her hands and up her nose. I only saw photos last time, as my sister likes to remind me. Marianna was the one who slept on a chair by her bed, not me. My mother wouldn't even video call, telling me we'd talk when I was finally by her side.

But I'm coming home now. I'm coming home.

The queue has turned into a mob and I'm getting jostled to the side. It's impossible to listen to my messages so I step into a shady spot and focus on my mother's voice.

'Ai, *hija*. Do you have the family Bible?'

What? I thought this was urgent.

'Your sister needs it, for the ceremony. And it really should go to her. Although you are the eldest, she's getting married first and will therefore have children first, so she needs the Bible.'

I think of the heavy white book with the rust-coloured stain on the spine. I should have thrown it away years ago, but some dark, sadistic side of me kept it. It's probably in one of the boxes in my room.

'You in the queue or not?' a man beside me asks, shoving past me towards the black-cab line. Two children scurry behind him. I move out of his way, back into the glare of the midday sun.

I can't hear what my mother is saying. I wheel my bag out of the way, people shifting to fit the space like a school of fish. I press the phone harder against my ear.

'Your sister wants to do the English thing for the wedding. Something old, something new,' she says in English. Her accent is so thick I can hardly understand what she's saying. All these years, and she never learned the language. 'You know the rest, something about borrowing something and something else being blue. Anyway, I thought the old and borrowed thing could be my necklace.'

Instinctively, I clasp the diamond hanging around my neck. The necklace I found inside my suitcase the day I arrived in London. My mother's necklace, the one that had belonged to her grandmother, the heirloom she told me would bring me luck.

'So, Marianna's dress is new. I made some adjustment – so

pretty. And the necklace will be the old and borrowed, and as for the blue . . .'

I think of what the necklace used to look like around my mother's neck. The different shades of blues and lilacs and pinks on her collarbone and cheek, bruises healing at different stages.

'I was also wondering if you wanted to wear your father's watch as you give your sister away,' she continues. 'As a gesture. It will be like he's there. It was Marianna's idea.'

Something bitter coats my tongue, but I have no water left to wash it away. I know which watch she's talking about. It was gold and heavy, thick, rectangular links that lost their shine a long time ago. In the summer it clattered when he spoke, slipping down his wrist and back again as he waved his hands about. I remember just how hard that watch was when it struck against my skin.

'So don't forget the Bible and the necklace. *Ai*, you and your sister are both going to look so beautiful walking down that aisle together. Text me when you're at the air-port. No need to call.'

As if I'd ever call her. She never picks up.

'*Por dios*, it's been so long since I last saw you, *hija*. Come home.'

I don't know how long I stand there, the sun beating down on the tops of my arms. They feel a little burnt already, but I like it, that sweet sting that reminds me of my childhood summers in Spain. Cold cream on pink skin. Rocket lollies, still in their wrapper, wiped over hot fore-heads. Ice in a tissue, pressed against a swollen cheek.

'Em?'

What am I going to do about the Bible? I can't go back for it. Maybe I can buy my sister a new one. How much does a Bible cost? Maybe Matt will post it to my mother's house. The wedding is on Sunday. How much does next-day delivery cost?

'Em?'

A hand takes my wrist and gently tugs me away from the crowd, which is growing thicker around me. I pull against it then realise who it is.

'Dante?'

My friend smiles and takes my suitcase for me.

'You look totally spaced out. You OK? What are you doing here?'

'Going home.'

I try to take the suitcase off him as he steers us into the shade.

'Hey,' Dante says, trying to catch my eye. 'You eaten?'

I shake my head. I gave him my lunch hours ago.

'Kate told me about your meeting with HR. Fucking Karen. Come back to the office, you can get out of your work clothes and drink some water.'

I sway a little and he steadies me.

'Em, you're going to pass out in this heat. Come on, I still have your baguette. You've got to eat.'

'I need to get to the airport,' I say. My voice is raspy, my tongue too big for my mouth. 'The Tubes and buses aren't running and . . .'

'I know,' he says, pulling up my suitcase handle with ease

and leading the way back to Swan & Swallow. 'Come on, I'll call you a cab from work.'

I fall into step beside him, Charing Cross falling away and the Strand nothing but a hazy grey blur ahead.

'Dante?' I say. His face is shiny from the heat, but it suits him. 'You sure they won't mind?'

He gives me a wry smile and shakes his head. 'Jesus, Em. Getting you back home is the least those bastards can do after the way they just treated you.'

I'm going home. My home. Always waiting for me with open arms and a clenched fist.

7

7

BBC Breaking News • @BBCBreaking

The female body of a 31-year-old lawyer, found
strangled to death near St Paul's Cathedral on
Wednesday, has been linked to Monday's St James's
Square murder and the drowning victim discovered last
night in the Thames. London police are urging the public
to remain vigilant.

I'm back in the big yellow chair in reception.

Kate has plugged in my phone to charge beside me and
got me a glass of cold water, and Dante has returned my
sandwich. He leans over Kate's desk, their faces inches
apart, her eyelashes brushing her cheeks. I nibble at the
crusty bread as I watch them flirt, but the sandwich has
formed a hard paste in my mouth and I can't swallow. All
I can do is scroll through my phone, checking transport
updates and flight information; calculating how many hours
I have left, even though there's plenty of time. I can't fuck
this up. This is my last chance.

Maybe I should text my sister, put her mind at rest, tell
her there's no problems this end. I don't. Instead, I continue

to scroll through Twitter. Everyone is posting about the same thing. Three dead girls in one week. All in central London. All found strangled with a blue stripy tie stuffed in their mouths.

The girl found in the Thames was initially presumed drowned until the autopsy report confirmed fabric fibres had been found in her mouth and the cause of death was strangulation. I'm sure the police wouldn't have investigated her death so thoroughly had another body not been found soon after. I wonder if three is the real number, or if there are bodies of other women scattered around the capital. Silenced. Waiting. Rotting away.

My hand is shaking as I bring the glass of water to my lips.

There's a montage: three photos of three smiling women. It's hard to imagine any of these happy people dead. Hanna Nilsson – we already know her: she was pretty, with long, chestnut hair and fair skin. But who are the other two?

Words will never hurt me • @Em_Dash_93
Say their names. Why is no one saying their names?

'Sorry about that,' Kate says, her Birkenstocks making a slapping sound as she rushes over. She squats beside me. 'I wanted to say hi properly, but today's been hectic. You know, SOM and all that.'

Oh yeah, the Stars of Marketing awards are tonight at The Savoy. How could I forget? It's all anyone has been talking about in the office lately. The hotel is opposite our building and Kate has booked all the directors a room there. Everyone is going to the big event. Well, all the account managers, designers, sales team and directors. Kate and Dante won't be there, even though she's done all the organising.

'I can't believe we've been nominated for the big one!' she squeals, grinning. She says it like it's *her* who will be thanked, like she's part of something grand and meaningful, instead of the awards being a mutual back-patting exercise.

'Sorry.' Her smile turns to one of apology. 'You're probably not in a very celebratory mood. Are you feeling better?'

I nod.

'You need to eat, Em,' Kate says, picking up the baguette from my lap. The bacon inside has gone brown and rubbery from the heat, the tomatoes flaccid and damp. I'm not hungry.

'Dante said you're locked out. Is that why you're heading to the airport early?'

I nod and breathe in deeply, the aircon hitting my lungs like ice. The sweat on my skin has dried so fast it's turned sticky.

'You should have called me,' Kate says. 'You could have hung out at my flat. Stratford is right next to the airport.'

I hadn't thought of that, although it's beside the point now there's a strike.

'The Tubes and buses are down,' I say, my voice raspy and low. 'And you may not even get home in time for me to give you back your keys. But thanks.'

Kate makes a face. 'I know. Nightmare. I called you a

cab and stuck it on the company account.' She lowers her voice and leans in. She smells of perfume and spearmint. 'Let them pay, eh?'

Yeah. Big revenge.

'So what's going on with you and Dante?' I ask.

Kate isn't the type to blush delicately; instead, she goes bright red. It never takes much, although this time even her chest has gone all motley.

'Do you think he likes me? He hasn't said anything.'

Dante is looking over his shoulder at us as he heads down the hallway. I know he likes her.

'He's a nice guy, Kate,' I say. 'And nice guys don't push. Tell him you like him.'

'He's going into a meeting,' she mumbles, her gaze following his retreating figure.

A few people from the sales team walk past me, heads huddled close, giving me surreptitious glances. Word will have got out that I was sacked. Is it being sacked if you don't get to stay after covering someone's maternity leave?

'I feel bad I didn't have a chance to say bye to everyone,' I say.

Kate shrugs. 'They all said it was outrageous they let you go, but you know what it's like.'

What what's like?

'I guess they have to give the job back to Abigail,' I say. 'When's she coming back from maternity leave?'

Kate adjusts her headset, fanning herself with her hand until her skin goes back to its usual pink. 'Oh, she's not. She resigned.'

I stand up too fast and Kate looks around nervously, like I'm about to start shouting. I don't.

'Can they do that? Can they sack and then replace me? I didn't do anything wrong!'

'They didn't sack you,' she says gently. 'You just weren't retained. I'm not saying it's right, but ... Hello, Swan & Swallow.'

Kate chirrups into her headset and I sit back down. The glass of water clinks against my teeth as I gulp down the last drop. They're interviewing people to do a job I did more than well just because Paul doesn't want me around any more. I wish Dante were still here. I need to talk to him. I need to hear him call them all cunts.

'That was your cab. It's a bit delayed,' Kate says. 'But you can stay here as long as you like.'

'No, you can't.' Caroline is standing beside the reception desk, hand on hip, the other hand holding an envelope. 'What are you doing here, Emily?'

That's not my name. She really doesn't know my name.

I look at Kate, but she's already scuttled back behind her desk.

'The Tubes and buses aren't running. I need to get to the airport.'

'And you're going to teleport from our office, are you?' Caroline asks, her lips curling in amusement. Her lipstick has worn off, leaving a faint line of orange. 'You know Swan & Swallow is out of bounds to anyone who isn't an employee or doesn't have an appointment with us.'

'I said she could rest for a bit while she waits for a cab,' Kate says.

'Did you now? And how are you getting on with tonight's guest list, seeing as no one can get in and out of London now?'

Kate keeps her head down and shuffles some papers behind her desk.

'I'm not hurting anyone, Caroline,' I say. 'I thought maybe I could use the loo and get out of these shoes.'

'Emily.' She walks over to me. 'I know it's all very embarrassing, but woman to woman . . .' She lowers her voice. 'Don't make this hard for yourself.'

Four people are looking over from their desks. I can see Paul through the glass of one of the meeting rooms. He's taken off his linen jacket, his light yellow FAMINIST T-shirt on full display. His arms are bronzed from his recent trip to Biarritz, the fabric stretching over his toned biceps. He catches my eye through the glass and rakes his fingers through his hair. A flicker of something crosses his face. Annoyance that I'm back, followed by the steely glare of someone who already knows they've won.

Caroline follows my gaze. 'I know you're angry.' Her voice has gone up an octave, the voice you use with a crying child. 'But this isn't the way. Don't embarrass yourself, Emily. You need to leave.'

I look over at the big-shot creative director again. The handsome, successful man with the beautiful children who will tell any woman in the office who'll listen that he's separated from his wife. Although by that he means he sleeps at the London flat during the week while she stays in whatever village they live in. I doubt his wife knows they're separated.

I liked Paul when I first started working at Swan & Swallow. He's one of those men who balances power with an air of nonchalance, the kind who actively listens and nods his head in all the right places. At first, I was flattered that someone as high up as him took an interest in me having started at the company. He was open, eager to know more about me, not at all intimidating. And he seemed genuinely passionate about women's rights, the environment and improving Britain's immigration policy. I probably shouldn't have told him how refreshing it was to hear a man say all the right things. I was only being polite.

He started wearing T-shirts emblazoned with strident slogans after I told him that.

I watch him as he scrolls from one slide to another. Can he feel my eyes upon him? Is that why the damp marks are growing under his arms?

If Caroline knew the full story, how all this started, would she have been more sympathetic? Or would she have still said it was my fault? Maybe it was.

We were in the Coal Hole, two weeks after I'd joined the company. It's a small pub on the Strand, dark and dingy, and never big enough to fit everyone who wants to drink there after work.

Paul liked to make a show of inviting everyone out on a Friday night; he said it was important to reward all our hard work. He thought he was bringing the team together, although the truth was most people went because they didn't have to pay.

The venue was chosen purely for practical reasons, as it was opposite the office. It certainly wasn't Paul's scene. With his organic cotton suits and suede loafers, he looked like he'd been superimposed at the bar. As if someone had cut him out of an article for a sustainable vineyard brochure promoting organic Pinot Noir from the Loire Valley. But Paul was good at faking it and making everyone feel like they were exactly where they were meant to be.

I was just happy to be there, my first after-work drink at a proper job. I was normally the faceless temp or serving behind the bar, not the one being handed a free, warm glass of Chardonnay.

'So you're Spanish?' Margery from Finance had asked.

'Yes,' I'd replied. 'And you? Where are you from?'

She'd frowned. 'Well, England of course.'

Kate had been sitting next to me, her perfume strong and her smile extra toothy. Because of her shift pattern, I hadn't spoken to her properly until now. She was already tipsy.

'I saw you talking to Paul,' she'd said. 'Don't.'

I'd only spoken to him a few times. He'd made a big deal of saying how important it was for me to feel part of the Swan & Swallow family, that he had big plans for me.

'He seems OK.'

She'd run the tip of her finger over a ring of water on the table, turning it into a sunshine.

'He can be a bit full on.'

She hadn't said the words. She'd stepped around them,

daintily, like she was avoiding puddles. I'd nodded. Five minutes later I was at the bar helping him carry some drinks and I got to find out what she really meant.

I look up, my baguette still in my lap, the office phone still ringing incessantly. Someone is standing next to me. A bright white shirt straining over a barrel frame.

Barry.

'Sorry, Em. But you have to leave.'

I look over at Kate, but she's deep into a call, her eyes wide and panicky. Caroline is leaning against her desk, a smirk flickering on her lips.

Swan & Swallow doesn't have security. Barry is the concierge; he takes parcels and signs people in. I guess he's the closest thing to a bouncer around here.

'Caroline, please. She's not hurting anyone,' Kate says.

'You know the rules. Only members of staff and approved visitors. It's a matter of client confidentiality.'

'Can I at least use the loo first?' I ask her.

She shakes her head. 'No. It's a security breach.'

'Are you fucking serious?' Caroline visibly flinches at my language. 'What do you think I'm going to do? Leak the latest *Love Island* celebrity endorsement campaign to the press?'

She gives Barry a pointed look that says 'See what happens when you're too soft on people?'

I really need a wee and I need to change my panty liner. This one is all bunched up and I'm due on soon. I go to unzip my suitcase, but Barry pulls the handle up without any trouble and wheels it away.

'Come on, love. You need to leave.'

'Five minutes.'

Caroline steps forward, her arms crossed so tight her bosoms are practically up around her throat.

'She needs to go *now*, Barry.' She turns her attention to me. 'I was very clear, three hours ago in my office, what our procedures are. Don't make a fuss, Emily. Don't make me call Management.'

'Management' means the CEO, Richard, who isn't in the office this week. So, who she really means is Paul, who's now watching our exchange through the tinted glass wall of the meeting room.

Don't make a fuss.

I get up, Kate giving me an apologetic look as she talks into her headset, and I follow Barry into the lift. He keeps his eyes on his shiny shoes, working his bottom lip between his teeth.

Don't make a fuss.

'I've ordered a cab,' I say. Barry nods slowly as the lift doors open. 'Can I wait in the lobby?'

'Sorry, love.' He pulls my suitcase behind him, opens the heavy glass doors and deposits us both back in the sun.

Don't make a fuss.

8

My shoulders sting from the sun and my cheap sunglasses are doing nothing against the glare. There's no shade here. The Strand is busy and thick with exhaust fumes, all cars and vans, but no buses. The heat has turned the air to treacle and even the traffic is struggling to wade through it.

I go to check the time on my phone. Shit. My phone.

'Barry!' I shout, banging on the glass door.

He gives me a 'come on now, give it a rest' look, and I bang harder.

'My phone is inside. It's plugged in, near reception.'

He shrugs in an exaggerated fashion.

Seriously? I can't do anything without my phone.

'Please!' I mouth through the glass.

Barry isn't a bad guy. He reminds me of my English grandad, my dad's dad, the one who died when I was eight. He has kind eyes, the watery kind, and a thick white moustache. What's he doing, working at his age? The expression on his face says he's thinking the exact same thing.

The lift behind him opens and I half expect Caroline to step out, arms crossed, thin lips pursed. But it's Dante, and he has my phone.

'Oh my God, thank you,' I gush, taking it off him. 'It feels like I've been waiting for ever out here.'

Dante tips his head to one side and gives me a long stare, his shoulders going up and down as he lets out a deep sigh.

'Karen's a cunt,' he says.

I laugh through my nose. 'Yeah, Caroline hates me.'

'She told Kate to cancel the cab, but when she called they said it's not coming anyway because . . .' His gaze goes from me to the busy road, hot metal and steaming tarmac making everything shimmer like I'm drunk. 'The roads are a mess, Em. Check it out.'

He nods at my phone, and I press the little blue bird.

BBC Breaking News • @BBCBreaking

Traffic nightmare: London grinds to a halt as London Transport unions walk away from Tubes and buses. People are strongly advised to keep away from central London today. Tailbacks reported to reach six miles in some areas.

I knew it was bad, but not this bad. I click on the image of the map showing disrupted routes in red. An abandoned bus in Tower Hill, issues at Limehouse and Piccadilly Circus. No wonder the cab driver refused to come here.

'How will you get home?' I ask Dante.

'I have my bicycle. Although they're saying the Tubes might go back to normal once it cools down tonight, like nine o'clock or something, so I might hang out with Kate for a bit after work. You know, make sure she gets home OK.'

He shuffles his feet and I try not to grin.

'That's great. Although my flight's at nine fifteen, so I can't wait for the sun to go down.'

'What are you gonna do?'

I look at Google Maps again. Eight point four miles. It's just gone 2 p.m. I have lots of time to think of something.

Dante is looking at my phone over my shoulder. 'I thought the airport was further away than that. You can walk it.'

I look at him like he's crazy and he bumps his shoulder against mine.

'Come on, Em. Says on here it takes two hours and forty-eight minutes to walk.'

Walk. Ha. Dante, with his thick arms and strong legs.

'You run marathons. I don't even run for the ice-cream van,' I say. 'Anyway, it's too hot and I'll get lost.'

'That's what Google Maps is for. You should have enough battery if you only turn 4G on to check your route.'

We both stand there, staring at my screen, the sun glaring off my phone, which is growing hot in my hand. My stomach gives a painful twist, and I don't know if it's hunger, stress, my period about to start or the fact that I really need to pee. If I can just get to the airport, I can sort myself out.

'Fine. I'll walk it,' I say. 'Not like I have much of a choice.'

Dante rubs his face, his palms coming away glistening.

'Man, I dunno, you're probably right. It's mad hot today. Dragging that suitcase about for hours is going to be tough. Maybe you should go chill in a café until your dickhead flatmate gets home, tell him to fuck off and change your flight to tomorrow.'

I talk about Matt to Dante. A lot.

He has a point. Maybe I *do* have another option. Maybe Rebecca isn't coming this weekend. Matt said he was meeting her at Euston station – he always pays for her train fare. But even with the trains cancelled, if she gets a flight the traffic will still be bad, so she may decide it's not worth the trouble. Maybe I can stay at home tonight after all and leave tomorrow.

I turn away from Dante and check Rebecca's Twitter.

Teachers rock! • @RebeccaMcGuire

So lucky I was already at a conference in London today because things are craaazy here right now. Can't wait to see my gorgeous man tonight. He says he has a surprise for me!

Bollocks.

'I can't miss my flight.' My throat is closing up and I blink three times until I can see again. 'It's my sister's wedding on Sunday and my mum, she's not . . . I haven't seen them in three years. I have to go.'

'Yeah. You do.'

I pull my handbag over my sore shoulder and rattle the handle of my luggage until it slides up.

'Wait!' he shouts, holding up a finger. 'One minute, yeah?'

He runs back inside, then reappears, holding up a bottle of water and some biscuits. 'For the journey, Frodo.'

I shove his shoulder again and laugh. 'Fool.'

'You know you're gonna miss me.'

I am.

'Look after Kate while I'm away,' I say. 'You two are the only friends I have.'

Dante presses his lips together. 'She says you have to text her when you get to the airport. You know, all that nastiness on the news about them girls?'

The girls. I'd forgotten about the dead girls.

'I'll be fine.'

'I know you will.'

Dante was right about the heat making everything harder. Within fifteen minutes my arm already aches and I've only got as far as Fleet Street. My mouth is dry and it aches to swallow, but I also really need to piss – which means I can't decide whether to drink my water or not. With every step my luggage grows heavier.

I look at my phone, now permanently welded to my hand.

2.37 p.m.

40°C.

41 per cent battery.

It's fine. I can do this. It's just a few hours out of my life. It's not like I have a choice.

The pavements are empty, but the road is full. Everyone's honking their horns, vans and cars so pressed up against one another even motorbikes and delivery scooters are struggling to squeeze through the traffic. One biker races along the pavement, but the girl he nearly runs into doesn't shout – she just leans against the wall of the bank and squeezes her eyes shut. I watch her as her chest rises and falls, the thin cotton of her white T-shirt transparent below her breasts where the sweat has soaked through. Her hair is dark and short, shaved on one side, with blonde tips.

I think of Nikki.

Is she working right now? This is the worst weather for flowers. Is she delivering bouquets to brides in this heat? Did she get around to getting the van's aircon fixed?

I grip my phone tighter, imagining what it would feel like to call her, to hear her voice. I want to hear her say my name one more time.

That day in her shop, when she asked me to buy her a drink instead of paying for the flowers, that day changed my life. I didn't know you could talk to someone like that – without stopping, or without saying anything at all.

She asked me about living in Ronda and Málaga, and at first I told her what everyone likes to hear. Yeah, the south of Spain is pretty. Yeah, loads of history and good food. Yeah, it gets really hot in Andalucía.

That's enough for most people. They like to feel they've asked the right questions, but they don't really want lots of information, just a summary. The abridged version.

But not Nikki. She swirled the whisky in her glass, the ice long melted, and looked at me with eyes that were neither blue nor green nor grey. She looked directly at me when I spoke – and even when I didn't speak. During the lulls in conversation, it was as if she was listening to my thoughts.

She didn't rush to fill the silence, she just kept swirling the drink in her glass, waiting.

'Do you miss home?' she asked.

I'd only been in London a few weeks at that point. What was there to miss? It still felt like I was on holiday. I had enough money in the bank to last me a month, maybe six weeks, although I'd already started enquiring about bar work and creating my website for freelance design work. I'd found a room in a house with a woman called Janet who had a teenage son at uni so was renting out his room for some extra money. I never did find out if he knew that some strange woman was sleeping in his single bed, beneath his geometric duvet cover and posters of footballers she didn't recognise.

'Yeah, I miss home sometimes,' I said.

'What do you miss?'

When I'm on the Tube and no one is talking. When I'm in the supermarket and none of my favourite food is there. When I'm lying in a boy's bed, in a house that smells of vanilla candles and pizza, and outside all I hear is wind and rain, instead of dogs barking and the whine of scooters.

'I miss the views,' I said. When I looked out of the window of my London rented room there was no undulating horizon made of misty mountaintops, it was just different-coloured wheelie bins, hedges and parked cars.

'You don't miss your family though,' Nikki said.

Just like that. Not a question, no judgement.

'How do you know?'

Her eyes crinkled at the corners. I soon learned it meant she was secretly smiling at me. 'You never mention them.'

'I only met you an hour ago.'

'That's long enough.'

But what about her? An hour together and all I knew was her name.

'Your turn,' I said. 'Tell me about yourself.'

'I'm boring,' she replied. Yet she wasn't. Every time I looked at her, I saw something new. 'Born here, studied here, set up my business here. Only child, raised by my mum after my dad died. She moved to Bristol thirteen years ago when she married Terry. They met on a Facebook group for miniature-village enthusiasts.'

'You're winding me up.'

Nikki smiled, a proper smile. 'OK, not the miniature-village part, but they did meet on Facebook. She's happy. Terry owns a newsagents', they spend their weekends in a caravan by the sea. Things were a bit rocky between Mum and me for a while, after I came out at eighteen and she moved away, but we're OK now. I visit her every couple of months.'

I glanced at her hand on the table. I wanted to ask about her dad – it was always the first thing I wanted to ask every woman I met, needing to know if my own father had been normal, if perhaps I'd been unrealistic in my expectations. I wanted to ask about her tattoo, the semicolon on her wrist, and if it meant what I thought it did. If it meant what mine does. I didn't know about the king of lions then.

Her fingers brushed over mine as I took a sip of my wine. I lowered the glass, placed it on the table, and she took my hand in hers, her thumb stroking over the inside of my wrist. My own mark.

I held my breath.

'I was in therapy for a long time. Trust issues. Being rejected by your only family member as a teenager can mess with your self-esteem, you know. But I'm all right.' She gave me a shaky smile and a wink. 'I mean, it gets dark now and then, but I'm getting better at finding the light.'

I closed my eyes at the touch of her skin on mine.

'Tell me *your* story,' she said, pulling me gently by the wrist so we were inches apart across the small table. 'What happened?'

I didn't want to tell her, so I kissed her.

9

Metro Newspaper • @Metro

Women in London have been warned not to travel alone at night. 'Three women have been murdered in central London this week. We believe they died at the hands of the same person,' Chief Commissioner of the Metropolitan Police warns.

My feet hurt.

Why didn't I change my shoes when I went back to the office? In fact, why did I even bother with this entire outfit, only to sit at my desk for an hour and then get fired?

I thought these wedge sandals were cute when I bought them. No thin stiletto heel to get caught in the cracks of the pavements or the grilles of the Tube station, nice open toe for summer, not too high. Except now they're rubbing raw against the back of my ankle and I've lost the feeling in most of my toes.

I have trainers in my suitcase. As soon as I find a shady spot, I'll stop and change.

My suitcase whirrs along the pavement. Each time it snags against a crack it yanks my arm back and the handle slides out. This is going to be the longest three hours of my life.

A trickle of sweat works its way down my temple and into my eye. I blink furiously. Fuck, that stings. I want to rub it, but it will only smudge my makeup, which will make my eyes sting more. I have makeup remover in my bag too. I can sort my makeup out when I change my shoes. With the knuckle of my right index finger, I wipe the smudged eyeliner as neatly as I can and keep going.

Ludgate Hill leads me to St Paul's Cathedral, each step making the church's roof climb higher, until it's looming before me. The sun bounces off the white exterior, its dome shining like a trophy, and I think of Paul and the awards ceremony tonight.

Saint Paul. Does every man think he's beyond reproach? Like he deserves a medal just for being himself?

That night in the Coal Hole, Paul bought us all drinks and told me how happy he was that I was working at the company.

'It's refreshing to have young blood like yours in the business,' he said.

Like mine?

He glanced at my cleavage when he thought I wasn't looking. I pretended not to see, to save him the embarrassment

'I'm not that young,' I replied with a giggle that came out of nowhere.

I helped him carry the drinks to the table. The bar was

busy, and he was shuffling so close behind me I could feel his chest against my back.

Kate saw me and whisked the drinks out of my hand, telling me to sit beside her on the bench. There was no room for Paul.

'Budge up,' he said, squeezing in next to me.

His leg pressed against mine, saying something about how our team felt like a family.

'This is special,' he said, gesturing around the table. 'Life is not measured by the number of breaths you take but by the moments that take your breath away.'

'Maya Angelou,' I said quietly.

His eyes lit up. 'Yes, indeed. A woman who truly understood our struggles.'

Our?

Kate made a face and I took a sip of my wine to hide my smirk. I'd found it funny. He was only trying to be inspiring, fun, bring us all together. I was sure he meant well. Back then, I thought I could tell simply by looking at a man's face which ones were trouble and which ones were just . . . misguided. Paul didn't scare me.

My feet throb as I get closer to St Paul's. I can't take it any more; I have to get out of these fucking shoes before the back of my ankle is cut to ribbons.

There's an archway with the words 'Ludgate Square' printed above it. It's a small side street leading to offices or houses or something. I don't care. I just need to get in the shade. My stomach is aching from my need to pee and I'm desperate to drink something.

Stepping into the shadows, I crouch down beside my suitcase and pull the zipper around.

'You all right there, love?'

A man wearing a dusty T-shirt and khaki shorts with more pockets than anyone will ever need stops beside me. He's holding a paper bag from the sandwich shop next door.

'I'm fine,' I say, rummaging through my clothes for my trainers. I'm conscious that he can see the bra I threw into my suitcase last minute, and my box of Tampax.

'Cheer up,' he says, beaming down at me. 'It might never happen.'

It already has.

I zip up my bag and stand. Then I smile at him. I actually smile. I don't know this man, I don't want to get to know this man, but I smile at him because he wants me to. Because he's having a nice day and the sun is out and he's about to enjoy his chicken-mayo sandwich and a woman he doesn't know looks grumpy and the world would be a much better place if only she'd look happy to see him.

'You on holiday?' he says, nodding at the suitcase that is now upright and beside me.

'No, I live here,' I say, telling a stranger my business.

'You don't sound English.'

'I'm Spanish,' I reply, sharing more personal information.

'Ah, I love Spain. I go to Alicante every year. El Campello,' he says, pronouncing it *pelo*, like 'hair'. 'Lovely beaches. You been?'

'I have to get going,' I say, glancing at my wrist as if I have a watch on, even though I've not worn a watch in years.

He doesn't notice.

'Here, maybe you can teach me some words. All I know is "*Dos cervezas, por favor.*" Go on, how do you say "You're very pretty"?'

'*Vete a la mierda.*'

He repeats it slowly, looking at me earnestly like I should pat him on the back for a job well done.

'I have to go,' I say, looking at my imaginary watch again. Smiling again. Walking away slowly, my feet throbbing, my bladder bursting.

The man waves as he crosses the road, as if we've known each other for ever, and I quicken my steps.

'You should smile more!' he shouts out. 'It suits you.'

Ludgate Hill is rammed with cars and vans, but this time there are people in hi-vis vests in the road directing the traffic. I take my sunglasses off and squint into the distance.

St Paul's and its grounds are beautiful. I've been meaning to visit since I arrived in London over three years ago. Nikki said we'd go one day, that she'd take me to the very top and show me the whole of London, that we could add our names to the millions of names scratched and scrawled into the stonework.

'My mother would kill me if she thought I'd defaced a church,' I'd said.

'St Paul's isn't Catholic,' Nikki had replied, showing me that dimple in her cheek again. 'The Anglican God is way more forgiving.'

I'd laughed because it was a stupid conversation, and because I knew we'd never end up going. The same as we never made it to the London Eye, to the Tate Modern, or seen the giant dinosaur skeleton at the Natural History Museum. Our trip to Covent Garden and my introduction to Mufasa had been an anomaly. Nikki had one day off a week, Sunday, and we liked to spend it together, sleeping and eating and fucking.

Something yellow flickers in my peripheral vision and I realise what I'm looking at. It's the same thing I saw at St James's Square this morning.

I slow down, along with everyone crawling past in their cars and craning their necks out of their windows. This is where the third girl was murdered. The one found near the gravestones, by the steps, thrown into the dry undergrowth.

I don't care if the god who lives here is Catholic or Anglican. Who kills in his house?

'Awful, eh?' says a woman next to me. Her hair is scraped back in a bun and she's wearing a light cotton dress and flip-flops.

'She was a lawyer, you know,' she says. 'I heard about it on the radio earlier. Farah something. Can't remember the surname, foreign, but I thought of Farah Fawcett when I heard her name. First that pretty one got herself killed. You know, the rich one from Switzerland or whatever. Funny, I expected her to be blonde when I heard where she was from, but she wasn't, she had all that long dark hair right down to her bum. Bit like yours, actually. What was her name again?'

Hanna Nilsson. Her name was Hanna Nilsson.

'Then that one what drowned. God, imagine finding that, eh? Poor love. No idea what her name was.'

Jennifer Buchanan.

'Then this one. Farah whatsit.'

Farah Mitri.

'Bloody awful. I keep thinking of my own daughters. You can't look away though, eh? I've been here fifteen minutes already, watching the police and all sorts come and go. I think that lot are reporters,' she says, pointing at a woman talking into a camera and a couple of men taking photos. 'Good God, I can't get my head around it. All of them young, too. Late twenties and early thirties, same age as my own girls. Not connected, you know, well . . . I mean, they weren't known to one another. But all killed in the same way. Bloody awful. Mind you, what was that Farah girl doing, walking around on her own near them gravestones?'

Working? Socialising? Living? Trying to.

I don't say anything. I don't think this woman needs me to.

'Innit hot, eh?' Her dress is tight and white with tiny printed flowers. I can see the line of her underwear and every curve of her body. She pulls the fabric away from her ample chest and fans herself with her hand. 'I've been at work all morning. Bloody nightmare to get home today, but my Derek is picking me up. I should have told him to meet me at Blackfriars. Probably less busy there. I forgot about all this murder stuff. You got a light?'

I shake my head as she feels about inside her bag.

'Why don't they make dresses with pockets, eh? Deep

pockets, not them bloody fake ones what you get with your jeans. Bloody impossible to find a lighter in your handbag. Anyway, nice talking to you. You look after yourself, eh?' she says.

Her gaze settles on the top button of my shirt. 'I weren't gonna say nothing, but . . . girls like you in this heat, walking about without covering up. You gotta be careful.'

I nod and walk away, past the reporters and the police vans and the yellow plastic tape that doesn't move in the thick, still air. My head is beginning to throb from dehydration and a desperate need to piss. I can feel my thighs dampening with every step, the tops of my legs sliding with sweat and sticking to one another. I hope it's sweat and not blood.

My pounding head competes with my aching feet and stomach. But I can't stop here.

I glance at my phone to check the time but get distracted by a text message from Kate.

Are you OK? If you get any weird messages from people at work, ignore them. Not everyone believes the shit Paul is saying about you.

What's he saying? That I got sacked because I was a stalker? That I was obsessed with him? What bunny-boiling crap has he been making up to cover his tracks?

I don't reply. I can't think about that right now. I've been walking for half an hour already. Thirty minutes more and I'll be at Whitechapel.

There should be less commotion there, less tourism. Less murder.

10

I'm lost. I'm not sure how it happened. One minute my phone had 37 per cent battery, and the next, it's dead. I should have listened to Dante and not drained it by checking Twitter. I know, when I get to Whitechapel, I'm meant to head through Shadwell, then Limehouse and Poplar, and then towards the Excel Centre. But I don't know east London; I've never been to any of these places. I can't even check to see how much time I have spare to charge my phone.

Also, if I don't piss soon, I'm going to wet myself.

I look around, attempting to get my bearings. Every place has looked the same for the last ten minutes. I turn into a narrow street with a Turkish restaurant on the corner and a fish-and-chip shop opposite. Both are shut. This heatwave is meant to last a few more days so a lot of people are refusing to go to work – especially kitchen staff. I doubt anyone wants to eat fish and chips in this weather anyway.

I walk further down, past shops with graffitied shutters pulled down and boarded-up windows. Money transfer, fried chicken, mobile phones, an off licence with a metal grille at the window. A few metres ahead is a small, tired café with a table and two chairs outside. I enter. The girl behind the counter is wearing a hair net and a dirty apron. She looks up from her phone.

'Can I use the toilet, please?' I ask.

'We don't have one.'

'You must do. It's an emergency.'

'Only for customers.'

I order a tea, the cheapest thing on the handwritten board behind her, and go to pay with my Visa.

'We don't accept cards for under a fiver,' she says, her fingers a blur as she continues to type on her phone.

'I don't have any cash.'

She puts the teacup to one side and I tell her I'll be back in a minute. But I won't. I haven't seen a cashpoint in ages and I'm not taking £10 out of the bank for a £1.75 tea I don't even want.

More fast-food joints, more boarded-up shops, a gate leading to a car park full of identical white vans. Finally, I see a pub. Actually, what I see are twenty-odd people standing on the street corner of Brick Lane holding gleaming pints of beer and glasses of Pimms. Maybe I can charge my phone inside and use the loo.

I push my way inside, but I can't see a toilet.

'What can I get you?' the guy behind the bar asks.

'I need to use the loo first.'

My thighs are damp, and I can feel my panty liner threatening to slip down my leg.

'The women's loo is out of order,' he says. 'Can I get you a drink?'

'Four pints of Guinness and a vodka and coke,' the man beside me says, sliding my suitcase back and taking my place at the bar.

The barman gets to work, and I stand there, like a ghost. What if I just piss on the swirly brown carpet. Would they even notice? What if I scream?

Two pints of dark brown stout are placed in front of me, their heads white and frothy. I can practically taste it. I really need to drink something, but not while my bladder is threatening to burst.

The sign for the men's toilet says it's down some steps and past the kitchen. No one will know if I quickly use it.

Hauling my case down the steep stairs, using both hands and unable to hold the handrail, I reach the bottom, push open the grimy door and step inside. It stinks. The cubicle is empty but there's a man at one of the urinals. He turns and grins at me.

'Don't mind me,' he says, wiggling his eyebrows, dick in his hand, a steady stream of urine splashing against the porcelain.

I mumble an apology and back out, dragging my case back up the stairs.

'Want a hand with that?' he says, jogging up behind me. I pretend not to have heard him and speed up, my shoulder aching with the effort.

Back at the bar, I stand beside the guy waiting for his order, as if we're together, and the man from the toilet goes outside. I'll just have to hold it in a little longer. I need to stay here and charge my phone; even 20 per cent is enough to get me somewhere decent with a toilet. I can charge it properly at the airport.

I feel around inside my bag for my charger, the easiest thing to locate in this sack of a bag as everything normally gets tangled up in the cord. But it's not in there.

Then I remember Dante handing me back my phone, but not the charger. It's still plugged into the wall of reception in Swan & Swallow.

I push my damp hair back off my face and shout 'Fuck!' out loud, earning me a look of disapproval from the man beside me attempting to balance all his drinks on a black plastic tray.

Back outside, the heat has grown more cloying, like sweaty hands grasping at me. My hair is plastered to the back of my neck, a thick cape covering my shoulders. I should have asked the barman for an elastic band. If I could just stop somewhere long enough to open my suitcase, I could get a scrunchie out of my makeup bag.

'All right?'

Two men are leaning against the pub wall. One of them is smoking; the other is the man from the toilet.

'Told you she was eager,' he says to his friend. 'I'm not interested, sweetheart. Leave me alone.' They both laugh.

'What's the time?' I ask the one smoking.

He looks at his watch. 'Nearly three.'

I still have six hours. Four and a half, if I factor in an hour or so to check in and find my gate. City's not a big airport. I'm about two hours away.

I think of my mother at home right now, looking at the

kitchen clock, counting the hours, like I am. I wonder what she's saying to my sister. Do they think I'm going to let them down again? I'm not. I *will* get home, whatever it takes.

'You know I was only joking, right?' Pissing Man says.

I smile, so he feels better about himself, and walk back down the way I came, back towards what I hope is the direction of Shadwell. The air is thick with the smell of doner meat and weed. A child, mouth sticky with ice-lolly juice, runs past me, chased by a mother pushing a buggy containing bare feet and a sun hat. There's no traffic here. The only people I can see are either outside the pubs or going in and out of the bookies. Where is everyone? Are they staying at home? Or in their air-conditioned offices? I think of Matt, and Kate, and Dante. Are they thinking of me?

To my left is a kebab shop, and next to it is a piece of empty land where a building has been knocked down, hidden from view by some wobbly boarding. Someone has spray-painted the words 'BEST KEBAB' on the side with an arrow pointing to a dirty window. Inside a man is slicing through a giant skewer of meat, wiping his brow with the same cloth he just used to clean the counter.

I push against the graffitied plywood. A piece of the board is missing, and behind it I can see a patch of waste ground littered with empty beer cans on scorched grass. I squeeze in through the gap, pulling my suitcase behind me, and step over the translucent skin of a used condom. I look around me. There are no cameras, just rusty stairs leading into the shadows and thirty square metres of rubbish.

Finding a spot near the fire escape, away from the glare of the sun, I lay my suitcase down and open the lid. I pull one of my trainers out, then rummage around for the other, which is tucked neatly into the side. I should probably wear socks too. It's too hot for socks, but the backs of my ankles are already red raw and one is bleeding a little. I don't need my trainers to rub too.

I ease my shoes off, sighing out loud with the sweet release of freeing my swollen feet, and wiggle my numb toes. I know I didn't pack any plasters, so I don't bother looking for them. If I pass a chemist later, I'll get some.

Slipping my socks on, then my trainers, I groan at the soft, springy sensation of shoes I can actually walk in. I contemplate leaving my heels behind but realise I don't have any other nice shoes for the wedding on Sunday – more pain to look forward to. It takes some manoeuvring, but I manage to squeeze them back into my bag.

Inside my toiletry bag is a scrunchie, which I use to pull my hair into a tight ponytail, and a pack of makeup-remover wipes. I carefully run one below each eye, then wipe the back of my neck and my sticky hands with them. With one last look behind me, I pull down my knickers and piss on to the dry grass with a satisfying groan.

Oh my God. I close my eyes and lean against the wobbly wall as I empty my bladder. At the same time, I search inside my handbag. I add my empty water bottle to the rubbish at my feet and take out the full bottle I've been carrying around for half an hour. It's no longer cold, but it's not too warm either. I take a large gulp, sighing as it fills my stomach. I splash my hands with it; I even pour a little on my head. My thighs are already aching from squatting, but I feel a million times better. I look down, watching the rivulets of urine and water snake their way around the discarded litter, the cracked earth sucking at it hungrily, then I notice my underwear.

Fuck.

No.

I've started my period.

My knickers are soaked in blood. They're beyond saving and my panty liner fell out as soon as I started to pee. I pull my skirt up higher and peer down. My thighs are stained red too. Fucking fuck. I stand up a little, kick my knickers off then use them to wipe myself, screw them up in a ball and pull another makeup-removal wipe from the packet. I pour water on it and use it to clean myself up, then wrap my underwear in it. I don't feel happy that I'm adding to the mess on this forgotten patch of grass, but neither do I have much choice.

I can't believe, just a few hours ago, I was at work, excited to hear that I'd be a full-time member of the prestigious Swan & Swallow agency, hours away from seeing my family and getting to finally be the woman they already thought I was – and now I'm lost somewhere in east London, no knickers on, blood all over my thighs, squatting in a puddle of my own piss.

I swear under my breath again. At least I have tampons in my suitcase and spare underwear. It could be worse. I add the applicator to the used wet wipes and soiled underwear on the ground and hunt around the many pockets of my luggage for a clean pair of knickers – but all I can find are socks, a bikini and my headphones, which are wrapped around something shiny.

I put them to one side while I locate a black pair of knickers, wriggle into them and straighten my skirt. Then I pick up my headphones and untangle them from the large silver object.

It's my keyring ... and my keys. My housekeys were in my suitcase all along.

'Are you fucking kidding me?' I shout out loud. 'Fuck, fuck, fuck!'

I let out a scream, no longer caring if anyone's walking past on the other side of the partition. I can't believe, after the hell I've been through already, that I could have got into my flat, had a shower and put some decent clothes on if I'd *just looked inside my fucking suitcase*.

I give a frustrated cry as I ram my keys into my handbag and zip up my suitcase, once again struggling to pull the handle up fully.

'That's quite a show you're putting on,' says a voice from the shadowy staircase.

A woman in a short black dress with a plunging neckline is leaning over the rails of the fire escape above my head. She steps into the sunlight, flicks her cigarette butt in my direction and descends.

11

I really don't need this right now.

The handle of my suitcase won't budge as I attempt to pull it up. I yank at it again, each pull in time with each step the woman takes down the stairs, until finally the handle comes away in my hands, the tips of the spokes sharp and dangerous. She's walking towards me now, but I can't get the tubes of the handle back into the holes. Fucking hell. She's going to ask for money or start talking about Jesus.

Why won't this handle go in?

In a matter of seconds, she's standing in front of me, watching me struggle with my luggage. Her hair is big, her lipstick a deep shade of maroon, the hoops in her ears so large they nearly graze her shoulders.

She makes a lunge for my suitcase.

'There's nothing valuable in it,' I say, jumping back. 'I don't have any money on me. Please, I just need to get to the airport.'

She looks up, the silver cross around her neck catching the light of the sun.

'You thick or something? I'm trying to help you.'

Effortlessly, in one swift movement, she slides the handle

back into the hole and clicks it into place until, although not fully extended, it stays put.

'There. Fixed it. So what was all that about, back there? You don't look like a skaghead.'

I duck through the hole in the wall and manoeuvre my bag through it, but she follows.

'Oh, you're ignoring me? You piss in the street, leave your bloody knickers next to all that rubbish, I help you with your luggage, and now *you're* ignoring *me*?'

I take a deep breath. It doesn't help. The heat of the air is stifling and dry, and I've already used up my only bottle of water. At least my feet and stomach are no longer aching. Each step in my trainers is like walking on a trampoline. Can't believe I waited this long to change my shoes.

I'm able to move a lot faster now, so I do. Yet the woman keeps walking behind me, the clip-clop of her boots beating a rhythm on the cracked paving stones. How is she able to keep up in such high heels?

'Why are you following me?' I shout out over my shoulder.

I don't even know where I'm going. Last time I looked at the map, it seemed pretty easy, one straight road from Whitechapel through Limehouse to Poplar before it got a bit complicated as you near the docks. One road. Except I veered off it to see if the pub had a toilet, and now I'm not sure if I'm going in the right direction or heading back west again.

The pavement is empty, no mums or drinkers, no one who can help me find my way. As if anyone could, anyway. It's not like I can ask a random stranger how to get to the airport on foot. Who walks to an airport?

The woman is still behind me. I can hear the flicker of her lighter and a soft laugh as I take a surreptitious glance back. At the main road I'm forced to stop. It's a crossroads. There's a sign for the Royal London Hospital pointing left, and Aldgate East station in the distance to my right. I passed the station half an hour ago, which means I need to go straight ahead if I want to reach the main road. But without Google Maps and a charged battery, I can't be certain.

I use the back of my hand to wipe my brow, my under-arms stinging where my shirt has been rubbing all day.

'You lost?'

The woman's beside me now. She takes a long drag on her cigarette and looks me up and down.

'Please, leave me alone. I have a flight to catch, and I've had a hard day. I don't want any trouble.'

'You saying I look like trouble?'

'No.'

Yes.

'I'm walking the same way as you.'

'What?'

She nods at my suitcase, then pulls something out of her handbag. It's a phone, a Samsung like mine. She holds it up to me. Google Maps is open.

'I live in Canning Town. It's not far from the airport. I went out last night with some mates, met some bloke and woke up fuck knows where.' She yawns, then holds her head like even that hurts. 'Anyway, public transport is fucked, so we are too.' She takes another long drag on her cigarette and blows it up to the cloudless sky. 'Fuck me, this is going to be the longest walk of shame in history.'

I look down at her feet, at her red leather boots with their spiked heels and her short tight dress, and I wonder if she's as uncomfortable as I am.

'Why are you looking at me like that? You think I'm lying? You think I want to mug you for your broken suitcase? Listen, we're walking in the same direction, and you look lost. Do what you want, but just know I'm not following you.'

She glances at her phone, crosses the road and disappears behind a stationary bus. Fine. If she'd wanted to steal from me, she could have punched me in the face and taken my bag when I was crouched on the ground cleaning blood from my thighs. But that doesn't explain why she was lurking in the shadows of a fire escape, watching me.

I can see her big hair bobbing up and down in the distance as she marches ahead of me, phone in one hand, cigarette in the other. I have no idea how she can walk so fast in those boots. Her feet must be killing her.

My suitcase whirrs behind me as I trail her, the handle no longer wobbling. I'll just keep her in sight until I figure out where I am.

A minute or two passes, me watching the woman, the woman completely unaware I'm following her, when the soft thud of footsteps behind me makes the hairs on the back of my neck stand on end. Someone is breathing heavily. I want to turn around and look, but I don't want to appear paranoid. I keep walking, but whoever it is remains on my heels, each step heavy and each breath laboured. I speed up, but they haven't taken the hint.

Why is he walking so close to me? I asked the red-booted woman why she was following me, but this is different. This is a man.

I look up. Now I've lost sight of the woman, the one who knows where she's going. Shit! I wait until the road is clear then cross to the other side, taking a subtle glance over my shoulder. Everything about the guy behind me is bigger than it should be – his neck, his arms, his workman's boots. He catches me looking, our eyes locking; he smiles and I look away.

He can see I'm walking faster – why doesn't he stop or cross over? Surely if a man senses a woman is nervous, he'll back off? Or is he enjoying the control? The power.

The man makes a sound like a chuckle, or maybe he's saying something. I'm not sure. I stumble as I mount the kerb. My suitcase is stuck, the wheels catching on the grooves of a drain.

The man stops and waits for a car to pass, looking like he's about to cross the road too. What was I thinking, brushing that woman off? Why would I think it's better to walk across London alone than stick with a woman who has a map?

I speed up, my shoulders tingling with the sensation of the stranger behind me again. Where the hell is she? I see a flash of red in the distance, her boots visible beneath a parked car.

'Hey!' I call out, running to keep up with her.

She doesn't turn around, but she does reply. 'Oh, *now* you're interested in talking to me?'

'Sorry.' I'm out of breath, my head swimming. 'You're right. I'm lost.'

I look behind me again. The man has gone.

'What do you want?' she says.

I remember the biscuits Dante gave me, wrapped in their individual foil packaging. I scramble through the contents of my bag, gritting my teeth as my fingers brush past my house keys, and pull one out.

I jog beside her, holding out the biscuit. 'Are you hungry?' It looks like the kind you get in a hotel, each one with a different picture on the front.

The woman doesn't slow down, but she takes it.

'They chocolate chip?' She rips at the packaging with her teeth and pulls out the biscuit. 'Raisins? Why do they do that? Why do they make a biscuit that looks like it has chocolate in it and put fucking raisins inside? Who the fuck likes raisins?' She throws it to the ground.

I like raisins.

'Wait. Slow down a bit,' I say, reaching out for her arm.

She shrugs me off but stops. I rest both hands on my knees as I try to catch my breath.

'I really need to get to City Airport. Can I walk with you?'

Her face remains stony, her plum-stained lips two dark, straight lines. She turns her head to one side, her earrings swaying. Then she laughs, a loud bark of a laugh that makes me lean back.

'You look well stressed,' she says. 'What time's your flight?'

I tell her and she shrugs. 'You've got plenty of time. Chill and enjoy the scenery.'

She waves her hand about, and I laugh. This street is just like the last one: boarded-up shops, graffitied shutters, a derelict plot of land surrounded by building equipment. There's no sign of the man I just saw.

'Oh, look, you can crack a smile. Well, that's going to make our walk nicer. You got any more biscuits?'

I hunt through my handbag and pull out a shortbread and another raisin one. She takes the shortbread and eats it in two bites. I nibble at mine. I need to eat, but I'm already too hot and I'm so thirsty my throat is stinging. It makes me think of Paul, of what happened a few weeks ago. I bat the memory away and focus on what the woman beside me is saying.

'How come you're lost?' she asks.

'The battery on my phone ran out.'

'What phone you got?'

'Samsung.'

'So do I.' She reaches into her bag and holds up a tangle of wires. 'I don't go anywhere without back-up. You never know when you're going to meet some fit guy – who was a lousy shag, by the way – who then ghosts you, forcing you to find your own way home like some desperate fool.' She laughs again. 'Here, you can see if there's any juice left in this power-pack thingy too. If we pass a pub or something we can stop for a drink and you can charge it properly, yeah?'

She passes me a black square and I plug it into my phone. I smile and mumble a thank you.

'You don't say much, do you? I'm a talker, so you're going to have to get used to that. What's your name?'

I tell her and she laughs.

'That's a bit of a mouthful.'

'Most people call me Em.'

She shakes my hand with a firm grip. She's wearing a chunky gold sovereign ring, her red nail varnish chipped around the edges.

'I'm Rose.' Something in my chest jumps. Another flower. Rose grabs the handle of my suitcase and pulls it behind her. 'Come on then, Em. Let's get going. You can tell me your life story on the road.'

12

Rose's power pack was practically empty, but it's given me 12 per cent on my phone battery, which is enough to check my messages. There's a WhatsApp from Kate asking if I'm OK (I reply with a thumbs-up emoji) and one from my sister reminding me to bring the family Bible (too late for that).

Rose is on the phone. It looks like mine, except it's encrusted with diamantes. She holds it clamped between her ear and shoulder, a cigarette in one hand and my suitcase in the other.

A Twitter notification pops up and I take a quick look as Rose continues to speak in short sharp sentences, five steps ahead of me. I can't tell who she's talking to, but she keeps mentioning some guy called Olly.

The Sun • @theSun

Serial killer on the loose! The Metropolitan Police have confirmed that all three women murdered in London this week were killed by the same person. The public is urged to be vigilant. Will the London Strangler strike again?

The London Strangler. A shiver runs up my spine. Why do they do that? Why do they give violent men fun nicknames like they're comic-book villains?

'What you making that face for?' Rose says, dropping her phone into her bag.

I show her my screen and she rolls her eyes.

'Aren't you worried?' I ask her.

'Babe, if a man's going to get you, he's going to get you. You can't lock yourself away. My mates last night were being all para like you, when the first two women were found, and I was, like, "You think I'm staying home watching telly, missing out on a fun night, because some fucking perv is on the loose?" I don't think so.'

'But it's so terrible.'

'Of course it's fucking terrible.' She takes a new packet of Marlboro out of her bag and unravels the seal. 'But do you know how many women are killed in the UK every year by men? One every three days. And double that are dead men killed by other men – but for different reasons. So, basically, a lot of men are murderers.' The flicker of her lighter makes me jump. 'But do the newspapers report on *all* these dead men and women? No. Men killing other men isn't clickbait. And the other women? Well, some of them work on the streets, or have shit husbands, or got caught up with the wrong kind of guy through addiction or whatever. But *this*' – she jabs my phone – 'this is *exciting*. Serial killers are *sexy*. A lone man hunting random women, and no one knows why. People listen to podcasts about men like this and movies are made about them.

'And why are they so sexy? Because they have their fun little brand – killing the women in unusual ways, or they have some tragic backstory, or, like this one, who has a thing for long dark hair and stripy ties. Men like that sell newspapers because, unlike the other dead women, these victims were *nice* girls, the ones that society has decided don't deserve it. Aren't we all brought up to believe that good girls die last? That's what the horror movies tell us. These girls weren't asking for it, not like the stupid woman who stays with her violent husband or the crack whore wandering the streets half naked at night. Which means, with a serial killer, it could be any one of us. Even us nice girls. Ooooh, the thrill!'

She waves her arms up in the air, jazz hands, and rolls her eyes again. With exaggerated motions she takes a long drag on her cigarette and blows the smoke in my face.

'But the truth is, Em, it can *always* be any one of us, no matter what we look like or how well we live our lives. Wherever. Whenever.' She pushes my phone down so I can't read any more of the story. 'Don't feed into the frenzy.'

I put my phone in my bag. But Rose hasn't finished yet.

'You know what *really* fucks me off about serial killers?'

I'm guessing a lot of things fuck her off about serial killers.

'I hate the way everyone's surprised that so many of them are not-bad-looking. Why wouldn't they be attractive? Like, why are all the baddies in the Bond films ugly? What are we saying? Don't trust some bloke with a pock-marked face, but if he's handsome and evil he's still worth fucking? You see it in books too, everyone fawning over the villain just because he has floppy hair and a crooked smile.' She flicks her cigarette butt to the ground and grinds it beneath her boot. 'I don't know. I swear people think men kill women because these poor souls are unwanted, like they're all fucked-up incels who haven't found true love yet. Like we should give them all a charity shag and keep them sated. Truth is, hot guys are the worst kind, because we always make exceptions for them.'

Each word out of her mouth is like a bullet. I wonder if she's aiming at anyone in particular. She takes another deep breath.

'It's that Beauty and the Beast bullshit we're all fed as little girls, where it's down to us women to love the monster's badness away. Nah. Lots of men are cunts because they're cunts. They just are. They're even cunts to each other. Problem is, we can't tell which ones are good and which ones want to kill us. We're like a bunch of rabbits hopping about in a field, looking cute, trying to get on with our boring little lives, trying to forget we can't get mauled by a fox at any given moment.'

Rose sticks a piece of gum in her mouth and chews on it hard, pulling out her diamante-encrusted phone and jabbing at the keypad, her jaw working ferociously as she squints at the screen. Then, with eyes trained straight ahead, she continues marching on like we're on a mission. Like we can't slow down for anything or anyone.

I scurry behind her. Are women *really* little bunnies? I'm not a rabbit. I don't think I fear men. I certainly don't hate them. I want to tell Rose that, but she's walking too fast ahead of me and I know it won't come out right anyway.

The first person I ever fell for was a man. Actually, except for Nikki, he's the only other person I've ever said 'I love you' to. At least, I thought it was love, until I felt it for real.

Juan went to the same college as me. I was studying graphic design in Málaga and he was studying accounting. He said it was boring but it would get him a well-paid job. Juan thought small, every one of his dreams within easy reach. Perhaps that's why he was always so content with his lot. With me. With the life he'd dreamed for us.

From a young age I knew I was bisexual, but I didn't have a word for it. I reasoned that God couldn't punish me if I settled down with a decent man, and maybe – over time – the rest of my feelings would pass. So I focused on finding a man that was nothing like my father. And that's exactly what Juan was.

Skin full of sunshine, hair long enough to cover the tips of his ears and strong hands big enough to hold me up. I did love Juan – in the way you seek out any source of warmth when you're cold. He was kind, gentle, understanding and couldn't look any more Spanish. He was everything my father was not.

I tried so hard to be good to him, to ignore the curiosities bubbling up inside me – refusing to think about the things I might be missing out on. Juan really thought I'd given him my whole soul. He had no idea I'd kept the brightest part for myself.

But he was a good man, and over time he taught me

that my father was not what most men were like, making it increasingly hard for me to go back home to Ronda on weekends. My mother accepted my excuses because Juan was a nice boy, and nice girls marry nice boys, and that's all she ever wanted for me. My family wanted us to get married and Juan wanted us to get married, and with each year that passed my true self got buried deeper and deeper beneath their expectations.

No one understands that treading water can be more tiring than swimming. How sometimes you fantasise about stopping, imagining how peaceful it must be to just sink.

I tighten my ponytail and try to catch up with Rose. She's marching along as if my suitcase is hers and she's forgotten all about me.

What she said about men, it's not true. I still trust them. It's not like we have any other choice. Life would be unbearable if we thought every man we met was out to hurt us.

I think of Matt this morning. His bony back and messy hair. The way he smiled at me when I got in from work last night, and the way he ignored me when I woke up beside him. Rose would call him a cunt, but it's never that simple.

For the last ten weeks, I've been fucking a guy with a girlfriend. He's been with Rebecca for nearly five years. Does he love her? He tells me he does all the time. Sometimes he tells me before we have sex, like I'm a priest at confession, forgiving him for his sins. For the things he's about to do anyway.

He'll be stroking the inside of my thigh while saying how difficult it is that he doesn't get to see Becca very often.

He'll tell me how pretty she is, how pure (he actually says 'pure'), and how she'll never understand his needs like I do. And while he's saying these things he's kissing my neck, his hands climbing higher up my skirt, and I'm closing my eyes and thinking of Nikki. Then trying not to think of Nikki. We're both there, me and Matt, skin on skin, tongues intertwined, going through the motions. But he could be anyone. Anyone at all.

And then there was Paul. Paul is nothing like Matt, but then none of them are ever the same. If they were, we'd know what to look out for.

Maybe we're all born bad. Men and women.

Rose stops suddenly and I stumble into her.

'My head is killing me. I need water and some greasy chips.'

She keeps chewing, her eyes screwed up against the sun. Her shoulders are bare. I wonder if she has sunscreen on. I didn't pack any. My phone beeps. It's running out of battery already.

'I can't see anywhere to eat around here,' I say. 'Maybe there's a supermarket nearby.'

'No idea. Where the fuck are we, anyway?' She looks around, every action sharp, almost violent. She points at a street sign then glances at her phone. 'Sidney Street. OK, my phone says there's a pub on Jubilee Street.'

I screw up my face. 'I really don't want to hang around here.'

'What?' Rose puts her weight on one foot and leans back a little as she studies me, her earrings swinging in tandem.

'You need to charge your phone, right? It won't take long. We're not far from Limehouse station, which means we're just an hour and a half from the airport. You've got time.'

She hands me the charger and points at the now-empty power pack in my hand. I give it back to her. She's helped me get this far and I do need to charge my phone. Who am I to deny the woman some food?

Her strides quicken as she heads towards the pub in the distance, leaving my suitcase in the middle of the pavement. I grab it and trundle behind her, alternating hands, even though both arms are already aching equally. At least the handle is staying in place.

'You've hardly said two words since I found you pissing on the floor.' She spits her gum out and pulls me by the arm until I'm level with her. 'You do understand me, right? I mean, your name and accent and that. I wondered if maybe your English isn't that great and I'm jabbering on and you've no idea what I'm on about.'

'My English is fluent.'

She laughs again, a brittle cackle. 'Wish mine was.'

We slow down once we reach the pub. It's a Victorian building with peeling paintwork and a row of hanging baskets full of brown, crunchy foliage. There are two wooden tables outside. A family is sitting at one table in the shade, sharing a bag of crisps. Rose sits down at the empty one with an exaggerated noise. I join her.

'These fucking shoes.' She turns back to the family. 'Sorry. Potty mouth.'

The mother gives her a tight smile and tells the kids to

drink up. The dad mumbles that he hasn't finished his pint yet but downs it in one anyway.

Rose has taken her boots off and is massaging her bare feet. 'I'm all right dancing in them, you know. But walking's another thing.'

'I have some flip-flops in my suitcase,' I say quietly. 'If you want to borrow them.'

She gives a laugh through her nose and leans in closer.

'No, thanks. I've got some standards.'

I look up at the sound of laughter. A group of people about my age are huddled together by the entrance of the pub, all wearing vest tops and shorts. One of them has a red nose that's peeling, and each one of them has shoulders that are tinged pink. They don't seem to care that they're getting pissed in the direct glare of the scorching sun. I think of how badly their heads are going to hurt tomorrow.

The family beside us leaves and Rose takes their table in the shade. The empty pint of beer on the table is still cold to the touch. I watch the remnants of the white foam slide down the inside, making pretty patterns like lace. Suddenly the thought of sitting inside and having a drink while I rest my legs and charge my phone fully is the most enticing thing ever.

I look at my screen, the battery symbol flashing red. It's eighteen minutes past four. We're only ninety minutes away from the airport. I have time.

'Thanks for letting me use your charger,' I say.

Rose shrugs. 'Us girls got to stick together, right?'

13

I've decided to go to the toilet, even though I don't need to go, because I have someone to look after my suitcase now, and who knows when I'll get a chance to go again until I reach the airport?

I change my tampon and at the sink use the paper towels to apply cold water to the back of my neck and between my legs. My thighs sting and I can feel the skin is raised where the damp skin has been rubbing. I should have taken some shorts out of my case to change into. I'll do that before we leave.

The reflection in the mirror doesn't even look like me. My skin is glowing, but my eyes are dead. What did Nikki used to see when she kissed me minutes before we turned out the light at night? What does Matt see when he looks at me? And Paul? I know what he saw.

I run my little finger beneath each eye in a feeble attempt at tidying up my smudged eyeliner and shake my hair out. My scalp aches from how tightly I pulled it back before, but it's better than having it hanging around my shoulders. I feel a lot better already.

Stepping back into the cool of the air-conditioned pub makes me shiver, but I instantly feel cleaner.

Two men are standing at the bar, watching me make my way back to the table where Rose is waiting with two pints of icy water.

'You all right, love?' one of them calls out.

I nod.

He shakes his bottle of beer in the air. 'Fancy a drink?'

'My boyfriend is on his way,' I say, using the only line that ever works. The man turns back to his friend, as if we had never had an interaction.

When I get back to the table Rose mutters something along the lines of 'You took your time. I feel like shit,' and scurries off to the toilet, leaving me with the bags and my drink.

I take a long gulp of my water, lean back on the fake-leather banquette and pick up my phone. Instinctively, I click on the little blue bird icon first. I've had a few likes on my latest comment, and one comment telling me that it's because of women like me that men kill.

Today's trending hashtag is #LondonStrangler. I click on it.

Holly GoHeavily • @HollyHenderson92

> Anyone else worried about walking through London
> on their own right now? I'm 28 with long dark hair.
> It's freaking me out! #LondonStrangler

> **David Tibbit** • @cryptodave3333
> Replying to @HollyHenderson92
> Statistically it's no more unsafe than it was last year.

> **Jackie Silver • @JackieBWSilver**
>
> Replying to @cryptodave3333
>
> Women are being murdered by a serial killer and
> you're talking stats?
>
> **Sophie Owen • @sofowenfilm**
>
> I don't live in London but I still don't go out on my
> own at night.
>
> **Michael The Wolf • @wolfmanmickie**
>
> Not all men are murderers, you know!
>
> #LondonStrangler
>
> **NAFC • @34994FKU**
>
> Sun comes out. Women start dressing like slags.
> Then a couple get killed. Are you surprised?

I keep scrolling.

Everyone's talking about the murders – there are already London Strangler memes. The Met police have confirmed that the three victims were murdered by the same person but at different times of the day and night. They're urging all women in London's zones one and two to stay safe.

Stay safe. That's our advice. They don't say how, just to be 'vigilant'.

I glance over in the direction of the women's loo. Rose didn't look too great when she ran off; I can't think of anything worse than a hangover in this heat. Maybe we should have gone in there together, dragged my luggage down the stairs and waited outside the door for one another.

Is she safe down there alone? Am I safe sitting here? Are we any safer together?

A notification is flashing on my phone. Three missed calls from my sister. I call her back.

'*Hola*,' I say with a smile. When I worked at a call centre, I was told people can hear your smile on the phone. Marianna is definitely not smiling.

'Finally! Mum's flipping out.'

'Why?'

'My wedding. What else?'

What else. There's nothing else.

'What's the problem?' I say.

'She thinks you're not going to make it. You haven't replied to her voicemails.' There's a pause, then her voice softens. 'You're definitely coming, right?'

'Of course.' I wonder if she knows about the transport issues in London. I'm not going to tell her; it will only stress her further. 'I wouldn't miss your special day.'

'You missed Dad's funeral.'

Another arrow. They never miss.

'I'll be there.'

'Did Mum tell you about the necklace? And the Bible? And the watch idea?'

I play with my mother's necklace, moving the diamond from side to side.

'Yes.'

Marianna's voice relaxes a little. 'I can't believe I've not seen you in three years.' She hasn't once considered coming to visit me in London. Just like my mother, she acts as if I emigrated to the other side of the world and not somewhere you could get to with a ninety-euro EasyJet return. 'You haven't even met Alberto yet.'

Alberto is her fiancé. The groom. She's right, I've never spoken directly to him, but I know everything there is to know about Alberto Alvaro Huerta, because Marianna has updated me every day since the day she met him.

He's five years older than her, twenty-six, and works for his family business – something to do with fashion imports and exports. She met him at a fancy-dress party two years ago. He was dressed as a banana and she was dressed as a giant bunch of grapes. It was fate. He doesn't like her wearing her hair up because it makes her neck look too long. He loves dogs, hates cats. He has big plans to make enough money so she never has to work. He's addicted to coffee but hates coffee-flavoured desserts. He can't wait to have children. They have already picked out names – all of them strong, Catholic, Spanish names, of course. He likes DC comics but not Marvel. He's very romantic. When she asked him whether she was too young to get married he said no, he was claiming her before anyone else did. She giggled when she told me that part. He's a Pisces. Sensitive. She likes that.

'I'm looking forward to meeting him,' I say.

'I wish you were bringing Nick.'

Who? Oh. Right.

'About that . . . things aren't great between me and Nick.'

The line goes quiet.

'Hello? Marianna?'

She says my name softly, like a prayer. It's so strange to

hear anyone say my real name in full, let alone my younger sister, who's injecting it with so much disappointment.

'Again?' she says.

She makes it sound like I do these things on purpose. As if I enjoy smashing hearts and trampling over the broken pieces. If that's the case, then why do I feel like it's me who has shards embedded in her chest?

I don't know what to say, so I stay silent.

Marianna sighs. 'You know it took Juan years to get over you. He's coming to the wedding, by the way. Him, Elena, and the kids.'

Oh, yes. Juan and his wife who looks exactly like me, and their three gorgeous children just one year apart from one another. I look forward to that.

'What happened?' she asks. 'Nick sounded perfect for you, like he really loved you, like you had a future together. Mama and I really wanted to meet him.'

And Nikki really wanted to meet them.

'I don't know why you do this,' she says, so much pain dripping off every word. My mother has taught her well. 'You always push people away. Juan, Papa, us, Nick. Everyone who has ever loved you.'

'I have to go,' I say. 'I need to leave for the airport.'

'I'll see you soon. And don't forget the family Bible,' she says. 'And the necklace.'

I hang up, put my phone on the table and take a sip of my water. Did I, though? Did I push Nikki away?

Being with her was easy, so easy it felt dangerous. I didn't know relationships could be so ... pleasant. I thought it was a sign it wouldn't last.

My mother's favourite motto is 'Nothing worth having is easy.' She means that about everything – family, love, dreams. For a long time, I had no reason not to believe her.

After my first date with Nikki, and hanging out at hers all weekend, I went back to my teenage-boy bedroom, told Janet I was leaving and a week later was living with this beautiful, energetic, kind woman I'd only just met. It was as simple as that. She had a one-bedroom flat in Palmers Green, close to the train station. She used to drive to her shop in Enfield, said rent and business was better in the suburbs.

The day I moved in I stood in her living room with my purple suitcase and an old holdall, taking in all the details I hadn't noticed before. The first time I was there, all I'd looked at was her; now I could see her in everything she owned.

'Are these orchids fake?' I asked. She had them lined along the windowsill, purple and pink and white.

'I'm not home enough to look after real plants and flowers.'

She wrapped her arms around my waist, kissed my neck and told me how beautiful I was.

'I have my own flower now,' she said. She was talking about me, my name. I closed my eyes and sunk into her embrace. I'd come to London with no plan, hardly any money, and I didn't have a secure job yet. Neither had I spoken to my family properly since they'd told me my father had died. I had no friends and no idea what the hell I was doing with my life – but I had Nikki.

Nikki held me up, told me I was perfect in every way and that everything was going to be OK. I wanted to believe her so much it hurt.

'Are you sure I can crash here?' I asked.

She made a face. 'You're not crashing. You're moving in.'

'But isn't it too soon?'

'For what? For two people who like each other to share a bed, cook together, wake up on Sunday mornings in one another's arms?'

Her grip around me tightened, and I didn't pull away. I let her hold on, like I was sinking and she was stopping me from drowning. This was my new start. This was the reason I'd walked out of my parents' home in Ronda and never looked back. Nikki became my reason to stay in London and start again.

It was that easy.

Every day for two and a half years I waited for it to not be easy. I waited for words that really meant something else, for a look that told me she knew who and what I really was, for the night she refused to hold me. I waited, but that day never came.

Perhaps my mother had been wrong all this time. All great things didn't have to be difficult.

My favourite thing about living with Nikki was that life was filled with the scent of happiness. Her cooking, our bed-linen, her. Nikki smelled of soap. Not the expensive floral type, or the bacterial kind, just simple and clean. Her hair looked different every day, her bracelets and rings changed with her moods, rattling as she prepared breakfast before the sun was up. She was never the same person twice – but she always smelled the same. Like home.

'Work with me,' she said, two weeks after I'd moved in with her.

I'd found bar work in a pub called the Hidden Fox – they'd even paid me a little extra to design their new menus. I'd signed up with a temp agency, simple admin work, hoping it would get me some design leads. Everything I read about freelance designers said it took time to grow a client list, that word of mouth was the best form of advertising. There was no such thing as being an overnight success, and I was happy to take my time. My dream was to work for a big London ad agency.

'You don't want me working with you,' I said to Nikki. 'I don't know anything about flowers.'

'Just on Saturdays, in the day. You're stuck at home on your own anyway.'

I liked being on my own. I liked watching Nikki dress for work while it was still dark outside, biting into the buttered toast she always passed me in bed, cleaning her house for her, preparing something nice to eat for when she got home. I'd lie in bed all morning, working on my website, dreaming that maybe ... all of this ... might last for ever. I'd laughed at the realisation that I'd finally become the kind of woman Juan had always wanted me to be, the kind who made a fuss of their partner. With Juan it had felt like playing at Housewife, a role I was being squeezed into, but with Nikki it was different. I wanted to make everything beautiful for her. I wanted to please.

'OK,' I said. 'I'll work with you.'

Wrapping flowers in brown paper and ringing them up on the till was easy work, it was a fair wage, and it meant we got to be together. We were always together. This way, every evening, and all weekend, we were together.

Words will never hurt me • @Em_Dash_93

Why do we never hold on tight enough to the ones that matter the most?

Two women have walked down the stairs to the toilet, waited outside the door, then come back up again. What is Rose doing in there?

My phone's flashing. It's another WhatsApp voice message from my mother. My sister must have told her we'd spoken. I hope she didn't tell her about my mythical break-up with the mythical Nick.

'*Hija*, Marianna says you're on your way to the airport. Do you have the Bible? What are you wearing on Sunday? You have the necklace, right? Don't forget I have your father's watch here for you. Will you be hungry? I know you won't get here till late, but I'll make you some tortilla. Nothing heavy. Maybe some albondigas. You want tortilla, albondigas, maybe some salad? OK, I will make you dinner. And you're staying for a week after the wedding? Nick and your boss don't mind you away so long? What good men you have in your life. You hold on to that man of yours, and you hold on to that job. I tell all my friends at church that my high-flying daughter is a bigshot in London. *Ai, mi niña*, it's been such a long time. Why did you stay away so long? You make sure, when you and Nick get married, that it's here in Spain. I will make the cake.' She goes quiet, then clears her throat. 'I will still be here, *hija*. I will.'

Marianna got engaged on New Year's Eve, seven months ago, and had planned a long engagement, but then our mother got even more ill, so my sister brought the wedding forward. Mama said she was making a fuss about nothing. She also agreed it was better for me to give my sister away, instead of her. Not because she was too weak, she insisted, but because she wanted to sit at the front of the church and watch us *both* walk down the aisle in case she'd never see me do it for real one day. She's still holding on to that dream though.

'You never talk about your family,' Nikki would always say. 'What's your mum like?'

'Strong,' I would reply. 'But also, too soft. Quiet. She doesn't take up room, you know? You can be in the house for an hour and not realise she's there.'

'And your sister?'

'Spoilt.' Maybe I was being unfair. 'She had a different childhood to me. Different parents. Well, the same parents, but the age gap is nine years so . . . she never stopped being their baby. The miracle baby.'

Nikki loved listening to me talk about my family. She lived far away from her mum and she missed her father. She said grieving for a parent was lonely when you have no siblings. She wanted to meet Marianna, she wanted to share my family with me. She'd create these elaborate stories about us holidaying together in the south of Spain, my mother cooking a paella at the villa and being the best of friends with her mum, while Nikki, Marianna and I hit the bars until sunrise. She just wanted my family to love her as much as I did. And I wanted that for her, I really did, but every time I tried to imagine that picture it would dissolve like smoke.

'What about your father?' she would ask.

She knew he was dead, but everything else I said about him was far from the truth.

Back in the pub, a shadow looms over me.

'What's a nice girl like you doing sitting on her own?'

I take a deep breath and look up into the craggy face of a man old enough to be my father. He places his pint on the table, frothy white beer spilling over the edge. His fingers are wet now, but he doesn't seem to notice.

'I'm waiting for someone,' I reply.

The man sits down anyway.

'Been watching you,' he says. 'You've been here at least half an hour and I said to myself, that's not right. A pretty girl like that, sitting on her own in a pub. It's not safe. Especially with all that on the news. Shocking. So I thought I'd keep you company.'

I don't want to talk to this man, but I know what will happen if I ignore him or I'm rude. I look around me. The two guys from earlier are still at the bar. They're glancing over. Neither of them does anything.

'What's your name?' the old man asks.

I look in the direction of the toilets. Where the hell is Rose?

'Daisy,' I say.

Stay safe. Stay vigilant. Lie to strangers.

'I'm Brian.'

I give him a tight-lipped smile and go back to looking at my phone. He doesn't take the hint.

'"Daisy, Daisy, give me your answer, do,"' he sings, then chuckles. 'Bet you get that a lot. So, your man stood you up?' He edges his seat closer to me. 'Young men nowadays. No manners. I blame them phones. How you going to have a decent relationship with a bird if you've only met her electronically, eh? These boys go out, get pissed, ignore all the women in the bar, then go home and pick one off some app. It's not right. You gotta talk to people face to face, get out there, be friendly.'

I really don't want to be friendly. My phone's at 65 per cent. That's enough. I unplug it, looking busy, placing it in my bag. He still doesn't get the hint.

'I should get going,' I say.

His chair is blocking my way. Why isn't he moving?

'Nah, go on, stay for another drink. It's on me. What you having? How about a Bacardi and lemonade?'

'I really need to . . .'

My seat rises and falls as Rose sits down beside me with a heavy thump. She stares at me, at the man, and back at me again.

'Let's get something to eat,' she says, grabbing my arm with one hand and my suitcase with another.

Neither of us look back at Brian as we head to the other side of the bar, where there are people eating at tiny tables and a large group of people ordering drinks.

'Lesbians,' I hear Brian mutter. 'Should have known.'

14

'Who was that?' Rose asks as we find a space at the bar beneath a sign that says 'Order food here. Remember your table number.' We don't have a table number.

'That was Brian. He wanted to keep me company.'

'Jesus. Why do they always have to be so creepy? Why can't we ever just sit quietly on our own?'

With a pained sigh she picks up a laminated menu, sticky with a splattering of various condiments, and runs her finger down it as she reads the options.

She doesn't look well.

'You were ages in there,' I say, meaning the toilet.

She makes a face and leans into me. 'Let's just say last night's tequila shots, mixed with a questionable kebab and a crap shag by some over-energetic bloke I wish I'd never bothered with, has not agreed with me. I need water and carbs and to get the fuck back to bed.'

There's only one barman. He's at the far side of the bar, busy taking an order from a group of men in suits. By the way they've all taken their jackets off and rolled up their sleeves, I'm guessing they're done for the week.

Rose looks like she's going to vomit.

I lean over the bar as far as I can, my feet lifting off the pub floor, and wave my hand in the air. The barman ignores me, but the men he's serving have seen me.

'Oi, oi. Hello, hot stuff. Wave back, lads!'

I roll my eyes and slide back down the bar on my stomach. The top button of my shirt has popped open, and I do it up again. Rose gives me a 'Why is everything so bloody difficult?' look, then with two fingers gives a piercing whistle. Everyone around us jumps, including the barman. His face is slack with shock as he looks around for the culprit.

'Did you just whistle at me?' he calls out to Rose.

She gives him a cheeky grin. 'Yeah, sorry about that.'

'I don't want any trouble in here, OK?'

'We just want to order some food. When you're ready. Wasn't sure you'd seen us.'

'Oh, we all saw you,' he mutters, going back to pulling pints.

The Suit Boys aren't done yet.

'You were whistling at us, right?' one of them shouts at Rose. 'Why don't you come and join us?'

I turn to my left. Brian, my valiant protector, is still sitting where I left him, nursing his pint with his back to us. And at the other side of the bar, watching the commotion, are the two men from earlier who offered to buy me a drink.

I say something to Rose, something stupid and inconsequential about our route back, hoping it will make the men in suits stop shouting out at us. It doesn't work; they've edged closer.

One of the men has tight curly hair and a goatee. He's

untucked his shirt and unbuttoned it so low his chest hair is showing. The dark hairs against his white shirt make me think of my unruly bikini line.

'Come on, ladies. Why the long faces?' he says. 'Sun's out. Let's be happy. I know *you* like a good time.' He directs the last part at Rose. Rose with her large, hooped earrings and tight dress and boots that are made for dancing not walking.

She turns her back to him and, with both elbows on the bar, holds her head in her hands.

The barman walks over and Rose points at something on the menu.

'Chicken pie, chips and peas, please. And a large lemonade. Plenty of ice. What you having, Em?'

My head is pounding. I should probably eat something, but I can't think with these guys edging closer to us.

'Diet Coke and chips?'

Rose pays, tells me I can pay her back later, and points to an empty table behind us so the barman can write down our table number.

'Table sixty-nine,' he says, eliciting raucous cheers from the men behind us.

Rose swings around. 'Seriously? How old are you all?'

'How old do you want us to be?' a blond one answers. They all laugh.

I want to sit down at our table, but they're blocking the way.

'All right, calm down. We're only having a laugh. Going on holiday?' Goatee says to me, pointing at my suitcase.

I nod.

'Might as well have stayed here. We've got more sun than anywhere else right now.'

'Listen,' Rose says. 'We've had a hard day and I don't feel great. We just need to sit down and eat our food in peace.'

Blondie holds his hands up and makes a 'wooo' noise. 'No need to be such a grumpy bitch. We were just being friendly.'

Who knew everyone in London was so friendly? Every man. So, so friendly.

'Did you just call me a bitch?' Rose says.

'Woah! We've got ourselves a little pocket rocket, lads,' Goatee shouts out. 'Love it when a girl gets feisty.'

'She's so teeny. Like a little doll.'

'A little *angry* doll.'

'Yeah, Chucky.'

The office workers laugh as they do their best impressions of a demented toy. Rose turns her back on them, facing the bar again. I can hear her attempts to breathe properly, but she's failing.

I look over at the two men to my left again. Surely they're going to say something now.

The barman brings my pint of Coke and Rose's lemonade. She picks up her drink with two hands and takes a sip, her glass shaking at her lips. I don't know if it's rage or the hangover.

'Just let us pass,' I say to the group of men. 'Please.'

A third man steps forward. He's older, hair speckled grey, wearing glasses that someone probably told him were 'funky'.

'I like your accent,' he says. 'Where are you from?'

I close my eyes and let out a puff of air through my nose.

'Don't tell me I've offended you,' he says with mock concern. 'Seriously, you can't say anything to a woman any more.'

Rose swings around. 'Why don't you just do that then? Say nothing and mind your own fucking business?'

The barman is hovering behind us. I can feel his agitation permeate the air. I've worked in enough bars to recognise what he's doing. He's waiting for trouble.

The truth is, some people like to fight. I've known that all my life. You can see the switch in their eyes, like a cat who's seen a bird. It's an opportunistic thing, a waiting game. The fight is already inside them, but what they're looking for is an excuse, a valid reason to let it out. I know how it feels to be that reason.

The barman's waiting for the switch. The switch I used to see in my father's eyes, in the eyes of the men I refused to serve at closing time, in Paul's eyes that night we worked late.

Goatee raises his chin and sticks his chest out further. 'And what are you going to do if I don't?'

And there it is.

I look to the barman, I look at the men to my left, I look over at Brian, who's still staring into his pint. Is no one seeing this? *Isn't anyone going to do anything?*

'That's what I thought,' Goatee says with a smirk, rolling his eyes at Blondie, who replies with a snort. Goatee shapes his hands into crab claws, opening and shutting them. 'Girls like you are nothing but little yappy dogs. Yap, yap, yap.'

In one swift motion Rose grabs our drinks and throws them in the faces of the two men. It happens so fast, yet the seconds immediately after are in slow motion. The men's faces morphing from smug to shocked. Lemonade and Coke dripping from the ends of their noses, making their shirts transparent, matting Goatee's chest hair. Their work friends, dry and unscathed, aren't sure what to do so they just stand there, shuffling from foot to foot. One of them gives me what could pass as an apologetic smile; the others don't know where to look.

A hand grabs the top of my arm and I can feel Rose struggling beside me.

'What the fuck are you doing? Get off me!' she shouts at the barman, who's frogmarching us out of the pub.

'I told you I didn't want any trouble from you two.'

'But we didn't do anything,' I say. I hate how whiny my voice sounds, how high-pitched and shaky.

'And none of you bastards said a word,' Rose shouts over her shoulder at the two men on the other side of the pub. 'Get off me! I want my pie!'

The barman mumbles something about eating our food outside, but I've lost my appetite. He's crazy if he thinks we're going to sit in this heat, happily eating greasy carbs, while those soaking-wet men are still inside wanting to teach us a lesson.

He lets us go and starts collecting glasses left on the wall outside. As soon as his back is turned, I run back into the pub.

'Em!' Rose shouts out.

'My suitcase!'

But it's not where I left it. It's by the tables, where Goatee is sitting, holding on to the handle of my case.

'Ah, come back for more, have you?' he says with a smirk, his face still wet from our drinks. I look behind me. Rose is checking her phone and can't see me inside the dark pub.

I reach for my suitcase, but Goatee snatches it away. His friends aren't surrounding him any more, they're back at the bar; it's just him and Blondie. I try to get the case again and he moves it out of reach. As I lean over him, he grabs me by the waist and pulls me on to his lap.

'Giddy up, giddy up,' he coos into my ear as he bounces me up and down. His fingers have crept up my blouse, to the skin just above my waistband. They press into my flesh, holding me in place, while his knee moves up and down in sharp motions, making my sore thighs rub together.

His friend isn't laughing; he's just staring at me.

'I think she likes it,' he says. 'I think she wants it harder.'

I should fight back – scream, claw at his face, bite his arm, but I don't. Instead, I go limp, because I know it will be less fun for him and he'll stop quicker. I'm right.

After a few seconds he pushes me off his lap, and I grab my case, scurrying back outside, head bent low, avoiding eye contact with anyone else.

Rose is already halfway down the street. I jog up to her.

'You OK?' she asks, the cigarette in her mouth bobbing up and down as she speaks.

She can see I'm not OK. I'm shaking, my teeth clamped together so hard I can't open my mouth to answer her.

'It's like I said.' She lights the cigarette and takes a long drag. 'Men are cunts.'

It takes a while for me to calm down, but Rose doesn't look as rattled as I feel. She's walking at a normal pace, checking her phone, not once glancing behind her, like I keep doing.

'Chill,' she says. 'No one's following us.'

There's something about her that reminds me of Nikki. It's weird how I feel safer beside her, even though she's five inches shorter than me. She walks through life like nothing bad can happen. Like she can say what she wants, do what she wants and not think about the consequences.

Does she not worry about being hated? I guess some people are too brave to be hated – or maybe they *are* hated, they just don't care. How do you stop yourself from caring?

'Forget about those twats, Em. Men like that don't bother me,' she says. 'I half expected it, to be honest. As soon as you see them in a pack like that, it's just a matter of time. It's like wild dogs. One mangey dog is normally shit-scared, but with a pack you don't stand a chance. And they know it. They feel that energy. You ever been to a football match?'

She takes another puff of her cigarette. She's not expecting an answer.

'Were you not scared?' I ask.

She shrugs. 'When are we ever not scared?'

I watch her suck on that cigarette like she's filling herself up with all the courage she's going to need until she's finally home and safe in bed. Sometimes I wish I smoked, just so I had something to do with my hands.

'Aren't you angry?' I ask.

'Of course I am.'

'What made you the angriest?'

'That I missed out on my pie. I'm really fucking hungry.'

15

We pass under yet another bridge, each one giving us a small burst of respite from the relentless sun. The thrum of the heat is like the bass of a stereo; I can practically hear it humming in my ears.

Traffic is at a standstill, groups of confused-looking people hanging around Limehouse DLR station wondering how they're going to get home. It's cold comfort to see that Rose and I aren't the only ones walking at a steady pace, staring at our phone screens.

We've been travelling in silence for the last five minutes. The heat is pressing down on me, and I think it's affecting Rose too, because she's not as chatty as before. I keep looking at the time on my phone, doing the maths, telling myself I have plenty of time.

'I'm glad we get to walk together,' I say.

She gives me a strange look, as if to say I'm being unnecessarily soppy.

'I mean, because it's safer and I'm less likely to get lost.'

She laughs softly. 'True. You know what? I reckon there's a reason why I was there when you were having a piss.' I wish she'd stop mentioning that. 'I believe in fate. You and

I meeting was for some cosmic reason, but we won't know what that is until after that thing has happened. What do you reckon?'

I think it's all nonsense.

'I don't know.'

'Yes, you do. You *do* know. Everyone has an opinion, Em.'

'Sometimes I don't.'

'Bollocks! Just because you don't say it out loud it doesn't mean you don't have one. If you keep your opinions inside, all them feelings and stuff, they fester. Rot. You gotta get it out, love. Make them someone else's problem.'

Her laugh turns to a hacking cough, and she stops walking. I should have bought a bottle of water in the pub. I would have, had Rose not doused those men in cheap lemonade.

She lights another cigarette.

'So, where you going on holiday?' she asks, tapping the base of my suitcase with the pointy tip of her boot.

'I'm not. I'm going home. Visiting family.'

'Oh, where you from? Wait. Let me guess. Italy. No. Greece? No. Bet you're Croatian or something. I don't know what Croatians look like but you're hot and got that shiny dark hair Mediterraneans have.'

'Spain.'

'I knew it. Which part?'

'Ronda, it's in Andalucía.'

'Oh, I love Andalucía!'

'Have you been?' This is the longest conversation we've had.

'Nah. I don't like flying. I've seen photos, though, and it looks lovely.'

I'm waiting for her to ask if I miss home. She doesn't. I wonder where her family's from, what her heritage is, but I don't ask.

My father used to say you don't know where you're going if you don't know where you're from. But watching Rose stride ahead, my suitcase gliding effortlessly behind her as she blows out a puff of smoke into the sky, I realise some people don't live in the past. Maybe they're the ones who arrive at the most interesting places.

We pass beige building after beige building. Another pub. A patch of green with a bench. Bridge after bridge. At one point the road forks into two and we take the left one, Rose is humming a Christmas song, the light of the sun glinting off all the rings on her fingers. I wonder who she was talking to earlier on the phone, who Olly is, what her job is, who gets to go out on a Thursday night and has all day Friday to walk the streets of London. If she's skiving off work, she doesn't look too bothered about it.

'What you going to do in Spain, then?' she asks. 'Got any plans?'

'My sister's getting married on Sunday.'

Rose raises her eyebrows. 'Older or younger.'

'Younger. Twenty-one.'

She turns and throws her cigarette on the ground. 'Fuck, that's young. You don't think that's young?'

'Of course I do. And her fiancé's a dick.'

'Have you told her that?'

'No.'

'What else you not spoken up about?'

I glance at my phone.

'You don't like it, do you?' Rose says. Her voice rises along with her chin. 'You know, people poking you until you have to push back. You think it's safer in the shadows, is that it? I didn't see you saying anything in the pub earlier.'

I grip my phone tighter, like a security blanket. Rose slows down. Neither of us moves. After a few seconds of tense silence, she holds her hands up in the air, as if I'm pointing a gun at her, and raises her eyebrows.

'All right, all right. My bad. I clearly touched a nerve.'

My mother had Marianna at forty-one. My sister, the miracle baby, the second child they never thought they'd have. She was born two weeks before my ninth birthday. My party was cancelled, but I didn't mind. That tiny, milky bundle was the best present I'd ever had.

I thought she was magic, because from the moment she made my mother's belly swell my father changed.

'It's a sign from God,' he'd said. 'He wants me to be a better man.'

My mother had instantly jumped to his defence, telling him he was already a good man. She'd placed her hand on his strong chest and whispered words about believing in him, about having faith in his goodness. He'd held her, placed his hand on her stomach and reached out for me.

This wasn't normal. It didn't feel safe.

Instead of joining them, I ran to my room and hid beneath my duvet, praying to the God my parents told me was all powerful and always looking after us, and I begged Him to give me a sister who would make my father as good as he wanted to be. I begged for better.

And for a while God listened. My father stopped drinking and he stopped shouting. He told me we had to look after my mother because sometimes God chose to take babies away. Like the other ones. But if I was a really good girl, then this time He would bring us a miracle, and everything would be OK. I believed my father and I trusted in this powerful God that even my father was afraid of. I behaved, did as I was told, and because I was a good girl my sister arrived.

But within two weeks the spell was broken. People will always find a reason to fight.

I glance at the time on my phone. We're making good progress.

There are eighteen notifications on my Twitter. Most are people liking my posts and there's even a retweet.

Joe the Hoe Mofo • @JoeyB123
Imagine being this cut up about your ex that you write simp poetry for all the world to see. Have a wank and get over it, sad loser.

My throat closes up and the gnarly rock appears in my guts again. I try to breathe it away as I keep scrolling. The #SaveThem hashtag is trending. I click on it.

The Daily Mail • @DailyMail
Should women be put on curfew this summer? With
attacks rising and a killer on the loose, leading figures
are advising women to stay off the streets after 6 p.m.
What do you think?

> **Laura Peterson • @LauraBPeterson1**
> Are you fucking kidding us?

> **Meredith Stonewell • @StonewellM**
> Replying to @LauraBPeterson1
> No, they're fucking KILLING us

> **Elizabeth Smith • @LizzieSmi1961**
> I think it's a good idea. I'd feel a lot safer knowing
> my daughter was at home in the evening rather
> than out with friends.

> **Portsmouth FC for life • @MichPFCFL**
> Women that go out accompanied by men should be
> exempt. If they're out with a husband or their dad,
> they'll be a lot safer

We need to stay safe. *We* need to stay safe. It's our responsibility to not get murdered. Ten tips on how to stop a serial killer picking you and picking someone else instead.

I take another shaky breath and put my phone away. I need to stop looking at Twitter and reading the news.

'The people on there aren't real,' Nikki would say. 'They don't represent the whole world. They're just a bunch of trolls.'

Except they *are* real people. Even the anonymous accounts are real, accounts like mine, representing people's real

144

feelings. There are live humans behind each post, spilling their guts out to strangers; needing to be seen, to be heard, to be wanted.

With every person that walks past us I wonder if they're on Twitter. Would they care about my posts? Would they empathise with me or laugh at me? Would they say nice things to me at work yet from the safety of their phones call me fat, or ugly, or say it was my fault I got killed?

The smart buildings have gradually turned into old, ter-raced housing, brickwork black and soot-stained, shops with dirty shutters and litter swirling in circles beside empty bins.

Three young lads are standing at a bus stop. They're passing a joint around, laughing at something they're watching on a phone. The air hangs heavy with the scent of weed.

'Check those two out,' one of them says to his friends. He's wearing a beanie, in this weather. 'They're well old, but still hot. I'd fuck them.'

Am I old at nearly thirty? They're young. Probably around my sister's age. I ignore them, but Rose is slowing down.

'Oh no, I think they heard us,' one of the others says, elbowing his beanie friend with a snicker. 'Probably likes it, though. They do say MILFs are better bangs, innit, bruv?'

'Leave it,' I say to Rose.

I don't have time for this. We're getting closer to the airport, to aircon, to having a chance to sit down. I just want this bloody journey to be over with.

'No, Em. I'm not taking this shit again.'

She lets go of my suitcase and it drops to the ground with a loud clatter, the handle dislodging as it hits the pavement. Fuck.

'What did you say?' she says, walking up to the three lads.

'Just saying you're hot. It's a compliment.'

'Yeah, he wants to bone you,' the other guy adds. His comment gets him a laugh from his two friends.

'Come on,' I say quietly. Too quietly for her to hear from where she is.

She's standing before the boys, legs hip width apart, arms stretched out. Fuck, *fuck*.

'If you want to have sex with me, you should say it to my face, *bruv*.'

'It's just a joke.'

'Is it, though? Is it only a joke?' Rose cocks her head to one side then glances over her shoulder at me. 'Oh look, Em. Another man joke we forgot to laugh at.'

Why is she bringing *me* into it? I don't want to be here. I'm not getting involved in whatever the hell this is. We just got thrown out of a pub and she lost money on food we didn't eat. Why doesn't she just ignore them?

A woman who was walking behind us earlier sees Rose shouting and crosses the street, while a man leans against the doorway of his newsagents' and watches us. Rose doesn't care that she has an audience.

'You think two women, walking down the road, minding their own fucking business on a really hot day, is a *joke*?'

146

she shouts. 'What? Because I'm dressed like this, I'm a slut? Because I have lipstick on, I want to suck your dicks? Yeah? Go on then.' She points at the waistband of one of the guys. 'Get it out. Let's look at your fat cock. You said you want me, right? You said me and my mate are hot? Well, come on then, fuck us.'

Rose is tiny, nearly a whole foot shorter than the three young men, but she steps up to them so close it makes them back up. They glance at one another nervously, the joint now smoking on the ground. They're waiting for someone else, anyone but them, to take the lead.

I look at my phone: we've wasted five minutes already. *Fuck's sake, Rose.* I lift my suitcase up from the ground as silently as I can and wheel it back. It makes enough sound for the four of them to turn to me.

'Listen, we never meant nothing,' one of the men calls out to me. 'Tell your mate to calm down.'

'Oh, I'm calm,' Rose says. 'It's just you said you wanted to bang us, so here I am.'

I'm expecting these young men to do something – to push her away, to take her up on her offer, to walk off – but they just stand there. Frozen.

Rose takes a step closer to the one in the beanie who started all of this. 'Oh, so you *don't* want us? What's the matter? Your little ickle willies shrunken up now that a real woman is up in your face?' He looks like he wants to cry.

There are three of them, they're all much bigger than her, and stronger. They could push her, hit her. I know how hard a man can punch. I know how fast she'd fall and what little I could do to stop it. But they're not. They're just standing there.

'Fuck off!' Rose screams in their faces, one by one. 'Fuck off, fuck off, fuck off!'

And they run. They run without even looking at one another and without a backward glance as Rose races after them, screaming for them to come and take her.

But the boots she's wearing are not meant for running. With a yelp she stumbles and falls to the floor on all fours. I grab my case and run up to her.

'Are you OK?'

Her hands and knees are grazed but her eyes are still flashing black. No one comes to help us.

'Shit. That stings,' she mutters, wincing as I help her up to her feet.

It's not until the boys have reached the end of the road that they stop. They're laughing and pointing, emboldened now there's some distance between us.

'Stay on the ground where you belong!' one of them shouts.

'Yeah, you ugly old hags!'

'Crazy bitch! Go back to where you came from.'

Rose ignores them, but I'm surprised to see she's half smiling.

'Don't look at me like that. What was I meant to do?' she says to me, straightening her dress. 'Little twats like that love it when you keep quiet; it turns them on. Look at the ones in the pub. We said nothing at first and they just cranked it up a level.'

I think of Goatee and his game of Giddy-up. I didn't tell Rose, I didn't trust that she wouldn't go back in there and smash his empty beer bottle over his head.

'But you know what they don't like?' she continues, leaning in closer, so close I can smell the cigarettes on her breath. 'They don't like a woman with a loud voice. You start shouting, bringing attention to them, and it scares the shit out of them. Why? Because these kind of men never *really* want to have sex with us. I'm not even sure they want to kill us. They just want to win.'

I don't care about winning or losing, all I care about is that I need to get to the airport and out of this damn sun. I look at my phone for the millionth time today.

'Fuck,' I mutter. It's already gone seven o'clock and we're still miles away. 'I'm going to miss my flight if we don't hurry up.'

'Go,' she says. 'I'm fine.'

But Rose isn't fine. Both of her knees are covered in blood and the heel of one of her boots is hanging off. I can't leave her like this.

'Does it hurt?' I ask, nodding at her knee.

She spits on her fingers and rubs at the scratches. 'Nah, it's fine.'

She takes a step forward and stumbles. I catch her.

'Don't worry, these boots were cheap anyway. I'll walk on my tiptoes. Let's keep going,' she says.

I can't see the group of boys any more; they ran in the opposite direction to the one we have to go in. Rose takes the packet of cigarettes out of her bag and flicks the lighter.

It isn't working. She tries again and again, then drops the packet of Marlborough back in her bag with a sigh.

She sniffs, using the back of her knuckle to rub beneath her eye. Her breathing is fast, her hair even bigger than before.

'You OK?' I ask.

She nods, her lips pressed together as if she's scared to speak. After a while she clears her throat and takes a wobbly step forward, then another, her gait lopsided from her broken heel.

'Boys like that don't bother me,' she says, her voice thick and wavering. 'I can look after myself. I've got three brothers, loads of cousins, God ... my sisters were even tougher than those little pricks when I was growing up. It's not that. What worries me is the idea that my son could end up being just like that one day. And I have no idea how to stop it.'

16

I've placed my phone in my bag, because glancing at the time every few minutes isn't making us go any faster. We're still over an hour away from the airport and my plane takes off in under two hours. I'm cutting it fine. Too fine.

I can see from the expression on Rose's face that every step she takes hurts. Her knees are bruised and two lines of blood, like a crimson number eleven, have dried on her right leg.

'Tell me about your son,' I say.

Her face lights up, but I can still see the exhaustion in her eyes. Not just from walking in those ridiculously high boots, or the pain from her injury, but that she's used up every ounce of energy she had on far too many men.

'Olly's just your regular eight-year-old boy,' she says. 'He's amazing. He slept over at my mum's last night. She's got him until Sunday, thank God.'

Olly. That's the person she was talking about earlier on the phone. It wasn't some guy she'd met that she was gossiping about with her friends, she was asking her mum about her son.

'You know, when I found out I was having a boy so many

151

people said how lucky I was . . . how much easier it was to raise a son than a daughter. I didn't get it. I loved the idea of a little girl; someone I could do all my favourite things with. Then I realised what they meant. Parents worry more about their daughters, their little bunny rabbits trapped in a field of foxes. But maybe it's their boys they should be focusing on. Yeah, I'd worry about a young girl of mine walking across London like we're doing, about running into the kind of men we've seen today – but I worry about my boy too. I worry because boys get punched, they get stabbed, they join gangs, they need to prove they're tough and strong and funny and it leads them into trouble. Or even worse . . . they turn into foxes.'

I wonder how many of these boys started off like rabbits, before realising they were safer being the ones with the sharp teeth.

'I can't imagine any son of yours will end up like them,' I say.

She gives me a sad smile. 'Not on my fucking watch.'

'What about Olly's dad? Is he a decent guy?'

I think I already know the answer.

Rose smiles. 'Gio was hot. You know, like what I said before, one of the attractive ones who can do anything to you and make it feel like you're special. Dark, floppy hair, a crooked smile, that smooth way they tell you that you're different to all the others and you believe them.' She laughs, a dry cackle of a laugh that turns into a cough. 'I don't know why I'm laughing, it's not even funny. Gio was a right . . .'

'Cunt?'

'Yeah. But I don't hate him, not really. I was obsessed with him. It was my first year of uni and I was a grade A student – which is rare in my family. I knew exactly what I was going to do with my life. Gio was an exchange student, Italian. I know, total cliché. Anyway, it's not a long story. He went back after a few months of us hooking up, I found out I was pregnant, he'd already blocked my number before he'd even landed back in Naples or wherever the fuck he was from, and I didn't even know his surname. By the time I knew for sure I was really pregnant I was at twenty weeks and I couldn't do anything about it. So I didn't. Olly is one hundred per cent mine, I'm his, my family helped me, and I made it work.'

'Your family sound amazing.'

She laughs, a short, sharp 'ha'.

'My family is big and loud and really fucking annoying, but they're always there for me. Because of them I got to stick to my career plans *and* raise my baby. They all live nearby. He's always at one of their houses. I'm lucky.'

'Sounds like you're *all* lucky,' I say, thinking of Marianna and her future and how I won't even be in the same country as her when she has her first child.

'I feel bad for Gio sometimes,' Rose says. 'He doesn't know Olly exists; he has no idea what he's missed out on the last eight years. I know us mums moan about how hard it is, being the ones who carry them, birth them, feed them, but at least we'll never be out there, completely unaware that we have an awesome kid somewhere in the world who looks exactly like us. I sometimes wonder what would have

153

happened if I'd been able to tell him. Whether he'd have broken my heart, and Olly's, somewhere down the line – or if we'd be one of those perfect couples living a perfect life.'

She sticks her hand in her bag, stops, remembering her lighter doesn't work, and closes her eyes with a sigh.

A single drop of sweat works its way down my spine, landing in the small of my back and my wet waistband. The inside of my thighs hurt so much I'm having to walk with my legs slightly apart like a cowboy.

Every time I speed up, she slows down, and I have to wait for her. This is killing me.

I take my phone out of my bag to check the time, even though I promised myself I wouldn't. A Twitter announcement flashes up and I click on it, instantly wishing I hadn't.

The Telegraph • @Telegraph

Are the police doing enough to catch the killer? Met police are under fire as the capital calls for more patrols on the street. 'Women deserve to feel safe,' Labour MP Patricia Laverne said today in Parliament. 'We need to increase police presence and catch this man.'

> **Travis Jones** • @JoneseyT
>
> Is it any wonder men are turning into killers when the media tells women we're all dangerous?
>
> **Lynsey Lancaster** • @LiverpoolLynsey
>
> Replying to @JoneseyT
>
> Wait, are you seriously blaming women for a man going on a murder rampage?

> **N A Weaver** • @NicholasAWeaver00
>
> You make it sound like police will HELP. Who's to say the killer isn't a pig?
>
> **Sarah Harrington #SaveThem** • @SarahHN6
>
> This is why everyone should be at the #SaveThem vigil tomorrow. The world needs to see we've had enough.

Nikki used to tell me to stop reading incendiary news articles.

'You want to make a difference? Then *be* the difference,' she would say. She helped deliver gifts to sick kids every Christmas, she donated to a women's refuge charity each month, she went to every BLM march and every gathering for every murdered woman. She recycled everything, even potato peelings and apple cores, and would carbon offset any flights she took.

It should have made me love her more, but it didn't. It made me angry, because she tried so hard and believed so much that what she was doing mattered, but it didn't make a difference. Things always get worse, no matter how much you care.

We're all carrying our version of guilt around, trying to erase it with good deeds and public declarations of support, when it's the big, rich companies and governments destroying the planet and refusing to keep the streets safe. Governments we trusted, but because we voted for them the blame is still on us.

'What's the alternative?' Nikki would say. Always calm.

Always kind. 'Do nothing? Stay quiet? Or do you think you've done enough because you inhale every news article, you inform yourself about every travesty, you share Tweets. But that's not making a difference either, that's just projecting your own anxiety out on to the world. Then you and all your followers can agree the world is a terrible place, but what can we do about it? And you're proven right, because everything stays the same, and weren't you the clever one, not getting worked up about it?'

But what can I do about three women murdered in the same city I live in? What can I do but make sure I'm not one of them?

I look around. The streets are empty, and the roads have gone from being gridlocked earlier to completely empty. Not one taxi or bus has gone by. I see a flash of white out of the corner of my eye. It's a police car, and it's slowing down as it approaches us.

Maybe Tweets *do* make a difference and that MP was right. Police on patrol. Hopefully their presence will stop groups of men shouting out profanities at innocent women.

The car crawls alongside us and the window slides down. There are two officers inside. I wonder if they're going to offer us a lift.

'Excuse me,' a female police officer shouts out of the window. We slow down and the car pulls over. 'We just received a complaint from three men who said they were verbally assaulted by two sexually aggressive women matching your description.'

Rose steps towards the vehicle. 'You have got to be fucking kidding me!'

The policewoman doesn't look like she does a lot of joking. Her colleague, a male officer, is behind the wheel but keeps his gaze straight ahead.

'We haven't talked to any men,' I say.

I feel Rose bristle beside me. I lay a hand on her arm, and she deflates a little.

'She's right. We haven't,' she says. 'But we'll let you know if we see any dangerous women out and about scaring groups of defenceless men.'

I pull Rose back, my mother's voice ringing in my head: 'Do as you're told and keep quiet.' According to her, it's important that every woman remembers that sentence wherever they are. At work, at school, at home. She says that's how she managed to stay married to my father for so long and hadn't failed, like so many of her godless, divorced friends she no longer speaks to.

'Your father had a difficult childhood,' she would say as she applied a cold cloth to her cheek or cleared up shards of glass. 'All he needs is love, *hija*. It's why I left college and focused on him. Make sure you love your man enough, and it will soften him. They'll look after you. They can't help the way they are. Men are different to us.'

When I was a child, she would sit me down and explain that strong men don't realise they're being intimidating, they don't know the power they have over us, but arguing with them only makes things worse.

'Let them feel stronger than you,' she would say. 'They stop sooner, then life can go back to being nice and peaceful.'

Sometimes she'd forget to take her own advice and she'd shout back at my father or try to defend herself. Sometimes I would grab a wooden spoon and lash out myself, shouting at them to stop, reminding them that they'd wake up the miracle baby.

During the times when keeping quiet didn't help, she'd be silenced in a different way. Having a fat lip makes talking a lot harder. Either way, she always ended up with her mouth closed.

'We're simply trying to get home,' I say to the policewoman. 'But thank you for keeping the streets safe.'

'Just doing our job,' she says with a grim smile.

Rose leans over me. 'Maybe next you could find the serial killer. You know, instead of kerb crawling beside innocent women battling to get home in a bloody heatwave with a murderer on the loose.'

I pull Rose away from the car and smile at the officer. 'Sorry. Yes, thank you.'

They drive away and I open up my suitcase.

'What you doing?' Rose says.

'We need to speed up,' I say, handing her two items.

'What's this?'

'Wet wipes for your legs and face, and my flip-flops.'

'I don't want—'

'Just put the fucking flip-flops on, Rose.'

And for the first time since I met her, she does as she's told.

17

Daily Mail Online · @MailOnline
'Trafalgar Square #SaveThem vigil is irresponsible,' says
Hillary Atkinson, Tory MP for Barnet. 'Stay home. Stay
safe.' As thousands of women plan to descend on the
capital tomorrow, here's how you can pay your respects
without putting yourself at risk.

Rose has hardly said a word in the last fifteen minutes,
clutching her boots while my flip-flops on her feet slap the
pavement like hot hands on wet skin. The suitcase feels
heavier by the second and my trainers are rubbing against
the sores on the back of my heel. We're still not walking
as fast as we were before.

I thought the day would cool down as it slipped into
evening, but the lower the sun gets, the hotter it burns. I
glance at the time on my phone again, but it's not helping
the tightness in my chest. I need to stop calculating how
long we have left and what time my flight leaves. As long
as I get there with an hour to spare, I'll be OK. I'm going
to make it. I have to.

Rose is quiet. Sullen, even. Her hair's all messed up since

she fell, and she looks a lot younger now she's taken her makeup off.

The silence is killing me.

'Did you have the day off work today?' I ask, because I can't think of anything more interesting to say.

'Yeah. I was owed holiday time, so I took a few Fridays off. Good job too. You?'

'I don't have a job.'

'Oh, rich girl. Nice.'

'No, I got sacked today.'

Rose stops. 'Sorry. What did you do?'

What did I do? I stayed quiet, that's what I did.

'Nothing.'

'I meant, what was your job?'

'Graphic designer. PR agency.'

'Fancy.'

'Yeah. I guess I wasn't really sacked, they just didn't keep me on after a three-month placement.'

'You'll find other work,' she says. 'What about Spain? You can't work there?'

I could. Not in Andalucía, not at the same level, but maybe in Madrid or Barcelona. Or maybe I should go freelance. When my dad died, my mum got a big life-insurance payout, plus his pension and the house paid for. I could live at home, have my mum pay for everything while I set up my own business again, or go back to school. Marianna hasn't worked a day in her life. She'll go from being at home with our mum to having her new husband support her. She's never cared about financial freedom; she's never found the idea of someone else holding the purse strings completely terrifying.

Yet me moving back home, to a town perched on the top of a forgotten mountain and cut off from anywhere that matters, would also mean looking my mother in the eye every day and continuing to lie about my life. Who I am, what I do, who I really want to be.

'I want to stay in London,' I say to Rose. 'My life's here.'

She looks around her and makes a face. 'You're mad. This city is a shithole. If it weren't for Olly and my family being here, I'd have gone a long time ago. So, what's the deal? You got a boyfriend? Husband? Kids?'

I shake my head.

Maybe I should tell her about Nikki. I haven't spoken about Nikki to anyone in months – unless Matt counts. Although he only wanted to hear the details of my past relationship while he had his hand up my skirt.

'Fucking shitballs. Look!'

Rose is pointing at a bridge. I can't see what she's showing me.

'Look!' she shouts again. 'A DLR just went by.'

'So?'

She pushes me playfully again and rolls her eyes. 'The DLRs are running. Poplar station is somewhere near here.' She looks at her phone. 'Three minutes, that way. You can get a DLR straight to the airport and I can get off at Canning Town. It's fifteen minutes, instead of another hour of walking.'

Rose starts to jog, more of a hobbling shuffle, and I chase

after her. She's laughing, and I can't help but join in. My suitcase bounces along behind me. It's no longer heavy, and my feet no longer ache.

We get to the station and Rose heads straight for the DLR map while I stare up at the electric board above our heads. Poplar is only three stops from Canning Town and six from the airport. The next train goes to both and arrives in two minutes.

'Thank you,' I say. I'm out of breath and my shirt is soaked from my armpits all the way around to my chest, but I don't care any more. I'm going to get to the airport with enough time to get changed, maybe even have a wash.

'Thanks,' I say again as the DLR pulls up on the platform and we get inside. The windows are open and the carriage is empty. As we pull off a light breeze hits my face and I sigh.

This is it. I'm on my way to the airport. I did it! Rose sits in front of me and grabs the phone out of my hand.

'I'm putting my number in your contacts. Chill – no need to look at me like that. I'm not saying we should be besties. I just want to know you got on your flight OK.'

She hands it back and I ring the number then hang up.

'Now you have my number too,' I say.

She starts scrolling through her phone and I do the same. Twitter is blowing up about the Save Them vigil. Some are saying that women should be more responsible and not take part in anything at night in central London; others that the victims of the London Strangler should be remembered and that women shouldn't be cowed into silence.

I know what Nikki will be saying about this.

As soon as we broke up I blocked her from everything. She said it was over and I knew there was no going back. I wasn't going to risk getting drunk and begging her at 3 a.m. She's not on Twitter, but I unfriended her on Facebook, took her number off my phone and blocked it. Everything hurt too much. The only way I could cope with her walking away was to pretend she'd never existed in the first place. But I could never wipe the memories of her from my mind. So far, I've managed to keep away from looking her up online. I've not been on her website to check out her latest bouquets or read her blogs about the weddings she's been working on this season, or even googled her name just to see it in writing.

But right now, after the day I've had, I need to see her face.

I click on her Instagram page – I don't have an account, but I bookmarked her url – and a strangled sob escapes my throat. I cover it up with a fake cough. There she is, my Nikki, looking straight into the camera like no time has passed at all. Like I'm still lying next to her in bed, staring into her clear aquamarine eyes. The sight of her is a punch in the guts. She's so beautiful. How had I forgotten Nikki was so beautiful? She's taken the selfie in her shop, with roses and gerbera behind her in a million shades of pink.

She's changed her nose ring, too. It looks like the one I bought her in Camden Market to celebrate a year of us being together. A tiny diamond stud. Her eyes look bright. Is she happy? She's not smiling in the photo, but that's probably because of what she's written beneath it.

#SaveThem – tomorrow night 8 p.m., Trafalgar Square.
No woman deserves to die at the hands of any man.
No woman should be scared to go to work, to sit in
a park, to go home. Hanna Nilsson was waiting for
her dad outside a restaurant. Farah Mitri was on her
way to a meeting. Jennifer Buchanan was going to the
Tube station after a night out with friends. Another
woman, Zhao Li, was found strangled to death early
this afternoon at Stepney City Farm. Zhao is a mother
of three and a nurse at Royal London Hospital, walking
home after a night shift. Her colleague said she normally
took the bus, but because of the strike she decided to
walk. It was daylight. DAYLIGHT. And she never made
it home to her babies. Police haven't confirmed yet if
she's another victim of the #LondonStrangler, but either
way she's another woman who wasn't safe to walk the
streets of our city. Don't stay home. Don't stay silent. Do
something. #SaveThem #MeToo #TimeIsNow #Enough
#SaveOurWomen

Another murder? I read it three times.

Of course Nikki will be at the vigil. Would I be there if
I wasn't going to be in Spain? No. Well, maybe ... if we
were still together. Nikki would have made a day of it,
brought a picnic with her to eat in the square and worn her
most feminist of T-shirts. We probably would have bickered
about it – her saying she was doing her part, me saying it
was futile. Then I would have apologised and said that what

I thought didn't matter, and she would have said what she always did: *All of you matters*.

Then after the sit-in we'd have gone home and made love and forgotten all about the dead women.

'Who's that?' Rose asks, craning her neck to take a closer look.

I scroll from one image to the other. Nikki with her mum somewhere sunny, a photo of the sea, Nikki holding a bunch of flowers. I go back further. Some cocktails, flowers, a wedding arch, a close-up of a kitten – so she got the cat she wanted in the end – two glasses of wine, a selfie with a flower garland in her hair, another selfie, us.

I stop.

It's us, smiling, wearing bunny ears. The last day of us being a couple. It was Easter and we went to the Cotswolds for the weekend. The local country pub had an Easter-egg hunt for adults. It was a stupid idea. It was wonderful. We drank Aperol Spritz in the pub garden, even though it was overcast and cold, our drinks curdling in our stomachs with the chocolate we'd eaten, then we went for a curry and declared we truly hated ourselves because we felt very sick but very happy.

The hotel room had a four-poster bed and a sunken bath, and allegedly more than one ghost. We were a bit pissed. It was close to midnight and I was just about to get into bed when Nikki announced she'd been waiting for the right moment all day but there was no right moment.

Then she got down on one knee and asked me to marry

her. Just like that, in her dressing gown, like one of the crap rom-com movies she loves.

I said yes ... and then we had our first and last argument. The fight I'd been waiting for since I realised how much I loved her.

The next morning, while she was still asleep, I walked out of her life for ever. I left my diamond engagement ring in a bowl next to her side of the bed, along with three tiny chocolate eggs. One for every year we'd been together. I took the train back to Nikki's flat alone, packed up my things, blocked her from everything on my phone and never spoke to her again. She has no idea where I am and I didn't even give her the opportunity to ask me. Maybe she didn't mean what she said, maybe she would have forgiven me with time, but I didn't want to be the reason for her pain. She'd had enough of that in her life already; I didn't expect her to forgive me. I simply added the weight of that along with everything I've been carrying.

I glance down at the phone in my hand. I can't believe she hasn't deleted all these photos of us. The one after it is the photo of me holding up the ring and her kissing me. It got over three hundred likes. The one after that is also me. And me. And me.

'You two make a cute couple,' Rose says. 'She seems nice.'

I bat at my eyes with the back of my hand.

'That's my ex. She wasn't that nice,' I say. But I'm lying. She was perfect. Too perfect for me.

'Right, I'm off.'

'What?'

We're pulling up to Canning Town and Rose is already standing by the doors of the train.

'Good luck,' she says. 'Get home safe.'

Home. I think of my mother and sister. Matt. Nikki. I don't have a home any more.

Rose swings around. 'Come here,' she says, opening her arms as the train doors open. I didn't have Rose down as a hugger. 'Sorry. I stink.'

'Me too,' I say, laughing into her matted hair.

'Shit, your flip-flops.' She slips them off, but I stop her.

'Keep them. Thanks for everything.'

'Cheers. We should do it again some time.' She gives another of her singed laughs. 'See you around.'

Maybe I'll call her after all.

She joins the swarm of commuters on the platform but doesn't turn around or wave. The doors slide shut and she disappears from view.

I look out of the window. Train tracks, pylons, building work, tower blocks, Nikki, dead women, Nikki, dead women. Everything flashes past in a blur of grey.

Words will never hurt me • @Em_Dash_93

She said all of me mattered, but she forgot about the broken parts.

167

18

The DLR platform is covered overhead; it's like being inside a stripy blue-and-white tube. It's crowded and full of people rushing – clearly, I'm not the only one who's had trouble getting to the airport. Someone stumbles over my luggage as I make my way to the exit and we both apologise. I look up. It's a man in a baseball cap. My heart quickens.

London Strangler, London Strangler. It's all I hear on the whispered breaths of fellow passengers. Every white man could be a suspect. Every woman with long brown hair is a potential victim. Every guy on this platform could kill me, in theory. Maybe more than one of them would, if they could. Rose was right: how do you know? How do you stop being the rabbit?

In the distance, the view of east London is bathed in a haze of grey fog. The air smells of summer in the city; heavy, tinged with smoke from barbecues. Canary Wharf shines on the horizon, railway tracks criss-crossing the cityscape, and the large boxy airport sits squat to my left. There are no houses nearby. Perhaps it's not barbecues I can smell; perhaps it's hot trains and the sweat of dozens of people barging into me.

The tunnel from the train platform leads straight into the airport. Strands of my hair hang like limp string over my face and I blow them out of my eyes as I check my phone: 7.39 p.m. Plenty of time.

I close Google Maps and smile to myself, a cool ripple of relief washing over me. Time to stop worrying. I'm here now, and everything is going to be OK.

I close my eyes, snippets of my day flashing before me like a movie trailer: waking up beside Matt, losing my job, getting locked out, fucking Paul and fucking Caroline, Rose, the comments from the men and the men and the men, and this never-ending bastard heat. But it's over now. I'm here. I'm going to walk my sister down the aisle and I'm going to make my mother happy.

My grin widens, a bubble of hysteria making me giggle, and I cover my mouth before I look totally crazy.

A row of little machines lines the entrance to the airport. I check in to my flight and weigh my bag. It's officially hand luggage, although it's ridiculously heavy, but I'm not paying to check it in. I've spent enough on this flight as it is thanks to the wedding date being changed and having to pay peak summer prices. One more hour of dragging this bag around won't kill me.

The airport is tiny but shiny; everything glass and chrome and brand new. I glance up at the departures screen. My flight is on time and I'm all checked in. No issues. It feels almost unreal.

The queue for security isn't too long. When it's my turn I struggle to push the handle of my suitcase to get it into the scanner. As soon as I get to Spain, I'm chucking this piece of shit away and buying a new bag. With what money? I shake my head, a futile attempt to rid my mind of a million questions, and smile at the security officer.

'I need to check your bag,' he says.

I nod and he pokes through my belongings. He takes out my box of Tampax, grabs handfuls of my underwear, looks inside my makeup bag. He takes a swab, runs it through his machine and nods at me before moving on to the next person. I'm already sick of opening and shutting this suitcase.

The first thing I do as I step into the departures lounge is head to the toilet. Everyone looks happier here, calmer, like the weight of the sun has been lifted off their sunburnt shoulders. I'm practically high with the thought of getting out of these damn clothes and putting on a fresh T-shirt. The queue snakes all the way out of the door to the shop next door, and I join it. A woman is talking in French on her phone. I pick out words. *Dangerous. Too hot. Crowded.*

I've been standing in this queue so long, the air conditioning on full blast, that my clothes feel cool against my skin and I don't feel so clammy any more. My stomach grumbles and I realise how light-headed I am. I add up what I've eaten today – a slice of toast this morning, a nibble of a BLT sandwich, and half a raisin biscuit. I've walked nearly ten miles on that.

This queue isn't moving anyway. Food is more important than getting changed.

The airport is small and from here I can see a pub restaurant that doesn't look too busy. I know I'll get stiffed £10 for a limp sandwich, but I don't care any more.

I find a table near the departures screen and sit down on a rickety wooden chair. As soon as I take the weight off my feet they start to throb, but I don't care about that either. I don't care about anything any more. I'm here, my flight is on time, and I'm checked in. Nothing can go wrong now.

Beside the departure screen is a TV showing News 24. The London Strangler is all they're talking about.

Two women, immaculately dressed, are sitting at the table next to me, staring up at the screen, commenting between bites of quiche.

'I said to my niece, this is why you don't want to move to a big city. It's full of awful people.'

Her friend nods. 'Foreigners. They said he's white, but that doesn't mean he's English. He might be Albanian, or Polish. They come over here, take our jobs, prey on young girls. It's because we hand out money left, right and centre.'

Her friend hums in agreement. 'And because girls nowadays have no self-respect. When I was young, we didn't walk about like that. Getting drunk, hardly wearing any clothes, dating strangers online and having sex with them on the first date. It was a lot safer in our day and that's because we didn't go around shouting about our rights and bringing attention to ourselves.'

The two women look like they're in their seventies. I do the maths. They were in their twenties during the late sixties and seventies. Miniskirts, LSD, the summer of love, psychedelia. It's not as if women and children were any safer then: Ian Brady, Myra Hindley, Peter Sutcliffe, Fred and Rose West. The names and faces of nostalgic murderers are famous – but what were the women and children called?

I don't notice the waitress next to me waiting expectantly until she clears her throat. I zone out the two women, and the television, and pick up the menu. It's all blurry. I must be hungrier than I thought.

'What would you like?'

'Are you still serving the all-day breakfast?' She nods and I order it with a full-fat Coke.

I'm tired. I'm so tired of women like the ones at the next table, tired that the actions of one man can make an entire city turn on one another.

All this time, I've been dreading going back to Spain, walking back into that house, that room, resurrecting the memories that have haunted my dreams for years. But surely Ronda will be better than this. Better than this relentless foreboding and stifling heat, squeezing every last drop of humanity from everyone crammed into a city that is never big enough.

I take out my phone and look at Nikki's face again.

Running my finger over the screen, I imagine her voice, imagine what she would say about the day I've had.

'It's not your fault,' she'd say about the transport strike. 'You weren't to know.'

'It's not your fault,' she'd say about work. 'Fucking Paul and the fucking patriarchy. You need to report him.'

'I like her,' she'd say about Rose. But then Nikki always did like beautiful sharp things. She liked her flowers loud, thorny but with large, soft petals that opened up as soon as you looked at them.

And what about Matt? What would Nikki say about him, and the fact I'm still lying to my family, and what I did all those years ago? Luckily, she doesn't know about any of that. I tried so hard to prevent her from hating me, but it happened anyway.

My stomach churns at the sight of the plump sausage and gelatinous egg the waitress places in front of me. Maybe I should have had a sandwich. I pick at the bacon, nibble the bread, and bit by bit work my way through the food. With each mouthful I feel myself calming down a little more, my head clearing.

I keep scrolling through the photos of Nikki. There are lots of comments below her Save Them post. People calling her inspirational. Women saying they'd see her at Trafalgar Square. Someone I don't know calling her a 'fucking queen' and following her comment with three purple hearts.

I look at Twitter and click on the #SaveThem hashtag. Then instantly wish I hadn't.

Clarissa • @CJettersonParker

There's a killer on the loose and women are
planning an all-night gathering a few minutes from
where the murders happened? Are they crazy?
They only have themselves to blame. #SaveThem is
dangerous ☹

Melt the snowflakes • @Rob39762

Wake up! All these woke lefties banging on about
women's rights and #SaveThem. Things are better
now than they have ever been for women!

E M Butler Author • @EmmaButler1

I can't believe my daughter wants to catch a train to
London to attend the #SaveThem vigil for murdered
women when the police are still on the hunt for this
monster. I blame social media.

$$$UPERHERO • @bethemandotcom

I know it's sick, but those #SaveThem girls were hot.
I do like me some long dark hair. Why can't killers
pick on the ugly ones and do us all a favour?

I pay for my meal and check the time again. We start
boarding in forty minutes. There are only ten departure
gates, so I don't have to hurry to the right waiting area. I
keep telling myself there's no rush, I can calm down now,
but I can't let myself believe it.

The queue for the toilet is still snaking around the air-
port. I spot a W. H. Smith's and my chest swells. Yes! That's
way more fun than standing in line. It's not like the airport

is so huge I can't get to my gate when they call my flight. And I can always change my clothes on the plane.

The magazine section is so crammed with glossy covers full of white teeth and bold lettering it's hard to tell which ones are about celebs and which are about keto or country-house decor. I flick through them, tallying up the coverage Swan & Swallow has secured for our clients. One of our ads is in a health magazine, the one I worked on for a toothpaste brand. I spot an article about the gender-equality campaign we ran in a magazine for women in business, followed by a logo I designed for a new online course our film-school client is running. A logo Paul ended up taking full credit for.

'That logo idea was mine,' I'd said to him quietly as we'd stepped out of the meeting room.

'There's no "I" in Swan and Swallow, Em,' he'd replied with a wink, his fingertips brushing mine.

'But there *are* two "wa wa"s for "wanker",' I should have said. But then I never said anything to him that I should have.

Whatever, that's still my work, in a magazine, in a London airport. That level of success is all I've ever wanted ... which is why I can't stay in Spain. I have to get back to London as soon as the wedding is over and find another job.

I move on from the bright magazines to the two-for-one book table, wishing I could afford to treat myself to something new to read – then reminding myself I have over fifty unread books on my Kindle.

Sitting alone on the shelf, wedged between Politics and

Self-help, I spot a simple white book with a faux-leather cover. I pick it up. It's a small Bible. The cover is pale and embossed with a silver cross, the spine decorated with foiled lattice work with the edges painted in silver. It's not as large as our family Bible. That one has five generations of names written in it, a list Marianna and Alberto are desperate to add their own future children's names to.

I fiddle with the pendant of my mother's necklace. The same necklace I'm expected to hand over to my sister tomorrow, as if I haven't had enough taken off me lately. My sister gets my mother's lucky necklace and the family Bible. Why? Why can't Marianna and her husband-to-be start their own fucking Bible? I'm the eldest; I'm the one who should be adding her name to the book next. Who's to say I won't have children one day?

I think of Nikki. I think of the diamond ring nestled in a bowl of chocolate eggs. I think of a future I turned my back on. It could have been her name beside mine in that book.

But maybe it's not too late. What if I told Nikki everything, the whole dirty truth, and she took me back? Tonight, in literally a few hours' time, I could tell my family that their precious Nick is actually a girl called Nikki. I could tell them how much I love her. Because I do. I really love her, and I don't know how to stop.

The little white Bible in my hand costs £42, and I pay, a small price to ease my guilt. I hold my breath as the card reader takes its time to process the payment, but it goes through.

I've been like this since I arrived in London, counting

every penny, forever weighing up my wants against my needs. All I do is worry about money, yet how much has my mother spent on my sister's wedding? Surely she won't mind lending me – *giving* me – the same amount? It would be more than enough to buy me time to turn my life around. Yes. I'll ask my mum for money, rent a cheap room in a nice house on the outskirts of London and find my own clients. There are plenty of independent businesses looking for freelance designers. I can do this. I can be the person my family already believe I am.

I stuff the Bible into my suitcase, having to sit on it to zip it up, and make my way to the toilet. My luggage won't be so crammed when I take some clothes out and get changed.

As I exit W. H. Smith's I feel a tension in the air, a buzz that wasn't there before. I wheel my bag past a row of seats and spot a group of people staring out of the giant windows facing the runway. The grass is a dull shade of yellow, with the river beyond shimmering as the setting sun beats upon it, and in the distance the tall buildings of east London are shrouded in a grey, hazy mist. People are pointing at something glowing red in the distance.

A large departure screen is positioned above the toilet entrance, the word 'DELAYED' flashing beside the first four flights. A couple joins me, muttering to one another and checking their phones. They're followed by more people crowding at the glass wall, their hands pressed up against the pane like children staring into a sweet-shop window.

A woman holding a baby sidles up beside me. 'What's going on?'

We're meant to be boarding now. I shrug. 'No idea.'

The tannoy clicks into action. 'This is a passenger announcement. Because of a fire at Royal Victoria Gardens, all flights have been delayed due to visibility issues. As soon as the fire is under control, we will update you.'

I don't know how long I stare at that screen – maybe five minutes, maybe fifteen – but slowly, one by one, the flights change from DELAYED to CANCELLED until every single flight on the screen is red.

Then all hell breaks loose.

19

The information desk is heaving. It's taken thirty minutes of being jostled from one BA staff member to another and then waiting in line until I'm finally in front of someone who can help. So many people are trying to talk to the one woman behind the desk that my stomach is getting pushed against the counter. I've lost my hair tie in the scrum, and I can hardly move my arms in order to push my hair away from my sweaty face.

'Hi,' I say to the girl in the British Airways uniform. 'I was meant to be on the 9.15 p.m. flight, but it's been cancelled. Are you able to help?'

She doesn't bother to reply, just hands me a piece of paper outlining the refund policy before turning to the man beside me.

'Wait, listen,' I say, trying to edge my way back.

The man blocks me. 'It's my turn now.'

'I haven't finished asking my question. I need to get to Málaga airport—'

'We all have somewhere we need to be,' a woman behind me says. The one with the baby. Her child is red in the face, emanating a thick stench of shit and a scream so high it's drilling right through my head.

'Can you get us on another flight?' the man asks.

I stand my ground, listening.

The woman behind the counter is sweating, her hair frizzing around her hairline and her cheeks dotted with red patches. She's trying to get the attention of her colleague, who's on the phone looking just as flustered.

'Apparently the fire is getting worse,' she says to the man. 'A wind has picked up in a northerly direction, meaning the entire runway is obscured. We can't fly until the airways are clear.'

Why does he get a full explanation?

'I understand that,' the man says, running his hands through his hair and beckoning a stressed-looking woman forward. 'I mean can you get my wife and me on another flight at another airport tonight?'

The British Airways woman taps at her computer and says there's one leaving Gatwick in two hours if he can pay the £342 difference. He hands his credit card over like it's nothing, and she processes his booking. How does this guy think he's going to get from London City Airport to Gatwick that quickly when the roads are all jammed and public transport has only just started running again? Whatever. Not my problem.

'Can you get us on a morning flight?' I shout out.

The woman with the stinking baby is trying to push me out of the way, but I need to know what's going on. If I stay at the airport tonight, I can get the first flight in the morning. I have to get to Spain tomorrow. I can't miss the wedding on Sunday.

'I can move you to tomorrow's 8.20 a.m. flight.'

'Hey, I was next,' says stinking-baby woman.

I ignore her. 'How much?'

The British Airways woman taps at her keyboard, her long nails clicking like a million scuttling insects. 'Twenty-three pounds extra,' she says.

I can do that. I hand her my bank card and she doesn't bother to smile as she processes my booking and passes me the new details.

'Is it OK to sleep here?' I ask. I can wander around the shops until they close. I can doze in a chair. It's not like it's cold right now and I need a blanket.

The woman makes a face. 'Of course not.'

'But people sleep in airports all the time,' I say, rooting my feet firmly on the ground as everyone behind me pushes forward.

The mother with the crying baby sighs so hard the condensation from her hot breath collects on the back of my neck. The woman behind the desk is running out of patience too.

'This airport closes at ten thirty in the evening, that's in one hour, and re-opens at four thirty in the morning. I strongly suggest you take the complimentary shuttle to the hotel down the road, have a good night's sleep, then come back in the morning. Next, please.'

I trip and stumble as I'm pushed out of the way, my suitcase caught among the legs of all the people trying to get on the same flight I just managed to get moved to.

OK. This is OK. I can work with this. I'll stay at a nearby hotel tonight, ring my sister, tell her I'll be in Málaga tomorrow lunchtime instead and in Ronda a couple of hours later, and I won't have missed anything but the final day of wedding panic. I'm sure Marianna will have something to say about me not being there to get my nails done with her, but that's the least of my problems. I'll be walking her down the aisle, as promised. I even have a fancy Bible gift for the happy couple.

The queue for the shuttle bus to the airport hotel is just as long as the one for the help desk. I calculate how many queues I've stood in today. How many times I've waited to use a bathroom, get into a taxi, get on to a train, get help.

I end up standing in the tiny bus, one hand holding on to the rail above my head and the other attempting to stop the handle of my useless suitcase from coming out again. I sway from side to side, my all-day breakfast swirling in my guts, acid climbing up my throat.

I'll be fine once I get into my hotel room. I can have a cool shower, wash my hair, get a few hours' sleep, ring Marianna. Actually, maybe I should call her now, in case my mum's waiting up for me. Spain's an hour ahead; it's getting late. Hopefully my sister hasn't already left to pick me up from the airport.

Using my knee, I pin my suitcase against the seat of the person beside me and with my free hand fish my phone out of my bag. I'm on 27 per cent battery. At least I can charge it back in my room. Shit! I don't have a charger. Maybe reception will have one.

The phone rings. My sister answers on the first ring.

'Did you land early? Don't tell me you're delayed!'

I take a deep breath, keeping my voice low, acutely aware of all the other steaming bodies pressed in beside me.

'The flight was cancelled. Wait, calm down, I'm still coming. There was a fire near the airport and I'm on the first flight out in the morning. I'll be with you by lunchtime. It's fine, I won't have missed anything. Is Mama there?'

There's a rustling at the other end. I can hear a low voice. It must be Alberto.

'Mama's asleep.'

She never goes to bed this early. I have a sudden urge to hear my mother's voice. I need her to tell me she's OK and that none of this is my fault.

My sister sighs. 'She made all your favourite food, you know. It's here getting cold. She doesn't have the energy to do stuff like that any more. Worrying about you has exhausted her. She needs to be well for the wedding.'

'Tell her I'm sorry,' I say, a fist of guilt squeezing tightly around my throat. I use the back of my hand to wipe at my brow. 'I'm doing my best.'

'That's what you always say. Well ... just get here as soon as you can. I'll be at the beautician's at one o'clock tomorrow, but Mama will be home.'

So no one is picking me up from the airport? A taxi is going to cost a fortune. Maybe my mother will pay when I pull up.

'I'm really looking forward to Sunday,' I say. 'Oh, and Marianna, I have your Bible.'

I can hear the smile in my sister's voice as she thanks me and says she'll see me tomorrow. There's more rustling. I think she's hung up, but she hasn't. I can hear Alberto's voice telling her I'm not worth getting stressed about. That Sunday is all about her.

'You don't understand,' Marianna says, her voice muffled and distant. 'My sister always brings bad luck.'

Then the line goes dead.

20

BBC Breaking News • @BBCBreaking

Flights are grounded as fires sweep through east
London. London's emergency services are stretched
to the limit as the heatwave has firefighters and
ambulances busier than ever, and police have increased
their efforts in the manhunt for the killer who has been
dubbed the London Strangler.

Another desk. Another queue.

They only opened the front doors of the shuttle bus, which meant those at the back, like me, were the last to get into the hotel. Which means I'm at the back of the queue this time. It's just past ten o'clock and the light outside has turned to a deep blue – not yet night, but dark enough to make everything look like it's been put through a filter. I can really smell the smoke now; the view of the airport and Canary Wharf is completely obscured by thick white clouds.

I'm not sure if the fire is making the air hotter, but according to my phone it's still close to thirty degrees.

An SMS flashes on my phone screen. It's from Kate. I

glance at it, but it looks long. I'll read it later. I turn my phone to flight mode to conserve the battery.

This building is exactly what you'd expect from a cheap inner-city airport hotel. The outside looks like a box, a prison, a giant 1970s radio set. The inside is just as bland, and far too small for the busload of people that's just descended.

From my place in the queue, I can see that just past reception there's a beige-and-red cafeteria, if you can call it that, and a bar. There are already people milling about, clutching cold drinks and complaining about the delay. Through the glass windows behind me smoke from the Royal Victoria Gardens is getting darker and higher.

Has someone started these fires on purpose? Or was it a discarded cigarette or a disposable barbecue left behind?

I don't know how many people have booked in before me, or how many rooms this cardboard box of a hotel has, but with each guest heading towards the lifts my stomach sinks that little bit lower. I just want a shower, and to get out of these clothes that smell of sweat and now smoke, and wash my greasy hair, and sleep. I really want to sleep.

The man behind the desk is called Neil and looks like he would prefer to be sipping a single malt in an oak-lined library than dealing with hot, irate customers who want the cheapest room he has.

'I'd like the cheapest room you have,' I say. 'Single bed. My flight was—'

'Cancelled. Yes, we know. It's been quite an evening. Our standard rooms are £44.99, not including breakfast.'

That's forty-five quid I wasn't planning on spending, but it's fine.

I fill in the paperwork, ignoring the impatient shuffling of those in the queue behind me.

Neil takes a photocopy of my passport and nudges the card reader over to me. I stick in my bank card, punch in my code and a big red cross appears. My stomach knots. What did my balance say this morning? I haven't spent that much today. Two sandwiches and some water this morning, an all-day breakfast dinner, and the extra on my new flight.

I try again. Nothing.

The Bible. The fucking Bible! This room costs the same as a stupid book I felt the need to buy my whining sister to pre-empt her tantrum about my selfishness.

'I have a credit card,' I say, rooting through my handbag.

The strap of my bag pulls at my sore shoulders, now tinged red with sunburn. I place it on the desk and search inside, pulling out my purse and dipping my fingers into each slot to try and locate the card. My hands are sweaty, my hair falling in my face. I try not to use my credit card as the monthly bills are always a nasty surprise. That's why it's buried so deep inside my purse.

I hand it over triumphantly and Neil taps it on the reader. It asks for my PIN.

The PIN? I don't know my PIN. A woman behind me tuts, making the hairs on the back of my neck stand on end. My PIN. Jesus, what's my PIN?

I hold one finger up, give a tight smile, and scroll through my phone. My hand is shaking. Come on, pull yourself together! I have my PIN in the contacts of my phone under C. C. Smith . . . or something like that. I search for CC and spot a name. C. C. Banco. Subtle. The number is on there: 4932 0 4932.

I type 4932 into the machine, and it beeps.

Why? This is the number. It's in my phone. It's definitely the number.

'I don't understand,' I stammer. 'Let me try again.'

The woman behind me whispers something to her husband, something that sounds like 'As if today hasn't been bad enough.'

'Let me insert it again,' Neil says, looking like he really wants that whisky.

He pulls out my card, rubs it, looks at the back, looks at the front. Looks closer.

'Madam, this card ran out last month.'

'What? No. I—'

He holds it up close: 6/23. June. It's now the end of July.

'Would you mind stepping aside, please?' Neil says, ripping up the form I just filled in and the photocopy of my passport. 'There's rather a long line.'

I yank at my suitcase, the handle loosening in my hand, and kick it to the side of the desk. I'm struggling to breathe. Now what do I do?

It's nearly ten thirty and I have nowhere to sleep tonight. I have to be at the airport for an 8.20 a.m. flight tomorrow. The airport opens at four thirty, but that's six hours away. What am I meant to do for six hours in the middle of the night in the middle of nowhere? Where am I meant to go?

I can't go back to my flat, even though I have a key, because it's the weekend and the rules are, when Rebecca is there, I'm not. Also, I can't risk going all the way back to where I started this morning. I'm not even sure if the Tube is running properly already. What if there are still issues tomorrow morning? I have to be at the airport by sixish. And I can't go back to the airport now, because what fucking airport shuts at night? And I can't stay here. And . . .

My breaths begin to come in long pulls, my hands trembling as I try to adjust the handle of my suitcase. The queue surges forward and I'm pushed to the side.

'Come on, move over,' the woman who was behind me says. She's tall, wearing a floaty dress, her hair impeccable. Why isn't anyone else sweating? And why are they all so fucking calm?

'Sorry,' I mumble, sidestepping towards the café. I'm in the way there too. Everyone wants a drink. Of course they want a drink. I would love a drink.

My eyes are filling with tears. My throat is closing. I can't breathe.

Images of the day fill my mind. The men in the pub – I can still feel the press of that man's fingers against my skin. Those boys, the things they said to us. The look Paul gave me this morning, like he'd won. A sob escapes my mouth at the thought of the lies he's been spreading about me.

I can smell smoke and I can't breathe. *I can't breathe.*

The taste of sausage and egg lingers in my mouth, saliva

pooling in the insides of my cheeks, the acrid sting of vomit threatening to climb up my throat. I can't be sick here. I try and swallow it down, but my throat is dry, and it hurts, and I can't breathe.

I know what it means to choke on air, to feel like you're dying even though it's your own body strangling you. Light is fading and everything is blurring, and I can't feel my hands or my feet. My tongue feels like it's made of wood, my throat too narrow for air. All I can see is black and all I can hear is the thud of my own heart.

I'm six years old again. Mama has burned dinner and my father is shouting. My dinner plate is smashed to tiny pieces at my bare feet – my favourite plate, the one with the flowers. And he's screaming and she's crying and I'm hungry. I want to pick the pieces of china out of my food and eat it. Mama says I can't eat food off the floor, but this is my dinner and I'm hungry. My mouth is full of tears and mucus, bubbles forming at my lips as I try to speak. But no one is listening. My father throws a glass. Green fragments like a dozen crystal leaves scatter along the cold tiles. There's blood on my toe. I go to cry out, but I can't breathe.

And I still can't breathe.

I crouch down beside my suitcase, wrapping my arms around it, drowning. No air is getting in. My mouth opens and closes but all I can taste is smoke and heat and dust and vomit.

Nikki used to hold me up. Nikki knows how it feels to drown on land. I'd never seen it, but she told me. If it weren't for her tattoo, I wouldn't have believed she had ever got close to wanting the world to end. I wish she were here. I wish I still had her to cling to.

I'm curled up in a ball now, crouched low beside my luggage, my arms over my head and my chest heaving. People walk past, some muttering, their feet silent against the dirty carpet. Pretty shoes, sandals, trainers, work shoes, pretty shoes, sandals, trainers . . .

Someone taps me on the shoulder. They're saying something, but I'm submerged in memories and I can't hear them.

'Are you OK?' a woman asks. She sounds so far away. She's holding something out and placing my hand over it. 'You're safe. Deep breaths. Drink this.'

It's water.

I go to stand up, but the room is swaying, and my legs are too wobbly. I can't get any air in. Everyone is staring. Why is everyone staring?

The woman is wearing a gold clip in her shiny brown hair; it's shaped like a feather. An angel.

'Don't get involved,' a man says. He's dressed in a white shirt, his tie loosened at the neck.

'I can't leave her like this, Bill.'

'She's a nutter. Not our problem.'

My hands are shaking so hard I can hardly bring the plastic cup to my lips.

The woman who was tutting behind me walks past and says something about young people today having no backbone. The woman who gave me the water disappears and then reception is empty again.

Neil looks over at me from behind the protective shield of his little plastic desk box like I'm about to wreck the joint. His hand hovers over the phone. Not the police, not again. I'm just trying to breathe here, mister.

I sit on my suitcase and sip my water, my breaths shaky, but at least I'm able to get some air into my lungs again. My eyes sting from the last of my mascara merging with my tears, my nose and lips are numb and swollen.

Where's the woman who was kind to me just now? I want to thank her for the water.

Neil is still staring. I get the message. Slowly, with legs made of crêpe paper, I pull my suitcase up and stagger out of the hotel into the thick night air. The hotel parking lot is well lit. It's safe. Maybe I can just hang about a bit tonight.

Stepping outside is like walking into a sauna. How is it still so hot? Through the glass doors of the hotel I watch a man not much older than me with his arm in a sling and a walking stick in the other hand hobble out of the lift. He's probably going outside for a cigarette. He glances at me standing in a pool of light, mascara coating my face and my hair a mess, and a look of disgust sweeps over his features. More people go into the hotel, a few people go out, someone goes to their car to collect something, returning a minute later. Is this how I'm spending my night? Watching people come and go outside a cheap airport hotel?

'You're a fucking dick, Bill!' I hear as the glass doors of the hotel slide open. 'How many times do I have to say it? Just leave me alone!'

It's her, the kind woman with the golden feather in her hair.

'Mandy! Where are you going?' Bill shouts from inside.

Neil is watching. God, I bet he really hates his job.

Mandy marches off into the night, an overnight bag slung over her shoulder. I never got a proper look at her before. She's in her late twenties, dressed like she's been at work all day too. Her shoes don't look comfortable and her bag looks heavy.

A man with short-cropped hair is leaning against the wall on the other side of the hotel door, like he's waiting for someone. He gives me a tight smile, one of those polite ones you do when you catch someone's eye but you don't want to look like you were staring.

I don't smile back; instead I pretend to check my phone. That's when I see Kate's message from earlier.

Hey, Em. Sorry I haven't texted sooner. How are you? Did you get to the airport OK? It was crazy at work after you left. Everyone was getting in a state about the awards. I'm just glad Dante stayed late to keep me company. Guess what? We kissed! EEEEK!! I'm on my way home now, Tubes are a bit slow but up and running again. Text me as soon as you land in Malaga. Whatever the time. I want to know you're OK.

I smile at the thought of Dante and Kate together. Wait. *Kate!* Kate lives in Stratford! Why didn't I think of her sooner?

My hands are still a little shaky as I take my phone off

flight mode and look up her address on Google Maps, checking the distance via DLR. According to my phone, the trains are running until 12.30 a.m. and her house is just twenty minutes away. I can be there by eleven. I breathe a sigh of relief. She'll let me crash at hers tonight; I stay there a lot at weekends. She's probably desperate to tell me all the gossip about her and Dante anyway.

But I can't just turn up this late unannounced – what if I get there before she does? I call her back, but it goes straight to voicemail.

Pontoon Dock DLR station is just down the road. I'll keep trying.

The handle of my broken suitcase is getting close to completely breaking, but it's holding out enough for me to drag it down the road. Everything is industrial and ugly around here, even if there's a giant statue of a woman with her arms thrown back in the middle of the roundabout. Yeah, like there's anything glorious and freeing about this part of town.

The roads are empty and the wheels of my suitcase echo along the pavement as I call Kate again.

A message flashes up.

Sorry. On the phone to Dante. Call you back in a min.

I'll try her again when I get to the station.

A pool of sweat is forming in the small of my back and I keep marching as fast as I can. I have a blister on the side of my little toe and one on my heel, and I'm all too aware I haven't changed my tampon in hours. God, I really need a shower.

It feels like I've been walking down the same road for an hour. I check my phone; the station is just a few minutes away. These tall, ugly buildings must all be office blocks as the windows are dark. I cross over a bridge and pass some wasteland. A DLR train glides by in the distance, and I silently pray the trains are regular. I normally don't mind being on my own; I'm used to walking alone around the West End at night on the weekends. It's busy there. There's a buzz there. But this place is dead.

What if Kate's on the phone inviting Dante over to her place? I can't just turn up at her house without speaking to her first and ruin their romantic evening.

I keep walking until I'm nearly at the station. A narrow road leads me straight there, but it's dark and unlit. I don't know this area, so I stay on the main road in clear view of the traffic, even if it adds two minutes to my walk. I can see from here that the platform is empty. Nope, I'm not sitting on my own on an empty train platform.

There's a bus stop coming up, bright lights and a red bench facing the road. It's a safe place to stop. Kate knows I need to speak to her so I'm sure she'll call me back soon, then I'll get on the next train.

I lean against the glass and wait.

Words will never hurt me • @Em_Dash_93
Shortcuts are a luxury reserved for men

21

The bus stop bench isn't a proper bench; it's a slanted piece of moulded plastic that I can neither sit on nor lean against comfortably.

I'm about to look up the DLR times on my phone when a car slows down in front of me. A beat-up Renault Clio, a man with a grey beard and glasses at the wheel. He looks tired. Beside him, in the passenger seat, is the man who smiled at me earlier outside the hotel.

He winds down the window and hangs out of it. 'Excuse me,' he says.

I'm not going to walk over. I stay where I am.

'Sorry. I was at the hotel earlier and I saw what happened ... You know, you looked upset and ... Look, I didn't want to say anything, but my dad just picked me up and ...' The old man next to him holds up a hand in greeting. 'Well, we wondered if you needed a lift anywhere.'

'No, thanks.'

'It's no trouble,' the driver says, leaning over his son. 'I don't like to see a young lady out on the streets alone this late at night.'

He has kind eyes. He looks normal too. But what does that mean? Normal?

'No matter how far,' the younger one adds. 'Honest, we don't mind.'

I think about it. No, not worth the risk.

'It's fine. Thanks. My husband is on his way to pick me up,' I say, waving my phone at them.

They hesitate for a second or two. It's obvious I'm lying, but what can they do?

'I appreciate the offer, though,' I say. Because I do. But every woman knows you don't get in a car with two strange men. Every man knows that too.

They drive off and I look up the DLR times. According to the latest updates, they're running every ten minutes for another two hours. I rub my eyes, my mascara so worn off it has been reduced to a smudge, and lean back against the glass of the bus shelter. It's still hot, and my entire body itches from the need to get out of these sticky clothes. But I'm safer here facing the road than I am at the train station.

I try calling Kate one more time and it goes straight to voicemail again.

Another text.

SORRY! Now work is calling!

I text back, asking her to call me when she can as it's important, then scroll through Twitter as I wait for her call.

Why is anyone from work calling her this late on a Friday night? What on earth could be so important?

Oh, yes. The awards.

It's a bad idea, I know it is, but before I can talk myself out of it I click on Swan & Swallow's Twitter profile.

Their page is full of photos: my ex-work colleagues clinking champagne glasses; The Savoy's grand River Room bedecked in hues of gold and blue; close-ups of the food and goodie bags. So many photos of people I don't know clapping, but no Dante and no Kate. They exist in the outskirts of work life, holding everything together, but they don't count when it comes to the prizes and self-congratulatory back pats. That's reserved for account managers, sales people, directors and creatives.

And there's Paul. Paul in a fitted tux, totally composed, his mouth stretched wide into a grin. Paul drinking, lips glistening and eyes unfocused. Paul staring at me through my phone.

I know drunk Paul.

That night in the Coal Hole, everyone had moved on from beer and wine to sambuca shots.

'Are you a fun girl, Em?' Paul slurred, banging his shot glass on to the table. 'You look like a fun girl.'

We'd all been drunk. Kate is a sleepy drunk, I'm a quiet drunk, and Paul is . . . Paul gets very earnest. He'd taken his jacket off; beneath it he was wearing an Amnesty International T-shirt.

'I come from a working-class background, just like you,' he said. My family wasn't working class; my dad had his own business and my mother never worked. 'It's hard being a person of colour in this world. People don't understand us.'

'What do you mean?' I said.

I couldn't help myself. We're both white, Paul earns six figures, he has two houses, he drives a Tesla. He gestured with his hands, as if I wasn't keeping up.

'My grandfather was Portuguese, but very tanned. He came over after the war. So I know the struggles immigrants endure day to day. It's why I hired you. You and me ...' He placed his hand on my arm. 'We're the same, Em. I recognise talent when I see it.'

He was drunk, and everyone knows people speak the truth when they're drunk. I was flattered he'd called me talented, and he could tell. He stroked my arm.

'"Life is never fair, and perhaps it is a good thing for most of us that it is not,"' he said. I recognised the quote. Oscar Wilde. 'The world *isn't* fair, Em, but we can make it better. You can see that, right? You can see how hard I'm trying to make things better.'

Paul inched closer, which I thought was impossible, seeing as we were already so squashed together on the banquette. He took a strand of my hair, rubbing it between his fingers.

'You know Swan & Swallow could make or break your career?'

I nodded. He didn't let go of my hair.

'Let me help you.'

I looked at Kate for a cue, but her eyes were drooping, and Caroline was laughing like a donkey at something Leonard from Sales was saying. No one was looking over at Paul, with his one hand on my arm and the other playing with my hair.

'I have to go,' I said, pulling Kate up by the wrist. It was the first time she'd said I could stay the weekend at hers and I was looking forward to it.

'Hey, it's late, it's not safe. I'll walk you both to the station,' Paul said, standing up but not moving far back enough from the table, so we had to squeeze past him. Kate was out of it; she didn't even notice. But I did. I could feel Paul's semi-erect cock against my thigh, heard the noise he made as my hip brushed his.

I didn't want him to walk us to the station, but Caroline said it was a good idea we weren't stumbling down the Strand alone.

'The world is full of perverts!' she shouted out. Leonard reached under the table and Caroline gave an exaggerated screech then dissolved into a fit of giggles. He kept his hand there and Caroline was no longer interested in where we were going.

It was fine. A five-minute walk, then we could get away from Paul and his life lessons. Kate was slow, staggering like the walking dead, as we crossed the short distance to Charing Cross station.

'You're a good girl, Em,' Paul said to me. 'I bet your boyfriend loves you very much.'

He knew I wasn't in a relationship because he'd asked me on my first day. I told him again and he gave me a slow smile. Maybe I should have lied and mentioned Juan, even though that was years ago. Or Matt. Anyone. Funny how men respect an invisible man more than a woman saying no to their face.

Paul slowed down.

'We have to stop pretending,' he said. 'This . . . thing . . . between us, Em. I know you feel it too. When two souls collide, nothing is strong enough to fight it. I've noticed how you look at me in the office.'

I only ever glanced at him when I could sense him staring at me. Paul and his open-door policy, the door that opened right out on to a view of my desk.

He put his heavy arm around my shoulders. Sleepy, drunk Kate was dragging me down on one side, Paul's arm pinning me in place on the other.

'I don't think this is a good idea,' I said, ducking out of his hold. 'You're married.'

The gates of Charing Cross came into view, the building lit up. As we turned into the station Kate reached out for the wall, leaning against it with both hands.

'I'm going to be sick.'

Then she vomited all over the pavement, too drunk to jump back fast enough and stop it splashing against her tights. I wanted to hold her hair up, I wanted to rub her back, I may even have had some water in my bag to pass to her. But Paul got to me first, spinning me around and kissing me hard. As Kate vomited, Paul prised my mouth open with his own. Thick lips, wet tongue, jabbing, swirling, pushing his groin against mine.

The more I resisted, the harder he held me. So I let him. I knew it would finish sooner if I didn't resist.

'You're right,' he said as he pulled away. 'We should keep this a secret. People wouldn't understand.'

And now there he is, watching me through my phone, his lips shining like he just kissed me.

I keep scrolling, and with each photo my all-day breakfast climbs higher up my throat.

Marketing Week • @MarketingWeekEd
@SwanandSwallow win best PR campaign award for
#RiseAndShine, supported by top model Celene Morian.
The leading agency was praised for its outstanding
achievement in raising awareness of gender inequality.

No. My hand is shaking as I stare at my phone. *They won?*

There's a video of Paul holding up an ugly glass sculpture. I press play, my throat stinging from the acid rising.

'We pride ourselves on being a diverse company full of passionate men and women who believe in equality,' he's saying. 'These values are reflected in everything we do. Our Rise and Shine campaign has already had a huge impact not only on how the world views women and, we hope, it will have an impact on history as a whole. Women need to be heard.'

What women? The only women Paul has ever listened to are those who want to make him money or suck his cock.

'I'm so proud of everything we've achieved as a company. Swan & Swallow is one happy family – our team, our clients and you. And it's that love which shines through every campaign we work on.'

Love? Is that what he thought it was?

The Monday after he kissed me, Paul stood at the water

cooler by my desk and mumbled a quick apology. It was a relief – his interest in me was over before it had started. I told myself we'd both been drunk, that these things happened sometimes, that I'd probably been too friendly and given him the wrong impression. He'd been trying to find common ground, that's all, and I'd liked the attention. I missed Nikki. Maybe I'd come across as too eager.

Everything went back to normal. Then, a week later, as I waited for the kettle to boil in the office kitchen, Paul told me he was madly in love with me.

'That kiss,' he said, placing his hands on my hips. I glanced at the kitchen door, but no one was outside. I tried to step to the side, but he followed. 'I've tried, but I can't keep away from you. We make a great team, Em. I have the power to change your life.' He rubbed his thumb over my hip bone, making a noise halfway between a sigh and a groan. 'Oh my God, you'll be the death of me.'

'No. Paul, this isn't right.'

He stepped closer, his hips flush with mine. 'I know it's messy, but we can make it work. The course of true love never did run smooth.'

A laugh escaped my mouth. I was confused, shocked, nervous, a little scared.

Laughing was the worst thing I could have done.

I'd never been stupid enough to laugh in the face of my father when he was being mean. It was one of the first things my mother taught me as a child: 'Never laugh at men. They don't like being ridiculed.'

But Paul was nothing like my father. He wasn't violent.

Paul was smart, powerful, respected and a man proud of always doing the right thing. He had a nice family; I'd seen a photo of them on his desk on the countless occasions he'd called me in to tell me something that wasn't at all important. His wife was elegant, his children cute, people liked him – he wasn't anyone to be scared of.

Yet Paul was also a man used to getting what he wanted, and it was too late. The moment I laughed I saw the switch in his eyes.

I blink back tears, thinking back to all the moments after that when he would corner me. How he'd whisper what he wanted to do to me when we were finally alone. Always reminding me of how he could help me rise in the company.

'You've misunderstood me,' I'd say.

'Sorry if I've given you the wrong impression,' I'd say.

I said all those things, firmly and loudly, just like you're meant to. But Paul never listened because he didn't like to lose.

He never tried to kiss me again or force himself upon me, he'd simply comfort me; telling me I shouldn't feel guilty about my feelings for him. That we'd find a way to make it work. There were days I was genuinely confused, wracking my brain as to what I was doing or saying that was making him think I was interested.

Or worse, he'd smirk and wink, saying he liked it when I played hard to get.

I'd go home and drink, replaying each day each interaction with Paul, over and over. Wasn't I making myself clear enough? I'd fuck Matt, to stop myself thinking of Paul, then fuck him harder so as not to think about Nikki.

As long as I kept drinking and sleeping with Matt, I didn't have to spend my evenings worrying.

I told myself everything would blow over. Everything would work out just fine. Paul would soon get bored. All I had to do was focus on my job and do it well, because this opportunity at Swan & Swallow was going to change my life and I couldn't mess that up too. As if success ever has anything to do with working hard.

Leaning against the bus stop, I push down the bile searing my throat, my eyes filling with tears. The job I worked so hard to keep is over now. I've lost it all.

But maybe not everything.

What if I could start over again with Nikki? If I finally tell her what I did before I met her, and why I acted the way I did, perhaps she'd understand. And if she knew everything that's happened since, how many times I drowned without her, maybe she'll take me back. She loves me. I know she does. It was the last thing she screamed out of the Cotswolds BnB window as I was leaving.

'I love you!' she'd shouted. 'You're a fucking idiot and I'll never forgive you, but I love you. That will never change.'

Kate hasn't called me back yet. I try her again. Maybe her phone has run out of battery. If she doesn't call back soon, I'll go to her house anyway. I can't stay here all night, with my shirt so tight it hurts to move my arms and my feet stinging with blisters.

Enough Twitter. I click on Instagram instead. I need to see Nikki again, our smiling faces side by side, the way we used to be.

But the latest photo on her grid isn't her selfie and the information about tomorrow's Save Them vigil. It's someone else. Someone I don't recognise.

The caption below reads, 'My rock. My queen. My love.'

There's more than one photo. I swipe and I finally vomit, turning just in time to coat the bushes behind me. My eyes sting and my nose runs, snot and sick sticking to my lips as I heave on to the dry soil and yellowing leaves. I think of Kate being sick all those weeks ago and Paul's lips on mine and Matt's back to me this morning and the things men have said to me today and my father on the ground reaching out to me, and I heave until my throat is raw and my face is slimy with tears and mucus.

But the image that shines brightest of all, the image that is never going to leave my mind, is that of Nikki – *my* Nikki – kissing another woman. Her final words are no longer strong enough to moor me.

I wipe my mouth with the back of my hand.

'Fuck this,' I mutter, reaching for the handle of my suitcase. 'Fuck today and fuck them and fuck everything.'

I'm going to Kate's tonight and I'm going to Spain tomorrow and I'm never coming back. Matt can send me my belongings. Actually, he can fucking keep them.

The handle of my case is stuck and won't pull up. I keep tugging, wiggling it, trying to control the trembling of my lips and the shaking in my chest. I push my fingers beneath the handle, attempting to prise it out with my short nails, my sweaty hands slipping.

Then, with a sudden screech of metal on metal, the

handle slides out in one swift movement and comes away in my hand, the ends of the spokes broken and jagged. There's no way of pushing the handle back in now, and my suitcase is too heavy to carry. I can't move the bloody thing without a handle.

'No!' I cry between gritted teeth, kicking my case, my phone in one hand and the broken handle in the other. 'No, no, no!'

I keep kicking the bag, and it feels good. I relish the pain in my feet and the burn of my tired legs and the buzzing in my head; my body, mind and heart all screaming at once. Nikki. Paul. Nikki. Paul. Images of them running through my head like a carousel.

I kick out again, my case toppling over into the bushes. I keep kicking and kicking and kicking. Then my luggage disappears completely.

There's the sound of rustling, dry leaves and loose earth, and something heavy sliding. I stick my head into the shrubs, using the torch of my phone to search between the branches. Behind the bushes is a sheer drop leading down to a patch of grass in the park below.

I look at Google Maps, the only thing I've been able to trust all day, and zoom in. I'm right in front of a place called Thames Barrier Park.

The bitter taste of sick coats my teeth and gums and I smell of sweat and smoke. I also need to change my tampon and I need to piss – but I can't go anywhere without my luggage. Gripping the broken suitcase handle and holding it out like a sword, the torch of my phone in my other hand leading the way, I walk into the darkness.

Once I reach the clearing, I calculate that my case has to be beneath the cluster of foliage to my right. I poke about, moving branches and tiny yellow leaves with the jagged metal of the suitcase handle, but I can't see anything. Maybe I got it wrong. Maybe it's further down.

Then I realise I'm not alone.

On a wooden park bench a few metres away lies something long, dark and lumpy. A holdall. And lying on the ground is a woman with a gold feather clip in her hair. A man is sitting astride her, one hand around her throat, the other loosening his tie.

I stop and stare. My chest tightens. I hold my breath. The buzzing in my head gets louder and louder as something surges through me.

I've seen this before. It's my father and it's my mother, her head swivelling out of his reach. It's me and it's Paul, the taste of his skin at the back of my throat. The woman isn't moving, I'm not moving; it's much safer not to move. Do nothing. Say nothing. Wait for it to stop.

But then I see Paul's slimy smile and Matt's back and my father's cruel sneer and a woman kissing my woman and I run. I run as fast as I can along the grass, the handle of my case still in my hand, its jagged edges glinting in the moonlight, my thighs rubbing and my shirt tight and my hair sticking to my forehead, and I drive the two metal prongs into the man's flesh.

And I don't stop.

22

The Mirror • @DailyMirror

Murdered nurse Zhao Li has been identified as the London Strangler's fourth victim. Li was found in Stepney City Farm at 7.53 a.m. this morning after a dog walker noticed a woman's shoe in the bushes. This is the first of his victims found outside central London. Is the serial killer heading east?

I'm running. I can't see and I don't know where I'm going but I keep running. The air is thick with the stench of hot pennies. My face is wet, my lips are dipped in molten iron. Something grey is on the horizon.

Water.

Melissa Dunbard • @MelissaJDunbard
What are the police doing to catch this man?

Dr Mark Evermore • @MEvermorephd
Replying to @MelissaJDunbard
How do you know it's a man?

Kamaria Brown • @MojitoMama
Replying to @MEvermorephd
It's always a man!

I'm at the edge of the river. Large metallic structures rise out of its surface like a long line of curved, scaly huts. Giant, hunched fish. The Thames Barrier, built to stop the water from getting too high. Built to stop London from drowning.

> **Maria, you gotta see her** • @MariaSalvatorre90
> So are we just expected to carry on like nothing's happening? Take our kids to school, go to work, enjoy nights out with friends? With a killer on the loose?
>
> **Kamaria Brown** • @MojitoMama
> Replying to @MariaSalvatorre90
> What's the alternative? Stay locked up at home?

I see a bench facing the water. I sit down. There's a knocking sound. A hard wooden knock, knock, knock. It's me. It's the handle of my suitcase in my clenched fist. Metal on wood. The handle is slick to the touch, covered in something warm and wet. I'm shaking. Knock, knock, knock. Something is sticky. I'm sticky. The air is thick, and it won't enter my lungs.

> **Barry M** • @BarryMaloney
> I'm not standing by letting this piece of shit run rampant around the city. I have a wife and daughter.
>
> **Steve Fisher** • @SteveFisher2
> Replying to @BarryMaloney
> What you gonna do, Caped Crusader?

Keep Fit Katherine • @RomseyGymKate

Replying to @SteveFisher2

He's right. We can't just stand by and do nothing!

Maria, you gotta see her• @MariaSalvatorre90

Replying to @RomseyGymKate

It's OK, the PM said we should stay 'vigilant'. That will stop us getting murdered

I curl up on the bench and wrap my arms around my legs. It's too dark to see colours, but my trainers don't look white any more. I pull my skirt up, get some air to my legs. My clothes are wet and warm. I still have my handbag on my shoulder. I still have my phone in my hand. I'm still clutching the handle of my suitcase. My suitcase. Where's my suitcase?

Sam Cooper • @SamICan

Anyone else noticed the dead women all looked the same – long dark hair, 28–32, smartly dressed? Creepy.

Fan of a Yoda am I • @StarWarsSimon

Replying to @SamICan

You seriously telling me a murderer has time to pick and choose? He's an opportunist!

Barry M • @BarryMaloney

I think there's definitely a pattern with who he's picking and the direction he's heading in.

Sam Cooper • @SamICan

Replying to @BarryMaloney

I'm going to tell my girlfriend to dye her hair
blonde or cut it shorter. I don't like this one bit!
Fan of a Yoda am I • @StarWarsSimon
How the hell do you murder so many women in
one week and not get caught?
Grate Britpain is sinking • @LastChanceSalLoon
You've clearly never been to London. There are no
police around.
Maria, you gotta see her • @MariaSalvatorre90
Replying to @LastChanceSalLoon
As if you can trust the police!

I saw a girl. Her dark hair was speckled with tiny yellow
leaves. Why was she on the ground? She had something in
her mouth. She couldn't breathe. I could see she couldn't
breathe. A red line of blood trickled down her temple and
her eyes were closed. I looked at her, but I didn't look at him,
or at what I was doing. I just looked at what he had done.

Sam Cooper • @SamICan
I wish we still had the death penalty for bastards
like this guy.
Barry M • @BarryMaloney
And what's that thing he's doing with the ties?
Strangled, not raped, then a stripy school tie stuffed
in their mouths. And why do the women all look the
same?
Maria, you gotta see her • @MariaSalvatorre90
He could be anyone. Our friend, our neighbour,

someone we work with . . .
Kamaria Brown • @MojitoMama
I'm so fucking ANGRY.

It was easy. Too easy. Is that how easy it is to stop someone? All those years, I stood there and waited. I accepted. Be quiet and do as you're told. It's safer to do nothing. Don't get involved.

But what I just did was easy. So easy. And now what?

I hold the suitcase handle up to the moonlight. It no longer shines. My body twitches and my hand trembles as I stagger over to the river's edge and look down at the still water.

The Thames is ancient. How many people have stood where I am right now, staring down into its depths? What secrets does it keep? I stretch my arm back as far as it will go and with more strength than I knew I had I throw the handle into the water.

There's no splash, no ripple of water breaking, but it's gone. One hand is empty, the other still holding my phone.

I sit back down on the bench and look up at the moon. What have I done?

Melissa Dunbard • @MelissaJDunbard
I don't want to go to work tomorrow. I'm so scared.
Is anyone else scared?
Sharon Louise Brown • @MojitoMama
Replying to @MelissaJDunbard
I'm terrified.

What have I done?
What have I done?
What have I done?
What have I done?
What have I done?
What have I done?

23

My dreams are red.

Marianna is gliding down the aisle, and I'm running behind her but I can't keep up. The tiles of the church floor are slick with blood, and I'm slipping, my knees hitting the ground with a crack. I put my hands out, bare feet sliding in the warm, thick puddles as I try to stand. But my sister doesn't turn around. I try to shout, but no words come out, and no air goes in. I look to my left. My mother's in the congregation, smiling up at the priest. I know that man. The priest is my father, his arms stretched out, preaching about love and forgiveness. My sister stares up at him, eyes growing wide with wonder. Everyone stares up at him. But I still can't stand, flailing on the ground like a new-born deer soaked in the blood of its own birth.

I see Nikki. I reach out to her, but she turns to the woman beside her and they kiss. A passionate embrace no one else can see.

There are others in the congregation. Caroline and Paul are there, laughing at me, fingers pointing. Kate and Dante, Moby and Rose, are behind them. They try to pull me up, their hands grasping like the desperate claws of rabid zombies, but they can't reach me. They're pinned to the pews. Their fingertips are inches from my own, their hands dry and clean while mine drip with blood.

I scramble on all fours, face down, reaching out for my sister's veil. It's so long it glides along the ground, the fabric cleaning the blood off the floor long enough to reveal white marble tiles before the streaks fill up again. I reach out, leaving red handprints on the gossamer veil, but the silky fabric slips through my fingers. The priest keeps talking, and Marianna keeps walking, her eyes fixed on the altar.

Jesus on his giant golden cross floats above my father's head. Jesus is bleeding. It's his blood on the floor that I'm slipping on, his blood that has soaked my hair and stings my eyes.

A man waits for Marianna at the end of the aisle. Alberto?

He has his back to us as she keeps walking, the aisle growing longer and longer. I reach out again, attempting to grasp the train of her dress. My cries are muted, my throat clogged with thick, bitter bile that tastes of abattoirs and death.

The groom turns around, and it's him. The man with no face. He's wearing a baseball cap and in his hand is a blue-and-white striped tie.

I wake up screaming and for a moment forget where I am. The bench is hard against my thighs and my hair is stuck to my cheek. But I'm not screaming; the sound I hear is the wail of police sirens in the distance. I look up, expecting to see a dying Jesus, but all I see is the moon shining down like God is searching for something. Like he's found me and shone a spotlight on what I've done.

My hands are stiff. Why are they black? I try and clench them, but they hurt and something dry flakes off them.

I look around me. Where's my suitcase? I have my handbag, but where's my luggage? Then I remember. I remember everything. And I start to shake.

I'm still huddled in a ball when I hear the rumble of a scooter approaching. I should sit up and look normal, but I can't move. It doesn't matter any more. Nothing matters.

The rumbling stops and I keep my head down. If I can't see them, they can't see me.

'There you are!' says a voice.

I don't move.

'I've been looking for you everywhere.'

It's Rose.

She sits beside me and places a hand on my arm. I flinch. This is another dream.

'Look at the state of you. You OK?'

I remain silent, waiting for her to disappear.

'Hey. Em. You're safe now.' Her voice is low, like I'm a little rabbit she doesn't want to scare.

Except I'm not a rabbit. I'm the fox.

'Do you remember calling me?' she asks.

I don't understand.

'Em. Talk to me.'

I shake my head. I don't think I know how to talk. I can't feel my body any more; all I can see is red and all I can taste is metal.

'Take your time,' she says. And we sit there, side by side, looking out over the water.

Rose's face is illuminated by the glare of her phone. She stares at it while I stare up at the moon.

When I was young my mother used to say the dead would climb up to heaven and sit on the stars. That the moon was their sun, and that when I was sad all I had to do was look up at night and know that millions of people were looking down at me and smiling.

The night frightened me after that. All those people, watching me.

Then, when my father died, I imagined him perched on the edge of a star. Cold. Alone. Far away. And I was no longer scared of the dark.

Is he up there now? Did he see what I just did?

'You feeling better?' Rose asks.

I try breathing again, and this time some of the air reaches my lungs. I nod.

'Where's your suitcase?'

I shrug, and she places a hand on my shoulder. 'They'll fucking steal anything. OK, at least you can get on my scooter easier.'

'Scooter?'

Rose is the first woman to speak to me since the one who gave me water at the hotel. Was that her? Was she the woman on the ground with the tiny yellow leaves in her hair?

'Yeah. You called me, about two hours ago. You said you were drowning and that I had to save you. I kept asking where you were and all you said was "The park, the park by the river, the park where the river stops the water rising." I didn't know what the fuck you were on about. I don't do riddles, Em, but I could tell you were in serious trouble. I've been riding about for ages. Did you miss your flight or something?'

I shake my head. 'Cancelled. Big fire.'

Rose makes a motorbike sound with her mouth as she breathes out. 'Jesus fucking Christ, girl. You've had a day. Are you hurt?'

I don't know. Am I?

'Let's get you back to mine and we can talk there. I'm only ten minutes away. Can you hold on?'

Hold on to what? I can't hold on. I've lost my grip on everything.

Rose picks up my handbag, loops it twice over the handle of her scooter, then comes back for me. I stand slowly. Everything hurts – my hand, my head, my heart.

'Come on,' Rose says. 'Easy does it. Will you be able to sit on my bike? Where are you hurt?'

She thinks I'm the victim. She thinks I'm the rabbit.

'It's OK,' I say, climbing tentatively on to the back.

'Hold on tight!' she shouts, and with one last look around she starts the ignition and pulls off.

She doesn't care that we're riding over grass and gravel,

bouncing over the kerb, tiny stones skittering under her wheels. There are no roads. How did she know where I was? Why didn't she give up?

Blue lights flash in the distance. Did they find the girl? Did they find the man? Will they find me?

With a jolt we drop down off the pavement and swerve behind a van. I recognise the road; that's the bus stop I was sitting at. My luggage is somewhere in those bushes. A suitcase without a handle.

We ride past Pontoon Dock station. Kate. I need to call Kate. I hold on tighter and close my eyes. Rose smells of cigarettes and mints. She's wearing shorts and a different top, a T-shirt, the kind you sleep in.

All the streets look the same, every window in every building black and empty. I have no idea what time it is. I have a flight to catch. The wedding. I can't miss the wedding.

We slow down outside a collection of apartment blocks jutting out like stalactites. Stalagmites. Sticks. Colourful boxes. Loads of them, pushed together, facing a yellowing patch of grass. Everything here is so clean and sharp and new.

'Come on,' Rose says gently, helping me off the scooter. 'Are you in pain?'

She keeps asking me that. Should I be?

I take her hand, but she doesn't say anything when she sees my own hand is black and sticky. She just holds it and helps me walk to her block. Amelia House. That's pretty.

We go up in the lift. She's humming a Christmas tune,

'Silent Night', pulling her keys out of her handbag, opening a door, ushering me in. Is this where she lives? I wasn't expecting this.

'Took a while to get my own place, but I got there,' Rose says.

London twinkles below us like it's made from black card and glitter, the bend of the river snaking between the lights. It's peaceful up here. Almost like nothing bad is happening below.

'Listen,' Rose says, locking the front door then sliding the Chubb lock in place. Her voice is quiet, her hand on my shoulder. 'You might want to have a shower, I get that, but if we're going to report what happened to you, it may be best to stay as you are for . . . you know . . . evidence.'

I'm rooted in the centre of her pristine living room. Everything is white and soft shades of grey, with splashes of colour like the lime-green and hot-pink cushions. It's all so neat. The living room is open plan, the kitchen brand new and white and gleaming. I'm the only broken, dirty thing in her home.

'Here,' she says, handing me a tiny glass. 'It's brandy. It will help with the shock.'

'Are you hungry?' she asks.

I threw up my dinner. My stomach is empty. All of me is empty. I shake my head and she presses an ice-cold bottle of water into my hand.

'Drink them both, then rest. If you want to talk, I'm here. If you want to have a sleep, I can make you up a bed on the sofa.' She looks at me, at the state of me, the red streaks on my arms and my clothes torn and stained. 'I'll lay some towels down. When we go to the police it will help if they see you exactly like this.'

The police. We can't go to the police. She doesn't understand.

I stay rooted to the spot, sipping my brandy, unable to open my bottle of water with one hand. Rose hasn't noticed.

She busies herself laying down towels over her light grey sofa, covering a pillow with another towel, pulling a side table over to place my drinks on.

I lie down, pushing my hair from my face. It's matted in clumps. I close my eyes. I'm safe now. This feels safe.

'Em,' she says. 'What happened?'

I open my eyes again. Rose looks different; hair tied back, no makeup, face soft, eyes searching. She's not a fighter tonight.

'Did someone hurt you?' she asks.

'Yes,' I say. 'So many people.'

24

This time I sleep like I'm dead. I don't know what time I finally passed out on Rose's couch, but when I wake up the sun is streaming into the room, bathing everything in shades of honey that make me think it's nearing the afternoon.

Tentatively, I stand, every part of my body aching, from my hair follicles to the tips of my fingers and toes. I'm dirty, and a lot of the mess has rubbed off on the towels I've been lying on, white cotton streaked with maroon smudges like old wine stains. Why did Rose use her best fluffy towels? I need to pay her back. I have no money, but maybe, when I get to Spain, I can ask my mother for some money and do a bank transfer and . . .

Fuck.

My flight!

I scrabble for my phone, which is plugged into the wall. Rose clearly had the foresight to charge it for me.

I can't hear anything. If Rose isn't here, then where the fuck is she? My heart hammers as I imagine her walking into a police station, telling them there's a woman in her flat covered in blood, that I . . . No. Wait. She has no idea what I did.

I'm not even sure *I* know what I did.

With shaky fingers I punch my PIN into my phone, I press 'mobile data' for 4G, and look at the time: 12.53 p.m. My plane will have landed by now. My heart has gathered speed again. I hold my hand to my mouth. I'm going to vomit. What have I done?

My phone starts to vibrate maniacally in my hand as message after message pops up on my screen. Three missed calls from Kate, three texts, and nine WhatsApp messages from my sister.

I text Kate back first, tell her I'm in Spain already and that my last message wasn't urgent after all. Then I read my sister's messages.

12.03 a.m.
What time does your flight land?

6.15 a.m.
I couldn't sleep. Let me know everything's OK.

6.37 a.m.
I just tried calling you so you don't miss this flight too.
Tell me you're up!

7.11 a.m.
Shall I make you a nail appointment too?

7.46 a.m.
Mama is panicking and needs to know you're OK. London is all over the news. Pick up!

8.01 a.m.
Tell me your flight is on time and you're at the airport. You're making me worried.

11.25 a.m.
SURPRISE! I'm at Malaga airport. Alberto gave me a lift. Can't wait to see you!

12 p.m.
Your plane landed 25 mins ago. Are you stuck in passport control?

12.45 p.m.
WHERE ARE YOU????????

I peer inside my bag and check that I still have my passport. Then I check flights to Málaga for today. There's one this evening from Heathrow, I could ask my mum to pay and get there with my Tube pass, except it's fully booked and ... that's it. I can't afford to get to the other airports; they're all at least a £30 cab ride and I don't even have any luggage.

Marianna's service starts this time tomorrow. Whatever I do, I'm not going to make it. I'm going to miss my sister's wedding. The one thing I promised I wouldn't do.

I close my eyes, picturing the scene. Right now, she's standing in the arrivals hall of Málaga airport, waiting for me. She's excited. She's gone out of her way, the day before her wedding, to meet me, and I'm not there. I've let her down. Again. Just like I made her get through our father's funeral alone when she was only eighteen.

Tears that I've been holding back since my meeting with Caroline yesterday finally arrive. Full-on, heavy, painful, wracking sobs. I howl. I bunch Rose's filthy towel in my fist and squeeze, and scream, and cry. I gulp back snotty tears, my eyes stinging from whatever filth is on my face, and rubbing them with my grimy hands only makes the pain worse. But I can't get up, I can't move. All I can do is lie in a foetal position and clutch my aching stomach.

I should have jumped that day in Ronda. The day my father died I should have jumped off that wall and let my bones get smashed to pieces on the rocks below. It would have hurt less than this. But I didn't. I ran and I never went back. Yet no matter how fast I run or how far I go, I can never get away from everything I hate. Because everything I hate is inside of me.

A thin film of rust coats my hands, my knuckles black. I use the already stained towel to rub at my face, then I pull myself up from the floor.

I don't know where the toilet is in this house, but I guess correctly and pee. My sodden tampon plops out into the bowl, and I curse, horror stories of toxic shock syndrome swamping my mind along with every other fear I'm trying to block out. Rose has drawers beside her toilet and I rummage about until I find a sanitary towel.

Her flat is stiflingly hot and I feel woozy, then I realise I haven't eaten properly in over twenty-four hours, as I threw up my dinner. With the water running, I stand there, my wrists under the taps, letting the cold travel up my arms and around my body.

I look up, and instantly wish I hadn't. Is that really me in the mirror?

The woman staring back at me looks like she's been dug up from a long-forgotten grave. My hair is matted and tangled, with tiny yellow leaves stuck in it, my eyes red, my nose and lips swollen from crying, my skin deathly white and streaked in red and black.

Blood.

I'm covered in the blood of a man. A man who was trying to kill a woman. Trying to, or perhaps had already succeeded.

I start to shake again as I scrub my hands until they're pink and raw, my entire body trembling until my teeth clash together, but my attention is diverted by the sound of a key in the lock. I brace myself. Has Rose brought someone back with her? The police? Her son?

'Oh good, you're up,' she says. 'Don't worry, I'm on my own.' She holds up a bright orange plastic bag. 'Just been to Sainsbury's and got us something to eat.'

I want to say something but my mouth hangs open like the corpse I resemble.

'I went back to where I found you last night, thought maybe I'd be able to spot your suitcase. The place was swarming with police, so I didn't hang about. What the fuck happened, Em?'

My jaw aches as I try to stop my teeth clattering together. I grip the rim of the sink, but it's slippery. I can't stay up. I'm falling. What the fuck happened? What the fuck happened?

Rose drops her shopping bag and runs over to me. 'It's

OK,' she says, placing a hand on my shoulder. She leaves it there until I stop shaking. Her eyes fall on the dirty towel at my feet, but she doesn't say anything. 'Come and sit in the kitchen while I make some lunch. Toasted cheese sandwiches and crisps?'

I follow her to the pristine kitchen and sit at the table. More white furnishings to dirty.

She looks at me, a long, hard look, her lips pressed together.

'You know, you're not the first friend I've seen get beaten up or . . . you know.'

Friend. She said 'friend'.

Rose busies herself cutting cheese and buttering cheap, bouncy bread. 'These things are never as straightforward as people think. Trauma, PTSD, guilt, regret, flashbacks, everyone's affected differently and they need to heal at their own pace.' She stops, butter knife in her hand, poised like she's at a lectern. 'What I'm saying is, you can go to the police if you want. I'll take you. Or you can have a shower, pretend it never happened, and we'll never talk about it again. Whatever helps you get on with your life. I don't know what happened to you, but—'

'I told you,' I say. My voice is hoarse, my words blurry around the edges.

Rose squeezes the lid of the sandwich toaster down.

'You didn't. You said lots of people hurt you then mumbled something about a sword. I'm happy to talk if you want.'

Fragments of last night come back to me. Paul and his

fucking stupid fucking award and stupid fucking speech. Nikki and the kiss. Kicking my suitcase and watching it tumble into the bushes and disappearing. A tangle of shadows on the ground. A broken suitcase handle like a dagger in my hand.

A man, on top of a woman, a tie in his hand.

Blood in my mouth.

Blood. So much blood. Sliding through flesh like a knife through warm butter, over and over and over again.

'You're shaking,' Rose says, rushing over to me. The sandwich toaster bubbles over, but she ignores it. 'Here, have a drink.'

It's an effort to get the glass to my mouth. Most of the water dribbles down my chin and wets my chest, but it helps.

'I should have got in the car with that man and his son. None of this would have happened if only I'd trusted them and accepted a lift. But how do you know who the good guys are? How can you tell?'

'You're not making any sense, love.'

I clear my throat and look up at Rose. 'No one hurt me last night.'

She unplugs the sandwich toaster and waits. Rose isn't stupid: she saw the police, the commotion. It means they found something. Or someone.

'I attacked a man.'

She doesn't move or say a word. What are her friends like? Her brothers and sisters? Has she been in many fights? Has she ever hurt anyone? It doesn't matter what she thinks. I may as well get used to saying it out loud.

I take a deep breath, but I can't find the words. Whichever way I say it, what I did last night is going to sound unreal. Like a lie. Like a story I read about in the news.

'Can you pass me my phone, please?'

I take it from her and carefully, with one finger, because I'm too shaky to hold my phone properly, I type in the name of the park I was at.

Immediately, a news story pops up, a familiar scene. Yellow tape, people in white suits, big headlines. But this time it's not a woman with long brown hair lying partially hidden in the bushes. They found a dead man. Just a man. No mention of his victim.

I pass the phone to Rose, who frowns at the headline, then, as she keeps reading, her eyebrows rise further than I thought was possible. She lets out a long breath as she starts to read out loud.

'A man in his mid-thirties was found stabbed to death at the Thames Barrier Park in the early hours of this morning,' she says. 'The man had no ID on him, although a number of items found at the scene of the crime are being investigated by police. Due to the unusual circumstances of his death, police are urging witnesses to come forward.'

Rose looks up and I stare back at her. Neither of us blinks.

'You did that?' she asks eventually. 'That's what all the police were doing at the park when I drove by?'

I nod.

'Why? Why did you stab him?'

'He was killing her. The woman. He had . . .' Except they

230

hadn't mentioned a woman. Maybe I was seeing things. Maybe he didn't have his hands around her throat. Maybe they were an innocent couple kissing in the grass. No. 'He had a tie in his hand.'

'Oh my fucking . . . Jesus . . . What . . .' She clasps both hands over her mouth. 'Where did you get the knife?'

I squint at what she's saying.

'The knife! The one you killed him with.' She drops her voice, mumbling something about Jesus Fucking Christ again.

'It wasn't a knife.' I swallow and close my eyes. 'It was . . . the handle of my suitcase.'

Rose's mouth hangs open, and I count five blinks until either of us says anything.

'The handle broke,' I add. 'You know, came straight out again, like it did when I first met you.'

'Yeah, I remember.'

'The metal spokes are sharp and . . . well, the man was choking her.' My eyes fill with tears and my voice goes thick. 'He was strangling her, Rose! And there was this tie. A stripy tie. And . . . I had to do something. I couldn't just stand there. So I went for him and . . . there was so much blood. So much. But I couldn't stop. Next thing, I was running, and when I reached the river I threw the handle into the water.'

'Fuck. I can't believe I went back to look for your luggage. Where is it?'

'I don't know. Somewhere in the bushes.'

'Jesus, Em! I thought you'd been raped.'

'Sorry about that.'

She breathes out heavily from her nose. Like a bull. 'Does your suitcase have any form of ID in it?'

I don't understand.

'Em, look at me. Does your bag have anything inside that might identify you as his killer?'

Killer. Murderer. I shake my head.

'OK,' she says. 'OK.'

Then she leans over and holds me ever so gently, like I might shatter into a million pieces. As if I haven't already.

25

BBC Breaking News • @BBCBreaking

Doctor saved from imminent death. 'He punched me
to the ground and had his hands around my throat,'
victim claims. 'He was taking off his tie and I was losing
consciousness. Then a woman appeared out of nowhere.
She saved my life.'

Rose and I are standing in her kitchen eating toasted cheese
sandwiches. I feel like I'm under water, like my head weighs
ten stone, and it isn't until I take my first bite that I realise
just how hungry I am.

Yet I'm strangely calm.

This must be how it feels to fall, once you've made the
decision to jump and you know you're going to die and
there's nothing you can do about it. I've killed a man. I've
missed my sister's wedding. I may never see my mother
again before she dies. I've lost everything. I'm falling and
no one is going to catch me. The wind may as well carry
me to whatever awaits.

'I take it you're not going to Spain now,' Rose says.

I chew slowly. 'No.'

'Tell me about your ex.'

'What?'

'Listen, I know we need to talk about what happened. What you're going to do next. But let's not ... for a bit. While we're eating. Let's pretend that the world hasn't just turned to fucking shit.' She nods at my ringless hand. 'So, tell me about that hot girl on Instagram who you were looking at on the DLR. What happened?'

I appreciate what she's doing, but small talk isn't going to take my mind off being a murderer.

'You said she was a bit of a dick, right?' she continues.

I shake my head. 'I lied. Nikki was – *is* – a really great person.' I hold up my phone, showing her Nikki's Instagram page. I can't look at it myself, but there she is, kissing a girl who's the very opposite of me. Tall, angular, blonde, not a murderer. 'But she's over me.'

Cheese dangles from Rose's mouth. She slurps it up. 'She dumped you?'

I nod. 'She proposed to me early April, after the most amazing weekend away. She wanted to start planning the big day straight away; she already had Pinterest boards and a list of her favourite flowers saved on her phone. She's a bit of a wedding expert.'

'And?'

'I freaked out.'

'Why?'

I sigh. I don't want to think about this again. I've done so well not thinking about Nikki until last night, and then look what happened.

'Because she wanted to ask my sister to be our maid of honour and fly my mum out to London and invite my Spanish friends I hardly speak to any more. She was talking guest lists and table plans. I had to tell her the truth.'

Rose waves her sandwich in the air, asking me to elaborate.

'That no one knows she exists,' I say quietly.

Rose gives me a look of pure disappointment, one she never gave me when I confessed to stabbing a man to death. I roll my shoulders, my shirt now hard and crunchy, the welts under my arms having already formed a dark crust. 'I guess us women can be cunts too,' I mumble.

Rose holds up a hand, like a traffic cop. 'Wait. You saying you never told your family that you're a lesbian?'

'Bi. And no. They only ever saw me date men, one guy I was with from eighteen to twenty-four, followed by a handful of relationships that never lasted. Then I moved to London. I don't even know why we're talking about this. It's not important. I need to—'

'It *is* important because I think this is the first time you've ever told anyone.'

I nod. It is. No one has heard my and Nikki's love story. And no one has ever heard the ending.

'I did mean to tell my family about my girlfriend, but once I realised how much they wanted me to be living some movie-type life in the Big Smoke I found myself creating some bullshit elaborate lie about a wealthy accountant called Nick. A man who was everything my mother wanted my future husband to be. It felt good to make her happy, for once. I could never find the right time to tell her the truth.'

'Maybe the right time was the day you got engaged.'

'Yeah, that's what Nikki said. And I said it was too late, that she would never meet my family. Then she got angry and upset. Nikki's had issues in the past with rejection and trusting people. I guess I let her down in the worst way possible. She called me gutless . . .'

My stomach is aching. I'm under water again. I take a tight breath, because there's so much to say. All the words are there. They always have been.

'. . . and I said it was all too complicated, that she'd never be able to be part of my life in Spain. Nikki was devastated and said I couldn't possibly love her as much as she loved me. I'd met her mum, and her stepdad, and all her friends. I was completely part of her life, but I hadn't made her a part of mine. The exclusion was killing her, she said, and the fact I'd been lying to her *and* my family all this time was too much to bear. I never meant to hurt her – I just wanted to keep her to myself. I didn't want to taint her, my future, with the mess of my past. She said it was over, that she could never trust me again. So instead of fighting any more, I left the hotel we were staying at and went back to London.'

'Did you talk about it after?'

I wipe my greasy mouth on Rose's unsalvageable towel and shake my head.

'That was the last time I ever spoke to her. By the time she got back from the Cotswolds I'd packed my things and left. I hated myself, and I couldn't stand the idea of ruining her life any longer.'

'You could have fought for her,' Rose says. Rose, who fights for everything and everyone.

I shake my head. 'No. She deserves someone better than me. The following week I landed a job at Swan & Swallow, found a room to rent and pretended I wasn't gay.'

OK. I'm done. This isn't helping. I killed a man last night and now I'm in Rose's kitchen covered in his blood. We're wasting time. I can't stay here any longer.

'Thanks for the sandwiches. I'm going to hand myself in now.'

She jumps up and blocks my entry into the hallway.

'Like fuck you will!'

'But you said you were happy to take me to the police.'

'When I thought you'd been raped or mugged or whatever. Not now. You'll get locked up.'

'No, I won't. He was killing her!'

'The police won't give a shit about that. This isn't a movie and you're not Bond. You can't go about killing people then expect to be let off because they're the bad guy.'

'You don't know that.'

'Yes, I do. This is a major clusterfuck, Em, and there's no easy way out of it.'

I start to shake again.

'Oh God. OK,' she says. 'Jesus, it freaks me out when you do that. Sit down.' She pushes me on to her bar stool. 'We'll work this out. Keep talking. Tell me about this Swan & Swallow place you worked at.'

'Why? I've done an awful thing, Rose. We need to sort it out.'

'No. You need to stop fucking shaking and pull yourself together. Now tell me about the bastards that sacked you. What was this Swan place? A pub?'

'A PR agency.'

'Oh yeah, that's right. So what happened?'

'I wasn't kept on after a three-month placement. It's part of the reason I was so angry last night.' I sniff and hiccup. 'I saw Nikki had a new girlfriend, and there was a video of Paul on Twitter accepting an award the company didn't deserve. He's not the good guy he thinks he is, and he was taking all the credit, when it's people like me who do all the hard work. Paul was talking such shit and . . .' I'm clenching my blood-encrusted fists again, my teeth clamped together so tight my head is throbbing.

'Who's Paul? Your new boyfriend?'

I shudder at the thought and pass Rose my phone. 'One of the directors at work.'

She squints at the video on the screen, zooming in, sound off. 'The smarmy-looking guy giving the speech?'

'Yeah. He's the reason the company didn't keep me on. I should have reported him for what he did to me, but he got there first.'

She places my phone on the counter without listening to what he's saying.

'What did he do?'

I can feel my cheese sandwich clawing its way back up my throat. I don't want to think about Paul again.

Rose edges closer to me. 'Let it out, Em.'

Acid is burning my throat.

'Say it!' she shouts. 'You want this man's poison to eat you up? You want whatever he did to you to burn a hole inside of you? Scar you? Why are you keeping it inside? Say it out loud!'

'He abused me!' I shout. 'He told HR I was obsessed with him, that it was an infatuation that had got out of hand, then he had me dismissed.'

'Fucking cunt.'

So I tell her everything, because she's right. It feels good to say the words out loud.

Things got worse after he told me he loved me. A lot worse. Paul was convinced the kiss had been the beginning of a fateful love affair. I made the mistake of getting in the lift with him a few days after his proclamation. Richard, our CEO, got in after me, so Paul and me had to back up against the wall. Before the doors had even slid shut I could feel Paul's hand skim the hem of my skirt, the tip of his finger making a line against my bare leg. I looked at him, made a disapproving face, and he winked at me. I edged away and he grinned, like it was a game. Richard had his back to us and was completely unaware. I was heading to reception but got out on the second floor along with the boss. Then, that evening, as I was getting ready to leave the office, Paul brushed past me and whispered, 'Just you wait until we're finally alone.'

I told Matt that night. I told him how creepy Paul was being.

His first comment was 'I'm not surprised he likes you, you're hot. I'd crack on to you too.' And when I told him how scared it made me feel he'd rolled his eyes and slipped my top over my head. 'Don't worry about that idiot,' he'd said. 'He'll get bored soon enough.' And he'd climbed on top of me and lifted the same skirt Paul had been playing with, pushing himself inside of me without waiting for me to get wet. I didn't mention it again.

Back at work Paul made sure we were alone as much as possible. I did my best to avoid him, but he always needed a cup of coffee the same time I did or called me into his office to ask me a 'quick question'. He kept telling me how smart I was, how he had great plans for me in the company, how lucky Swan & Swallow were to have me.

Then, two weeks before my meeting with Caroline, I was working late, just me and Kate, and as I shut the toilet door behind me Paul pushed in after me and locked us in.

'You can't be in here,' I hissed. 'It's the women's bathroom.'

'Baby, we have to stop playing games. I can't wait any longer.'

He pinned me against the sink, a hand on either side of me, and started kissing my collarbone.

'Oh god,' he panted, his hot breath making my neck wet. 'I've been waiting so long to kiss you again.'

I tried to get past him, but his arms were clamped hard, locking me in.

'We could be a dream team, you and me. We're electric together. You know I have the power to make you very successful in this company,' he said, running his tongue from my clavicle to behind my ear. 'The Dalai Lama says the purpose of our life is to be happy. You make me so happy, baby. Let me make you happy too.'

I turned my head away from his mouth, kept still, kept silent.

'Don't make a scene,' I heard my mother say.

'He'll get bored eventually,' I heard Matt say.

'Kate is outside,' I said. 'I don't want to do this.'

His eyes were dark with desire, his lips shiny. 'Yes, perhaps a hotel would be better.'

'No.'

I said no. I did. I said the word 'no'. *No!* I couldn't have been clearer. I pushed him back, gently, but he liked it. He rubbed himself up and down against my hip, releasing a guttural groan. It was all still a game for him.

'Please, Paul. I don't want this any more.'

I shouldn't have said 'any more' because I'd *never* wanted it. I'd never ever wanted it, from the very first time he'd squeezed into the seat beside me at the pub and pushed his leg against mine.

Paul eased off me and smoothed down his T-shirt. This one had a rainbow on it.

'What are you saying? You've wanted this for weeks, we both have. You've made your feelings for me quite clear.'

'No. You don't understand.'

'Don't play the fool, Em. You're not a silly schoolgirl, you know exactly what's happening here.'

'Paul, please, get off me. This isn't what I want.'

He sniffed, looked away, adjusted his trousers.

'This is why office liaisons are ill advised. You're clearly

241

not mature enough to handle our relationship in a responsible way.'

'We were never in a—'

He placed his finger at my mouth to silence me.

'Shhh.' Slowly, he traced the outline of my lips, then pushed two fingers inside my mouth. He let out a light groan, and I just stood there as he grazed my molars with his fingertips. Then, slowly, his eyes boring into mine, he pushed his thick fingers down my throat, and up again, and down, and up again, his gaze daring me to look away.

'Stupid girl,' he whispered. 'You could have been someone.'

And then he left.

'I cried,' I say to Rose. 'I was so scared to leave that toilet. I kept washing my mouth out with tap water, but all I could taste was his skin, and all I could feel was where his fingernails had scraped my throat.'

Sometimes I can still feel him. Taste him. See that switch in his eyes.

The light under the toilet door was dimming and I realised Kate was getting ready to lock up the office. I ran outside and caught her just as she was leaving.

'Oh my God, Em,' she said. 'I thought you'd left. You scared the living daylights out of me!'

I couldn't talk, I was just looking at her, urging her to guess what had happened.

'Why are you here so late? You're really pale. Are you ill?'

And I told her what Paul had done, and she held me, making me promise to report him. But I couldn't do it, I didn't know how to. Every time I tried to write an email or imagined what I would say to HR, it always sounded like it was my fault. Why did I leave the pub with him? Why didn't I say anything earlier? Why didn't I shout out when he locked me in the bathroom?

Paul took annual leave the next day, went back to his family for a week, and I told myself it was over. He'd got the message. Then the week after that, at my end of contract appraisal, I was told that office liaisons were ill advised. Caroline used his exact words.

'HR said my obsession was unprofessional and I lost my job.'

Rose hasn't said a word during my entire speech, but her eyes have grown wider and wider with each revelation. She picks up my phone again and holds it up to my face.

'This piece of shit did all that to *you*? *This* guy, the one who looks like an extra from a 1980s cop movie?'

I can't help it, I start to laugh, then I instantly feel ashamed. I'm in no position to be finding anything amusing.

'I'm sorry,' I say, clamping my hand over my mouth. 'There's nothing funny about any of this. My life's ruined, and I've no idea what the hell I'm going to do next. I'm a disgrace.'

Rose laughs, a burnt-dry cackle.

'Nah, you've got it all wrong,' she says, grabbing our plates and heading for the sink. 'When I found out I was pregnant with Olly it felt like the end of the world. Like I'd lost everything. Then I realised it wasn't the end of anything – just a different beginning.'

The only new beginning I'll be starting will be a life behind bars.

'I killed a man, Rose.'

My lunch swirls and solidifies in my guts. I killed a man. I stare at my hands and the black creases on my palms. I'm a killer. A murderer. I'm no different to the London Strangler.

'I have no job, no money, no belongings, my family and friends have no idea where I am, and I'm wanted by the police. How the fuck is any of that hopeful?' I say.

Rose looks at me – really looks at me – and I stare back. Her eyes are black, and for the first time I notice the dark smudges beneath them. She hasn't slept because of me. Me, a woman she only met yesterday. A violent woman covered in a killer's blood. A woman she's allowed into her home, who she's fed, and she's listened to and she's trying to help.

'You're right,' I say slowly and quietly. I stand up straighter. 'You're right.'

Something is swelling inside of me like a wave gathering momentum, an idea that isn't quite fully formed, but it's big. It's dangerous. And I can't stop it.

'I'm invincible.'

Rose waits. She can feel it too, that surge of something moving between us. The rising waters, the way the world has tipped a little on its axis.

'I have nothing left to lose. For the first time in my fucking life, I can do exactly what I want because things can't possibly get any worse.'

Rose's eyes narrow and the edges of her lips twitch,

until we're smiling at one another, then grinning, and then laughing until we can't stop.

She nods her head once and crosses her arms. 'Too right, sister. And you're going to start by telling the world exactly what that bastard Paul did to you.'

26

Words will never hurt me • @Em_Dash_93

Yesterday I was sacked from **@SwanAndSwallow**. Last night they won a **@StarsOfMarketing** award for their #RiseAndShine campaign for gender equality. Let me tell you about their creative director **@PaulWAWilkes** and how he sexually abused me.

A thread . . .

I pour out the entire story. My excitement at joining the company. The night in the pub. The unwanted kiss. The number of times I said no. How Caroline had been there, how she believed him over me and how she did nothing.

My thumbs fly furiously over the keypad of my phone as I spit out every last ounce of venom I've allowed to fester inside me. I spit it out as hard as I spat out the taste of him in my mouth. And as I sit cross-legged on the carpet, on my dirty, bloody towel, my grin stretches wider and wider as the post slowly goes viral.

> **Emily Patterson** • @EPPR81
> Replying to @Em_Dash_93
> Paul is why I left that company three years ago. He
> called me a 'pretty little slut' at the Christmas party,
> and I know it was him who bought me a thong for
> Secret Santa.

> **Nadia Zoya Khan** • @NadiaZKhan
> How are men like this getting away with this shit
> still? Sack **@PaulWAWilkes** and prosecute him for
> sexual abuse!

> **Emma Dlamini** • @EmmaDlamini
> Replying to @Em_Dash_93
> Are you aware of this **@MarketingWeekEd**
> **@Adage** and **@AdWeek**? Look at the replies.
> **@Em_Dash_93** isn't alone.

And so it goes on. And on. And on.

Three trade magazines and some websites private-message me, asking for the story. I give them everything they want. A few men call me a liar. A few women share their stories. Not all the women with similar stories worked at Swan & Swallow, not all of them worked in marketing or PR, but all of them are confessing for the first time and sharing the relief of finally saying it out loud.

'You want to get changed?' Rose calls out. She's cleared away the dirty towels and cleaned up the kitchen.

I look up from my phone. I've already plugged it in to charge again.

'I just want to see where this goes first.'

It's addictive, every reply making me feel stronger. I watch the numbers keep rising, read the comments, click on the little heart symbol, let each woman know I acknowledge her story. An hour passes, and Rose is back on the couch, staring at me.

'Sorry,' I say, putting my phone down. 'Do you need me to go?'

She throws her hands in the air and looks at me like I'm crazy.

'No, you're just filthy as fuck and making the place look messy. Do you want to borrow some of my clothes? Have a long, cool bath, figure out what you want to do next. My boy comes back tomorrow morning so you can't stay here tonight, but I'm happy to give you a lift home on my bike. I have a spare helmet.'

Home? Oh, she means Suffolk Street.

'You've been so good to me, Rose.'

She rolls her eyes. 'Shut up. You saved a woman's life last night, and who knows how many more he might have killed? You did a bad thing for a good reason. Forget about it.'

How do I forget anything? I know from experience guilt only gets heavier to carry over the years.

'Any more news?' she adds.

I've been checking my phone between notifications and Rose has the BBC News channel on mute, but so far all they're saying is that a man was found stabbed to death and police are following up leads about the London Strangler. Maybe I was wrong. Maybe the two men aren't one and the same.

'Isn't the news saying the London Strangler had a walking stick or something like that? You know, I think he was at the airport hotel,' I say to Rose, pointing at the park on the TV. That same patch of grass surrounded by yellow crime-scene tape. 'I saw some guy with his arm in a sling, using a crutch, come out of the hotel lift and walk outside. I presumed he was going for a fag or had left something in his car. There's nowhere to go to around there. I nearly offered to help him, but then some woman, I think the same one who helped me when I had a panic attack, she had a row with her boyfriend and stormed out. I think her name was Mandy. She said she was going home. The killer must have got her into the park somehow. Maybe they were both at the DLR station, the one I was heading to.'

'That could have been me,' I want to say. Would he have picked me?

'Did you see the walking stick when he was trying to kill her?'

'No. I don't know. Her bag was there, but it was dark.'

Rose stands up. 'I'm calling the police.'

I frown.

'Not about you. If this guy booked into the hotel, they might have his details. It might help the police piece together all the info quicker. I'll make an anonymous call.'

I nod and wipe my forehead. Rose has opened the window, but all that's coming into her flat is warm air. My bra is scratchy against my nipples. All my clothes are beginning to itch now.

'About that bath,' I say.

Rose jumps up.

'Good. Yes. Finally. You stink.'

I can hear Rose talking on the phone as the bath is running, the scent of something floral floating down the hallway. I turn my attention back to my phone. The numbers are still climbing on my post.

Dante • **@DanteTheITBoi**
Wish I'd known, @Em_Dash_93. I got you, girl. Ain't keeping nothing quiet no more.

I'm grinning as a private message on Twitter appears. It's from the Swan & Swallow Twitter account. My heart starts to thunder in my chest.

Em. Are you OK? It's Kate.

I let out a long breath. Kate's not on Twitter, but I forgot that she manages the work account.

Just want you to know that what you did was very brave. It's all kicking off at work, I've been told to upload a press release and all staff just got an email saying not to speak to the press. Fuck that, I'm going to tell them EVERYTHING. Enjoy Spain xxx

I go on the Swan & Swallow account.

Swan & Swallow, PR and Marketing • @SwanAndSwallow
We take all allegations of sexual misconduct seriously at
S&S. Creative Director Paul Wilkes has been suspended
until further notice while we work closely with the
police and investigate further. In the meantime, we urge
anyone who has been affected to contact us.

An official press release is attached, with an email address and telephone number for other victims to come forward. You can always depend on an award-winning PR agency to know how to handle a crisis, even if it means throwing key staff members under the bus.

My grin widens. Fuck you, Paul. Try getting a job now.

'Em!' Rose is calling me from her bedroom. 'I've found some clothes for you to change into.'

Her bedroom is as pristine as the rest of the house, everything white and rattan with lush green plants. On the bed is a collection of clothes, all bright, tight and glittery. Rose is tiny; none of this is going to fit.

'Try them on,' she says.

'There's no point. I'm at least two sizes bigger than you.'

'But ...'

I place my hand on her arm and smile.

'You've already done so much for me. It's fine. I'm going to have a bath then put my nasty clothes back on and change at home. I need to get back.'

Rose nods and heads for the living room, no doubt to check for bloody marks on her upholstery, and I peel my clothes off in the bathroom, letting out a sigh of relief as I sink into the lukewarm bath. The grime on my skin comes off in a second, but it takes three rounds of shampoo to get my hair clean and it's still tangly. I pull the plug and use the shower head instead, rubbing at the sides of the bath, which are now coated in reddish scum, scraping my scalp with my broken fingernails. But no matter how much I scrub at my body and hair, I still don't feel clean. I keep the water running on my head until the warm water turns icy cold, but it won't run clear.

The TV is on in the living room. I hear the volume being turned up, followed by a gasp. Then Rose starts screaming.

'Oh my God. Em! Get in here!'

I reach for yet another towel, this one thankfully dark pink, and wrap it around me. Water from my hair runs down my back as I scramble into the living room, where Rose is pointing at the TV. It's me. Well, not all of me. It's the back of my head in the hotel, curled up into a ball, crying. You can't see my features properly. Then it's me again, at the airport, but my hair is covering my face. Then me throwing up near Pontoon Dock station.

'Turn it up,' I say.

The news reporter is wearing a bright blue jacket and a serious expression.

'The woman the police are looking for in relation to the death of the man found dead in Thames Barrier Park has long, dark hair and is believed to have been wearing a distinctive pink-and-green sleeveless blouse and pencil skirt. She was carrying a small lilac suitcase. If you have any information about this woman, please call the following number.'

My phone is buzzing, shuffling along the carpet. I scoop down and pick it up. There are too many notifications to count and ten direct messages.

I read the first comment.

> **Save the NHS** • @EmmaSmithCOYS
> The London Strangler's killer is a woman! I recognise
> that blouse, it's the same one **@Em_Dash_93** was
> wearing yesterday morning. Look!

There's a screenshot of the photo I posted as I left the house yesterday. My cleavage spilling out of my bright shirt, my long black hair covering my shoulders. Not my face, but you can even see the skirt.

My hands start to shake and I drop my phone.

'Rose,' I say.

She's still staring at the television screen.

> **Eva Labatinni** • @EvaLabatinniPR
> Isn't that the same woman **@SwanAndSwallow**
> sacked after she was sexually abused?
> **Paul C** • @PaulCC01
> Replying to **@EvaLabatinniPR**
> Man, that's one pissed-off lady!

'What the fuck?' I mutter. 'Rose!'
A text message from Kate pops up.

Em, please tell me you're in Spain. Please tell me you caught your flight last night. Have you seen what people are saying about you on Twitter?

'Rose!' I shout.
She turns to me, her face three shades lighter than before.
'We need to go. Now!'

27

The Mirror • @DailyMirror
Man found stabbed to death at the Thames Barrier Park
has been identified as William Hennington, 36, from
Essex. But who killed him? And how is he connected to
the London Strangler?

Putting my filthy clothes back on feels worse than not having washed at all.

'Where do you live again?' Rose asks.

'In town. Right in the centre.'

'You shouldn't go back.'

'I need to. It won't take long until someone recognises me and gives my photo and name to the police.'

'Exactly. Get the fuck out of London. You have your passport; you need to get as far away as you can.'

'I have to get out of these clothes.'

'Here,' she says, handing me a man's shirt. I put it on over my blouse. The cotton is cool against my skin, the light blue fabric turning dark where my long hair is dripping all over it. My fingers tremble as I do up the buttons. Did this once belong to her ex or a one-night stand?

'And I need to pick up a Bible,' I say quietly.

Rose makes the exact same face I expect her to make. 'A what?'

'I want to go home. To Spain,' I say, my voice wavering. 'My mother and my sister, they need the family Bible.'

'This is madness. It's not worth it, Em.'

It is. It's the least I can do. Marianna deserves that book more than I ever have.

'Do you have enough money to get away?' Rose asks.

I shake my head. 'None.'

'OK, well, lucky for you, I always have cash on me.'

'I don't know when I'll be able to pay you back.'

'Shut up,' she says quietly, disappearing down the hallway and returning with a fist full of red and purple bank notes. I don't count them, but I'm guessing there's at least £300.

'It's not much,' she says. 'But it's enough to get a train out of London and a cheap one-way flight to wherever the fuck you can. I'll take you back to your place. Pack light and fast, destroy anything that can identify you, then run.'

'How do you know this is the right thing to do?'

She makes a face. 'If life has taught me anything, it's that sometimes the right thing to do is the wrong one. Just get as far away as you can.'

'Seriously, thank you so much.'

'You've got to stop saying thank you,' Rose says. 'This is what women do. We stick together, we help one another out and we cover for each other.' She continues talking under her breath, as if she's trying to convince herself more than me. 'You'll be fine. It was dark when we came back this morning. No one will have seen us. Put this on.' She passes me a bike helmet. 'Cameras won't recognise you with that on and the shirt. Go straight into your flat, grab your shit, and get out as fast as you can. Oh, and put a hat on when you leave your place, tuck your crazy long hair into it. No one has hair that long. I've not got a hat, or I'd give it to you too.'

I nod at everything she's saying, but none of it is sinking in. I'm on the run? But where will I go? How do I get to Spain? Oh god, I haven't even spoken to my sister yet.

My feet sting as I push my dirty trainers back on. It's suffocatingly hot under the helmet, but I need to keep moving.

Rose is holding the front door open, my handbag in her hand.

'Fuck,' I mutter.

'What?'

'I don't think my flat's empty. I forgot Matt's girlfriend is staying over.'

'Who's Matt?'

'Flatmate. We kind of had a thing going. Wait a minute.'

I take my bag out of her hand and pull out my fully charged phone. I ignore the five new WhatsApp messages from my sister, the voicemail from my mum and the million Twitter notifications. I click on to Rebecca's account.

Teachers rock! • @RebeccaMcGuire

I said yes!!!! My amazing man put a ring on it last night and whisked me away to a luxury hotel. I'm the happiest person in the world.

There's a photo of Rebecca holding her hand up to the camera, a large round diamond on her ring finger. What? That lovely, sweet teacher is marrying Matt, the spineless, cheating bastard?

OK, well, at least they're not going to be home.

I feel around my handbag, check my passport and keys are still there and nod at Rose.

'Let's go.'

The sun is relentless as it beats down on my heavy bike helmet and two layers of clothing, but the hot weather is doing us a favour as there's no one around so we exit the block of flats unseen. I climb on the back of the moped, wincing as the hard leather of the bike seat rubs against the chafing sores on the inside of my thighs.

Rose pulls off in a spray of dust and the fresh air on my body feels good. My hair and wet shirt are dry in minutes, although I wish I'd put some deodorant on.

'Where did you say you live again?' she shouts as we pull up at a traffic light.

'Suffolk Street,' I shout back. 'It's around the back of Trafalgar Square.'

'For real? I didn't think anyone actually lived there.'

I won't be living there after today.

Rose has a special clip for her phone on her scooter and she's connected the wireless speakers to her helmet, so the GPS gets us there with no issues. The scooter zips past any traffic and within forty minutes we're outside Matt's apartment.

Unlike Canning Town, the streets are busy here. There are groups of people milling about, all bare legs and painted toes. Some are taking selfies; others talking on their phones. I squint against the glare of the orange sun, trying to read what's written on a large piece of cardboard someone is holding. #SaveThem is scrawled in big black letters on one side, the names of four women on the other. Those that aren't holding placards are clutching bunches of floppy flowers and candles.

Of course. The vigil for the dead women is tonight.

'What's the time?' I ask Rose as she turns the ignition off. I don't remove my helmet until a group of chattering women walks past.

'Ten past four.'

The vigil starts at eight tonight. I'll be long gone by then.

I clamber off the back of the scooter. 'I guess I'll never see you again.'

'Being a bit dramatic, aren't you?' she answers, but her eyes are full of tears.

She presses her lips together and we nod, neither of us saying anything. I keep my back to the main road and the people walking by, sheltered by the dry, pretentious bay tree outside my front door.

'You'd better go,' I say. 'Olly's home soon, right?'

I notice how her eyes light up at the sound of his name. 'Yeah, but my mum isn't bringing him over until the morning, so I might hang around town for a bit. Calm down a bit, you know.'

I thank her again and turn to go, but she pulls me back

and holds me close, a full hug, with her whole body. All I can think about is that my clothes are filthy and I haven't brushed my teeth, but she doesn't care. The more I try and pull away, the tighter she holds me.

'Don't you ever let those fucking bastards catch you,' she says into my matted hair. She pulls back and holds my face in her hands. 'You're a hero, Em. A motherfucking hero. You stopped a woman from dying and you may have saved many more. Fuck Nikki's new girlfriend and Paul and your family's expectations and your stupid brain telling you any of them matter. You use that money I gave you to get the fuck as far away from this rotting city, and you live your life, you hear me? Live it fully.'

Tears stream down my face, but all I can do is sniff and nod and smile.

Then she turns on her heels and walks away without a backward glance. I take a deep breath and open the door to my building and Matt's flat.

The communal entryway is cool and for a second I press myself against the marble wall, gathering my strength and trying to remember where the Bible is and what I need to pack.

I have a rucksack, not a huge one, but one big enough for the book and whatever clothes I can find, some underwear and any toiletries I hadn't already packed in my suitcase. I think I even have a spare toothbrush somewhere.

I let myself into the flat. It's quiet inside and I breathe a sigh of relief, then stumble into the wall. A large brown box in the centre of the hallway. My box. And six more, stacked in a triangle in the hallway. I run to my room, except it's not a bedroom any more, it's an office, complete with Rebecca's suitcase by my single bed and a bookshelf where I imagine all her favourite children's books will be displayed. Where the hell is my Bible?

'Motherfucker,' I mutter.

How long has Matt been planning this? When I was leaving for Spain and he said maybe I should move out, this is what he meant. He was going to propose to Rebecca this weekend, turn my room into a study while I was away, and then what? Wait for me to get back from Spain and announce I'm homeless? Change the locks? Legally, there's nothing stopping him – no contract, no lease, no proof I even live here.

It seems stupid to care about it now, seeing as I'm about to skip the country, but I'm furious. Who the fuck does he think he is?

I wrestle myself out of Rose's shirt, throwing it to the floor, then unbutton my now famous blouse and rip if off too. I'm so angry I don't even savour the feeling of getting out of that top or note how many of the buttons have flown off. I throw it on top of the shirt and rub at the marks under my arms. One of the scabs has come loose and is weeping. I need to deal with this.

I open the bathroom door; the room looks empty. Where are my towels? Matt has packed everything, even my toiletries. I open drawers and cupboards: no deodorant or spare makeup anywhere. All I can see is Matt's expensive aftershave on the sink. Did he pack all my things away while I was at work yesterday? Was he lying about being on a train?

As I turn, I catch sight of myself in the mirror. My hair must have been dirtier than I realised, as rusty brown trails cover my forehead like a metal toy soldier left out in the rain, and dry blood has collected in the creases of my nose and lips. My once white bra, my favourite lacy one that was meant to make me feel confident at yesterday's meeting, is now a dark red too, and my chest is mottled pink where the dirty fabric has touched my damp skin.

Using my fingers, I attempt to rake through my knotted hair, but my hand catches in the tangles. My hairbrush was in my suitcase and there isn't even a comb in this fucking bathroom. I guess Rebecca hasn't fully moved in yet. She only has her overnight things with her, whereas everything *I* own is in a bush or in those fucking boxes blocking my bedroom. No, sorry, Rebecca's new office.

I open the bathroom cabinet that doubles as a mirror, hoping Matt has some deodorant I can use, but I use too much force and the edge of the door scratches my forehead. Fuck! I clutch at my head, my fingers coming away red. Blood. More blood. Will I ever not be covered in blood?

I shut the door and catch sight of myself again. I look like someone from a horror movie: bloody face, wild hair and stained bra. The mangled victim ... or the killer.

With a piercing scream, I throw Matt's aftershave at the mirror, then jump back as sharp chunks of glass smash at my feet. A million versions of me grimace back. Which of those versions is me? All of them. And none of them matter any more.

The mirrored fragments crunch beneath my trainers as I head into the hallway full of boxes. I need to find my clothes and that Bible, which means I need scissors.

Clambering over the mountain of boxes, I search inside each empty drawer of the new desk in the now-office. Nothing. I scream. I can't get changed or collect my belongings or find a fucking backpack if I can't get into these fucking boxes.

The kitchen has also been cleaned out, including my drinks in the fridge and my tins in the cupboard. Bastard! And why are there no scissors in the kitchen either? Won't Matt and Rebecca need scissors in their newly married life together?

I slam open a drawer and pick up a knife. It's wide and silver, the kind TV chefs use to expertly dice onions.

That will do.

Stalking back into the hallway, wiping the blood from my eye with the back of my hand, I start to attack the boxes. With each stab and drag I try not to think of the man in the park and how much easier it had been to slide the metal into his flesh. How silent each blow had been. How I hadn't once looked at him or thought about what I was doing.

I rip back the cardboard flap and delve inside. Winter coats and scarves. I kick the box to the end of the hall and work on the next one. It's full of paperwork, books and notebooks. I pull each item out one by one, stuffing anything into my handbag that has my name on it. I don't know how long it will take the police to track me down, but I'm not going to make it easy for them. As I near the bottom of the box my hand closes around something large and cold. It takes two hands to lift it out.

My family Bible – the last thing I packed when I left Spain. I couldn't leave it there, not after what happened, and now it needs to go back. Complete the cycle.

This Bible is a prized family possession; the only thing spared at my father's grandmother's house during the Civil War before it was all burned to the ground. On the very first page is a list of every member of my family dating back to 1898.

I run my finger over the spine, the brown stain less visible now and its edges not as bent as I remember. Inside, its rice-paper pages are embossed with gold, each faded name in a different script. So delicate. So precious. I fucking hate the thing.

Fuck God. Where was he last night?

It's too big for my handbag so I put it to one side, continuing my search for a backpack and whatever summer clothes weren't in my suitcase.

Five boxes to go.

I plunge the knife into the duct-taped seal of the next box. This one is full of pots and pans, most of them new. I'd bought a lot from Ikea when I'd moved out of Nikki's flat, not having wanted her to accuse me of taking anything from her. Then I never used any of it. Matt has even thrown my groceries into this box, a half-opened packet of rice spilling grains all over my chipped glasses.

He's used a million miles of tape to seal these boxes, but he couldn't even close a bag of rice? A hot, hissing rage engulfs me as I imagine his fingers on my food, his smile as he smugly packed my life away as if it didn't matter that I no longer had anywhere to live. Why would he give a shit? He never asked me where I went on weekends. It was like I didn't exist outside of his bed, his grasp.

One by one, I throw my drinking glasses again the wall, rice and glass raining down upon me, shards nicking at my skin. My very own wedding. *Viva los novios!*

The next box has clothes and toiletries in it, all mixed up, most items missing their lids. One of my shampoo bottles is oozing transparent goo over my good jeans. I rummage around and pull out handfuls of knickers and a box of tampons. I stuff them into my handbag so I don't lose them as I sort through the few salvageable items of clothing that I can take with me. My handbag is full. I need a clean bra, T-shirt and shorts, and a bag to put the Bible and the rest of my clothes into, then I can get out of this fucking place.

I'm about to plunge the knife into the next box when the crunch of a key in the front-door lock makes me jump. I look up. The door's two metres away. My head swivels from side to side, searching for a good hiding spot. Hide? Where? This apartment is tiny, and I've already blocked the hallway with all my broken shit.

The door opens slowly, a woman giggles, and then she screams.

28

Rebecca looks a lot younger in person. Round hips, round breasts, round face. A face drained of colour and twisted in horror.

I try to see myself through her eyes. A woman with a face covered in fresh blood, wearing nothing but a skirt, dirty trainers and a filthy bra, standing in her apartment surrounded by broken things – and holding a really big knife.

'What the hell are you doing here?' Matt shouts, the whites of his eyes growing larger as he takes in all the chaos surrounding me – shattered glass, the smashed mirror, rice and torn paper. 'You're meant to be in Spain.'

'Surprise!' I say, deadpan, waving my hands in the air.

'You're mad.' He steps in front of his fiancée, puffing out his pigeon chest and raising his voice. 'Get behind me, Becca!'

I tip my head to one side and study him. Did he always look like this? So slight, so feeble, so . . . scared? *I* should be the one who's scared right now, standing half naked before an angry man, but once again I feel calm. My mind is clear. I can't believe I ever let this runt come anywhere near me.

'That's not her name, Matt.' I point the knife at Rebecca,

and she whimpers. 'She doesn't like being called Becca. Isn't that right, Rebecca? You say it all the time on Twitter, that you hate that nickname. I know Matt's not on social media, so you probably think it's safe to say it on there. Have you told him to his face? You probably have. I bet he didn't listen, though.'

'Do you know this woman?' Rebecca stutters.

Matt pulls his shoulders back and lifts his chin. 'That's Emmy.'

'Wrong,' I say. 'My name isn't Emmy. It never has been. *You* call me Emmy, because you said my weird foreign name was too hard to pronounce and Emmy suited me. That's not my name though.' I step forward, and Matt steps back. 'In polite society, knowing the correct name of the women you're fucking is considered good manners.'

'What is she talking about, Matty?' Rebecca says. He pushes her behind him again, but Rebecca struggles against the barrier of his arm and stands by his side. 'Isn't this the lesbian you used to live with? The one you said was moving out next week?'

'Oh, yes! Congratulations,' I say, giving them both a thin-lipped smile. 'Engaged! How exciting. Wedding. Babies. Happy ever after. Tick, tick, tick that list, *Matty*. Make sure you get it all in the correct order. So where did I come into this? Where exactly did you think I was going to go when I got back from Spain? Or didn't that matter? I guess it's harder to get a blow job off your flatmate once your fiancée's living with you.'

Matt has blanched to a shade of white paler than his

267

pristine shirt. His eyes keep darting to my own dirty blouse on the floor, then back to my breasts spilling out over my bloody bra.

'What are you talking about?' Rebecca says.

Matt turns to her, grasping the tops of her arms tightly. 'We need to get out of here. It's her.'

'No! Get off!' She squirms away from his hold. 'Tell me the truth.' She turns to me. 'Were you two sleeping together?'

Poor Rebecca, with her ill-fitting orange sundress and her hair in plaits and her ugly flat shoes. The smattering of freckles on her nose jumps around as her face flickers from one emotion to another then another. So innocent. Even the dab of lipstick she's applied is the exact shade of lightly bitten lips. Sweet summer child.

I throw the knife behind me and it clatters against the dining-room chair. I show her my empty hands.

'Don't marry him,' I say. 'Look, I'm no angel, and I certainly shouldn't have allowed myself to feel flattered when he paid me attention – but Matt's a piece of shit.'

I brace myself. I have nothing left to lose.

'I was going through a break-up, I was stupid and vulnerable, so I gave in when your boyfriend tried it on with me. We've had sex, a lot, and that's a stupid decision I made. But *you*? You really love your life in Manchester. You love your job and the kids you teach and your friends there. You don't have to make a bad decision.'

My heart squeezes as I watch her bottom lip tremble. She stays silent, but I can't.

'He talks about you a lot, Rebecca – but mainly while he has his fingers inside me. That's fucked up, right?' I look at Matt. '*Right?* You have to admit that's wrong.' I turn back to Rebecca. 'Did you *really* have no idea your boyfriend was such a cunt?'

Rebecca visibly recoils at my use of the C word.

'It's all lies, Becca. She's crazy!' Matt shouts, his feet shuffling as if he's not sure in which direction he wants to run. 'Look at her! She's completely deranged.'

I fix my gaze on Rebecca, marvelling at how her eyes are swimming with tears yet none have rolled down her cheeks yet. She's waiting for more, for proof. So I give it to her.

'He has a mole on the base of his cock.'

She gives a strangled whimper. She knows I'm telling the truth. Another life saved.

'No!' Matt's flapping his hands between us. 'Becca, don't listen to her. She's dangerous. Look!' He points at my blouse on the floor, moving it with the tip of his shoe like it's a curled-up tarantula that may pounce at any minute. 'She's the madwoman who killed that man in east London. See? That bright shirt and the long dark hair, like the footage on the news earlier.' Spit is collecting at the edges of his mouth, a blue vein pushing against the side of his temple. I've never seen him look so ugly.

'I knew you were evil, you dirty Spanish slag!' he shouts. 'Get out of my flat. Get out!'

I should probably defend myself or pick up my blouse, which is covered in another man's blood. Or at least finish packing. But I don't. I simply hook my handbag over my shoulder and walk towards them to the open front door. They part, as if I'm still holding a knife, and it's not until I'm back outside and have turned the corner of the street that I start to hyperventilate.

I'm dead, and that was the final blow. Matt knows it was me; he has the evidence crumpled in a heap on his glass-strewn carpet. And I have nothing. Not even my family Bible. My entire life is now scattered around their feet.

I need water, and I need to get as far away from here as I can.

Pret is still open, sandwiches that never sleep, and I catch my reflection in the shop window as I enter. I have barely any clothes on. I'm walking around in nothing but my dirty bra and too tight skirt, dried blood on my forehead and cheek. People are looking at me, some edging away – but no one says anything. This is London. The city where you don't get involved.

Using one of Rose's £20 notes, I pay for my water and walk as confidently as I can out of the shop towards Trafalgar Square. The streets are teeming with people, the busiest I've seen it since the sun came out. Usually, in the summer, the square is full of happy tourists taking photos of the lions, posing in front of the National Portrait Gallery and its dramatic columns. I've got used to seeing it empty lately, the fountains dry, the heat keeping everyone off the streets, but this afternoon it's buzzing. This is different.

Groups of women, many of them quite young, are milling about. Some are sitting cross-legged on the warm pavement, talking and taking selfies; others are laying down flowers by the fountain. I don't know who decided this would be the memorial site for four murdered women, four innocent lives lost at the hands of the man I killed, but tonight Trafalgar Square is the shrine these women are choosing to pray at. The atmosphere is charged, like the static before a storm, the air electric. This feels dangerous – too many emotions gathered in one place, too many things left unsaid.

A man is selling London-themed souvenirs on the edge of the square. Has he always been there, or is he expecting extra business from the hordes of grieving women tonight? Among the plastic snow globes of Big Ben and Union Jack pens is a stack of lurid T-shirts.

'How much?' I ask, pointing at one with the word 'London' written on it and covered in pictures of crowns, phone boxes and double decker buses.

He eyes me up and down, his gaze settling on the torn trim of my bra.

'Twenty-five quid.'

'For a T-shirt?'

'Beggars can't be choosers, love. How did you lose your top? Wind blow it away?' He laughs at his own lame joke. 'You don't wanna get cold.'

A trickle of sweat joins the puddle collecting between my breasts.

'I'm fine, thanks.'

'You really gonna walk about in just a bra?' he says. 'All them women what got murdered, and you're walking about like that? Not very respectful, eh?'

I stare at him. I imagine jabbing a Union Jack pencil

271

into his ear until blood trickles down his neck. I imagine smashing his Princess Diana mug and slicing the jagged ceramic across his throat. I imagine screaming at him, punching him, spitting in his face.

But I don't do any of that. I just stand there.

The man makes a face at me. 'What you doing?'

I just stand there.

'You funny in the head?'

I just stand there.

Eventually, he goes quiet, looking around for someone else to serve, but I'm the only one at his stand. He counts the money in his apron. Clears his throat. I don't move. Minutes pass.

'Sorry,' he mumbles. 'About what I said. I just worry about women.'

'And they worry about men like you,' I reply, turning on my heel and walking away until I've crossed the road and entered the Strand.

My phone tells me it's 5.48 p.m. Just over two hours until the vigil. Groups of people are already approaching Trafalgar Square from all angles. This gathering is going to be a lot bigger than originally planned.

It's not the atmosphere I imagined, though. It's charged, yes, and teetering on the edge of something darker, yet on the surface women are laughing, practically dancing along the street like it's Pride or Notting Hill Carnival. There's no anger or sadness on their faces. Is that because everyone believes the man who killed those women is dead now? Is that because of what I did?

A white woman with locks and a bar piercing through her left eyebrow slows down beside me and points at my chest.

'Strong statement,' she says, assessing me like I'm an unusual sculpture. 'Bloody face, messy hair, dirty bra. Says it all. Good job, sister. What these women went through should never be forgotten. This is gender war.'

No, it's not.

'I'm going to do the same,' she says, whipping off her top and revealing a grey sports bra. 'Because it's not about *burning* our bras; it's about showing them sullied and tainted by the hand of man.'

What the fuck is she talking about?

'Do you have any more blood on you?'

Probably. I shake my head and walk off.

'Wait!' she calls out. 'Can I get a selfie?'

What the actual fuck! What am I doing, wandering around talking to people? The police are looking for me, and after what I just did to Matt's flat, he probably is too.

I speed up, even though it's not easy to run in this skirt. My feet sting from blisters I haven't attended to and my skirt is so tight I'm shuffling more than running. Before I know it, I'm back at Charing Cross station.

It's the fourth time in two days I've stood at its gates, staring up at the medieval-style monument looming outside the train station. This structure is apparently a replica of a seventeenth-century cross depicting eight different versions of Queen Eleanor. It's ugly and out of place and I don't even know who that queen was – but I do know women

273

don't get worshipped like this any more. No crosses for our women, just shallow graves and wilting flowers on gallery steps.

What are my options? Charing Cross is a train and Tube station. Although, if I get a train from here, the furthest away I can get is Kent and then I'd have to change. I search my phone again, looking at all the possible escape routes.

Ferries to France leave from Dover and Portsmouth, and one goes to the Netherlands from Harwich. No one knows my name, so using my passport to get out of the UK won't be an issue. Then, once I'm on the mainland, it will be easy to travel through Europe to Spain undetected. A lead ball drops to the pit of my stomach. Oh God, I need to speak to Marianna, tell her I'm not coming. But what do I say?

I keep jabbing at the links on my phone, my dependable Google friend.

Alternatively, I can get a ferry from Holyhead to Ireland, but a train ticket to Holyhead will cost nearly as much as the crossing. Or I can go one stop on the Tube to Piccadilly Circus and get the Piccadilly Line all the way to Heathrow airport, using my travel card, and use Rose's cash to buy the cheapest one-way ticket to wherever.

Too many decisions; everything is blurring and spinning around me. The heatwave is meant to break tomorrow, but it's still pressing down on the city, squeezing every last drop of moisture from its people. Needing us all to remember it was here – and that it won.

There's been no rain for weeks. I can't remember the last time I didn't feel like I was walking through molten lava, hot, sticky wax, warm treacle sucking me down down down.

As I head towards the shade of the train station entrance I spot a familiar blue cap.

29

The Big Issue • @BigIssue

Homeless in danger during heatwave. With rising temperatures, a record number of homeless people are being admitted into hospital with heatstroke, severe sunburn and dehydration.

'Fancy finding you here,' I say.

Moby grins up at me. His face is redder than it was yesterday, his eyes like dark hollows.

'I thought you were going on holiday,' he says.

'Change of plan.'

He doesn't ask why I'm standing in front of him in my bra, my face bloody and my hair making me look like I've been dragged through a hedge backwards. Were the London Strangler's victims dragged through a hedge backwards?

'Do you mind if I sit down?' I ask him.

He looks momentarily surprised by my question then taps the cool pavement beside him.

'I'm in hiding,' I explain.

'Then you've come to the right place. I'm invisible, and now you're sitting next to me you are too.'

He laughs. I've never heard him laugh before. He sounds like a boy. He starts to cough, and I pass him my half-drunk bottle of water, which he gulps down gratefully.

He's right. At least twenty people have filed past in the last minute, and not one of them has looked at us.

He hands my bottle back.

'Finish it,' I say.

'Who you running away from?'

I don't know how to answer so I show him my phone. The notifications on Twitter have gone wild, and my account has gone from two hundred followers to nearly eight thousand in the space of six hours. People are calling me brave for speaking out against Paul, they're calling me crazy because of my one-line posts, a hero because they think I killed a murderer, and a dangerous fucking bitch because . . . well, maybe I am.

Moby scrolls through my phone and I wait as he reads everything slowly. My post about the abuse at work, the camera footage of me having a panic attack, my unhinged posts, the things people are saying about me. I don't rush him; I just stare at all the shoes rushing by. Sandals, flip-flops, trainers, sandals, flip-flops, trainers.

'That's your suitcase,' he says, pointing at the camera still of a lilac suitcase beside a bus stop. 'I remember it from yesterday. And that shirt you were wearing. You looked very smart.'

There's no agenda behind his comment, no sideways glances or judgement. My bra, although no longer white, is quite transparent. You can see the form of my nipples pushing through the lace, but he hasn't looked once. I'm practically naked, sitting beside a homeless guy I hardly know, yet I feel safer right now than I have since I was at Rose's house.

'Did you kill him?' he asks quietly.

I nod.

'Good.'

And we stay like that for a long time, on the cold, hard ground, staring at Queen Eleanor's ugly cross.

'I'm leaving London,' I say.

'Where you off to?'

I shrug, thinking through my options. Plane, train, boat, Ireland on one side, the rest of Europe on the other, anywhere that Rose's three hundred quid will take me. The more options I think of, the less I move.

Moby is holding out something red in his hand.

'Do you want to wear one of my tops?' he asks. 'They aren't too dirty.'

'No, I'm fine. Thanks.' I know he can't spare any clothes. 'Hey, Moby, do you remember what you said to me yesterday?'

He shakes his head slowly, resting it against the grimy station wall. He's looking up at the ceiling of the walkway as if it's the night sky.

'You said it's the little things that kill you, because they sneak up on you while you're busy holding on to the big things.'

He grins. 'I said all that? How deep. Was I drunk?'

I think he's joking. I've never seen Moby drink anything stronger than water.

'You were right,' I say, watching the ever-growing crowds of people with placards and flowers file past. 'In the end, it was lots of little things that got too big. I couldn't carry it. I got crushed by the weight of it all.'

Moby and I sit side by side, neither of us speaking. I'm too hot and scared to move and too wired to make a decision.

My phone has been buzzing in my hand for so long my fingers have gone numb, but all I care about are the notifications from my sister. I keep going to reply, then stopping, then deleting my response. I wonder if Marianna is watching the three little dots appear and disappear. Relieved I'm still alive, then wishing I were dead.

I'm staring at my screen, my notifications rolling like a news ticker, and suddenly there's Matt. His face flashing up on my phone with a headline under it.

I let out a strangled yelp and drop my phone on to my lap like it's on fire. It's a BBC news post on Twitter and people are already tagging me.

BBC Breaking News • @BBCBreaking
Em for Murder. 'I know who killed the London Strangler,' son of Tory MP says.

Tory MP? What!?

I click on the video link and turn up the volume. Moby stirs beside me.

The video shows the fuzzy footage of me having a panic attack in the hotel, me in the airport, me vomiting on a bush, then a photo of me smiling. A full photo, staring right at the camera – my entire face.

Fuck. Fuck. Fuck.

I know that photo. It was a selfie Matt took a few weeks after I moved in with him. He'd bought a fancy bottle of champagne to celebrate something, I can't remember what, and we'd got a bit drunk and taken photos of one another. This one was of us both, but he's cropped himself out of the shot. The others were worse – because in the others I'm naked.

I wait, expecting to see the nudes next, but instead it cuts to the reporter standing outside Matt's building in Suffolk Street. Yellow tape flutters behind them, and men in white overalls walk back and forth carrying boxes. *My* boxes.

This is live, it's happening right now, five minutes away from where I'm huddled half naked and covered in blood outside a train station.

'I'm here with Matthew Atkinson Carter, son of Tory MP Hillary Atkinson and TechNow founder David Carter,' the eager news reporter says to camera. She turns to Matt. 'Matthew, please tell us what happened.'

This is the first time I've heard Matt's surname. He said his father was a businessman and he never mentioned his mother. I didn't know his parents were a politician and a tech billionaire! Well, of course. You don't own an apartment in the centre of London unless you're rich or important – or both. And you don't get to your early thirties without a nine-to-five job unless your parents are financing you.

The reporter's eyes are hungry. She has the scoop of the century. She knows it, and Matt knows it, which is why he's taking his time to answer, savouring the suspense.

'I came home, and there she was. My flatmate, Emmy. The girl the police have been looking for.'

Girl? I turn thirty tomorrow.

'Are you sure it was her?' the reporter asks. 'The woman from the video footage?'

Matt nods. 'That vile shirt she was wearing was on the floor and it was stained dark red. With blood.'

The reporter feigns shock, as if she didn't know he was going to say that. As if that's not the reason why she's there.

'That must have been terrifying. What did you do?'

'I was with my fiancée and . . .' As if on cue, Rebecca steps out of the building behind him, pulling her little black suitcase. She gives Matt a measured look as he glances over his shoulder. Matt's torn. He's on live television, but the woman he apparently loves so much is walking away. She waits – I count – three seconds, then he turns back to the camera. 'And there was Emmy, in my house, brandishing a knife!'

Moby is fully alert now and watching over my shoulder.

'A knife?' he whispers in my ear.

I sigh heavily. 'He'd packed all my things up and I was opening boxes.'

Moby lets out a light laugh, which reminds me of something Rose would do. I wonder if she's watching this. If she stayed in town or went home.

The reporter keeps looking from the camera to Matt. 'A knife? What did you do?'

'I protected my woman, of course.'

My woman. Fucking idiot.

'Emmy came at us with the weapon, snarling and spitting like a demented demon. She smashed glasses and threw her belongings everywhere. It was terrifying. I already knew she was one of those feminist women who hates men, but I never imagined she was evil enough to kill one in cold blood. You can imagine what was going through my mind when I saw her standing there. I thought I was next. So I wrestled the knife off her and told her to leave. I must have scared her because she ran away.'

'Can you tell us where she went?' the reporter asks.

Matt looks straight to the camera and narrows his pale eyes. 'Probably back to Spain, where she came from. This is why the government is working so hard on immigration, why we have to have stringent checks on those crossing our borders.'

The reporter takes the mic away from him quickly and turns back to the camera.

'Scary scenes here in central London. Police are on the lookout for a woman who answers to the name of Em, or Emmy, in connection to the death of a man found early this morning in Thames Barrier Park.' The cropped photo of me flashes up on the screen again. I'm smiling, a bit drunk, the face of a woman who has just had sex with the man who would one day tell the world she was crazy, and dangerous, and didn't belong in her own country.

'If you see this woman, do not approach her. Call the number at the bottom of the screen.'

'Wow,' Moby says. 'What a nasty posh twat.'

'I didn't threaten him. Or smash his place up.'

'I know. But he missed out an important detail.'

'What? That he was cheating on his fiancée with me?'

Moby shakes his head. 'He forgot to mention you're the only woman walking around central London in just a bloody bra.'

'Ah, but I'm not.'

I nod at a group of women outside the station. One of them has locs, the woman who spoke to me earlier. Her shirt is tied around her waist, and all she's wearing on top is her grey sports bra. The others are taking their tops off too.

'Fuck,' Moby says. 'You've started a new trend.'

'My new summer collection,' I say. 'It's called Dress to Depress.'

But none of this is funny. It's fucking terrifying.

'Moby?' I say under my breath. 'Everyone has seen my face now. I'm on the news.'

'Yeah,' he says, looking back at the phone in my hand. 'But, no offence, you don't look anything like that photo right now. I wouldn't recognise you. Nice to know your name though, Emmy.'

I rub my eyes, my skin dry and rough beneath my fingertips.

'I'm not called Emmy. Stupid idiot doesn't even know my proper name. He rented out a room to me – clearly Daddy's allowance wasn't enough – but he was so arrogant he never even asked for my passport. If he had, he'd have seen it was a British passport, and the police would have my details by now.'

'What's your name then?' Moby asks. 'Don't worry, I won't report you.'

He gives another boyish laugh, and I believe him. Moby's invisible, and so am I. For now. I tell him my name, my full Spanish name with both surnames, and he grins.

'That's a very cool name.'

'A lot of people call me Em though, because they can't remember my real name, let alone pronounce it.'

'Yeah, I have that problem too,' he says.

Moby? That's not a hard name. Then I realise that's not his name. I made it up, to add some humanity to the poor homeless man I saw every morning. Just like Matt decided who I was and what I was to him.

'Sorry. I don't know your real name either. You must think I'm so rude, calling you a nickname you never asked for.'

'I like Moby,' he says with a grin. 'But my actual name's Sam.'

My turn to laugh. 'Right, so you were being funny. Yeah, I bet people struggle with the spelling of your name all the time. OK, Moby Sam, so tell me why you always have that book with you.'

I point at the empty McDonald's cup balancing on his well-thumbed copy of *Moby Dick*.

He shrugs, licking at the sore on the side of his mouth.

'Do you want me to say that the book helps me ponder on the existentialism of life and the concept of one final truth?'

I'm impressed.

'You're impressed, right?' he adds. 'You think the only thing I read is the back of a fag packet?'

'No.'

Maybe.

'Nah, I'm messing with you. I've never read the book. I found it by the bins a few months ago and it was a good sturdy thing to rest my cup on. Also, people give more money to homeless people if we have a pet or we're reading a book. Did you know that? Maybe it makes us look more valid or interesting. More worthy of their pity and money. I mean, no one wants to help someone who can't prove they're kind or smart, eh?'

Fucking hell. I rub my face again. I'm tired, but not like I need sleep . . . like every bone in my body has been filled with cement and every itchy inch of my skin is crying to be ripped off.

'You want a hit?' Moby asks.

Drugs? Maybe that's the answer.

He pulls out a can of Red Bull. 'I keep it for emergencies. Sometimes it's not safe to sleep.'

I don't know what face I'm making, but his lips set in a straight line.

'You thought I was gonna shoot up, eh? I've never done drugs. I don't even drink or smoke any more.'

I accept the energy drink and we take turns sipping it. It tastes of melted strawberry jelly, flooding my mind with regretful nights and hung-over days. I nearly gag, but it's helping.

'Been on the streets long?' I ask.

'Nah. Just this summer. Lost my job, got proper low and stayed at my sister's until we had a big row and she chucked me out. Then I pissed my mates off after months of couch surfing and being a dick, so I figured the best thing for me and everyone around me was to get away. Being on your own means no more excuses, right? You sort yourself out or die trying.'

'Do they know where you are? Your friends and family?'

He shakes his head. 'They probably think I'm dead. I thought I *was*, for a while.'

I think of my own sister, my mother, wondering where I am the day before my birthday and the big wedding. Are they worried about me? Or do they hate me even more than they already do?

'I've seen you around,' he says. 'I mean, not just when you give me food and drink on your way to work. Which, by the way, is well nice of you. Not many people do that. I mean at night, on weekends. I see you walking about and reading on your tablet. You hang about Trafalgar Square a lot.'

He means Nelson's Column and the lions. I wait for the sun to go down and I climb up, thinking of Nikki as a child and Mufasa protecting her. I hide in the shadows, leaning against the great iron beast, and I read my Kindle until the sky goes from black to navy. London isn't safe at night, but there are plenty of places to hide and plenty of parks in which to sleep in the day with the rest of the sunbathing tourists.

'Yeah, I live near here during the week, but not on weekends.' Hearing myself say it out loud reminds me of how messed up the entire arrangement was from the start. Why did I ever think that was acceptable, to be told to stay away from my own bedroom on a weekend and wander the streets of London alone? Fucking Matt. 'I had a flat-share just up the road there, where that reporter was interviewing Matt. I just wasn't welcome much.'

Moby nods and we sit in silence a little longer.

'So, what you gonna do?'

I look up, but I don't answer.

'Em, everyone knows what you look like now. Where are you going to hide? Because running in that skirt is out of the question.'

Perhaps London doesn't have that many places to hide after all. And he's right, I can't even sit down in this skirt without pulling it right up or sitting on my legs, which is giving me pins and needles. I also need deodorant. I wonder if Moby can smell me. Mind you, he doesn't smell so fresh himself.

'I'm going to the toilet,' I say. 'There's one here, right? At the station?'

He nods. 'Careful they don't catch you sneaking in though. You don't have to pay any more, but they still don't like ... certain people ... coming and going.'

I get what he's saying. I look crazy, possibly drugged or homeless, certainly like trouble.

What if, once I'm inside the station, I keep going? What if I just keep running? I can get on the Tube and head for Heathrow and . . .

But everyone has seen my face properly now. Everyone knows what I look like. I can't go anywhere, at least not while it's still daylight.

'Here,' Moby says. He's holding out a big pair of scissors. How many things does this guy have in his tatty bag?

'Why do I need these?' I ask, taking them anyway.

'Your skirt. So you can run faster.'

He's right.

'And for your hair.'

30

Daily Mail Online • @MailOnline
Jilted civil servant William Hennington, 36, was murdered
by a female illegal immigrant still on the run. Will she
strike again? Is he connected to the London Strangler?
Ill-advised #SaveThem vigil is still going ahead.

> **Jeffrey Gillingham** • @Jeff_G
> So now we have foreign women out there stabbing
> English men to death and that's OK?
>
> **Charles** • @CharlesMWhite
> If she can do that to a murderer, then she could kill
> any man. I'm nervous to go out now.
>
> **Nadja Kalinsky** • @NadjaK10
> Replying to @CharlesMWhite
> Oh, YOU'RE scared to go out alone in case some
> random person kills you for no reason? Hi, welcome
> to the World of Women.
>
> **Don't Feed The Trolls** • @CharlottSH
> Jilted? How is being a sadistic serial killer his ex-gf's
> fault just because she didn't want to be with him
> any more?

> **Charles** • **@CharlesMWhite**
> Replying to **@CharlottSH**
> No one said he was the London Strangler.
>
> **Don't Feed The Trolls** • **@CharlottSH**
> Replying to **@CharlesMWhite**
> Either way, he was still trying to kill a woman. And
> he would have succeeded if **@Em_Dash_93** hadn't
> stopped him!
>
> **UKIP** • **@UKIP**
> See what happens when you let foreigners into the
> country?

I sit on the toilet, scrolling through my phone, waiting for two women to leave the cubicles so I can sort myself out without being seen.

According to the latest news, I killed a thirty-six-year-old man called William Hennington. Bill to his friends. William worked in planning control for Basildon council. Dr Amanda Chambers, the woman he attempted to kill in the Thames Barrier Park last night, was his ex-girlfriend. She'd managed to escape their domestically violent relationship five months previously, but he'd been harassing her since, eventually tracking her down at City Airport and following her to her hotel after her flight had been cancelled.

I look at the photo of Amanda. Long dark hair, smart clothes, my age. It's her. The angel who tried to help me.

So was he killing women who looked like her until he eventually found her?

The news isn't reporting on why ties were found in the

victims' mouths, but someone on Twitter is saying they remember William Hennington from school. He was a bit of a loner back then, apparently, and the uniform they had to wear included a blue stripy tie.

Poor bullied boy couldn't take any more rejection as an adult so goes on a killing spree. Yeah, that sounds like an acceptable response. I wonder how much of a pitiful backstory they'd give a Black or Muslim guy who killed all those women?

Two toilets flush, two taps turn off, then silence. I rush out of my cubicle, grab a handful of hand towels, run them under the cold tap, squeeze some soap on to my hand then go back to the cubicle to wash between my legs. I throw my knickers and sanitary towel into the box by the loo – leaving my soiled undergarments around London is becoming a habit of mine – then insert the tampon before replacing my underwear with a clean pair.

It's not much, but I already feel a million times better.

The scissors are heavy in my bag. I take them out and look at them. They're big kitchen scissors, the type you use to cut through chicken bones. Sharp enough for what I need.

Slowly, and trying not to think about how expensive this skirt was, I cut twenty centimetres off the hem. Then a bit more. The line isn't straight, but the fabric is good, so it holds and doesn't look too bad.

Back outside the cubicle, I look in the mirror. OK, maybe a bra and mini skirt aren't the best combination, but I feel a lot less hot – in more ways than one. The freezing-cold water feels good against my face as I gently wipe away the dried blood, the cut on my head smarting at the touch. I also scrub under my arms with plenty of soap, but I can't remove the haunted look around my eyes.

All the hand towels are finished now, but I look and smell a million times better.

Now for my hair.

Someone is approaching, so I rush back into a cubicle and wait. I can't have anyone seeing me do this. I can't bring any more attention to myself. While I wait, I watch a silent tutorial on cutting your own hair on YouTube. I may be crazy, but I don't need to look it.

Once I get the all-clear I position myself by the mirror again and start to hack at my hair.

My father used to say it was my most redeeming feature.

'Thick and glossy,' he'd say, helping me brush it every evening. 'Your hair is just like your mother's. You must look after it. Hair is the first thing a man notices when he's choosing a bride.'

Taking a fistful, I hack at the tangled bunch and hold it up, as if it's the head of everyone who has wronged me. Forty centimetres of hair gone. I keep doing the same all around my head until I have a bob level with my chin, but I can't stop. I cut myself a fringe and neaten up the edges, and much like my skirt, it's not straight but it will do. I feel so cool and light, the heat leaving my body the more of it I display.

I stare back at my reflection. That's not the same woman who put on these clothes yesterday morning, dreaming of landing a full-time job at the company of her dreams. The woman too scared to return to Spain, pissed off that her sister's wedding day fell on her thirtieth birthday, the woman who thought sleeping with Matt, and quietly avoiding Paul, was a good idea.

The woman in the mirror has a friend called Rose and a friend called Moby Sam, and they have known her all her life – because her life started yesterday. And this is what the future looks like now.

I bury all my chopped-off hair as deep as I can in the bottom of the bin, beneath the mountain of dirty paper towels. Then I straighten my skirt and tuck my hair behind my ears. Today is the last day of my twenties, and tomorrow I will be starting afresh. Maybe I'll choose a new name and a whole new past, too.

'Excuse me.'

I swing around, waiting for handcuffs or a beating. A woman in her early twenties is standing in front of me, her arms hugging a stack of white boards. She's wearing shorts, trainers and a bra, with drops of blood painted on her face.

'I take it you're here for the vigil too,' she asks.

I nod.

'Would you like one of these?'

She hands me one of her signs. It has a hashtag on it, big and bold, in neat red letters.

'#SaveEm', it says.

'It has a typo,' I point out. 'Isn't it meant to say "Save Them"?'

The woman gives me a lopsided smile to match her one-shoulder shrug. 'Yes, but we're not just here for the women he killed. We're here because of the woman who saved the last one and stopped it happening again. Em. She's all over the news. Have you seen the latest? What a badass.'

I nod, the hair on the back of my newly exposed neck standing on end. She knows. She knows who I am.

Except, she doesn't.

'Em needs to be protected at all costs,' the woman says, handing me a board. 'If only more women were as brave as her.'

I don't jump on the Tube, and I don't run away. Instead, I skip back to Moby, because I can. I can finally move my legs, and it feels good. I smell of cheap bathroom hand-wash, which is better than blood and body odour, and my underwear is comfortable. Nothing is rubbing anywhere any more. The breeze on the back of my neck sends a shiver down my spine and I grin.

'What you got there?' he asks as I return his scissors and sit back beside him, the giant white board covering my face.

I pull it away and he mock-gasps.

'Ooooh, trendsetter strikes again. You look like that kid in that film *Leon.*'

'The film about a murderer?'

He grins and wiggles his eyebrows. I show him what the sign says, and he raises his eyebrows even higher.

'Fuck. Things are getting out of hand, don't you think?'

'I don't think it's even got started yet.'

I follow his gaze to the street, where the crowds are getting thicker, everyone heading up the Strand towards

Trafalgar Square. I'm not the only one holding a #SaveEm sign. Some have created new ones; others have simply crossed out the TH of 'them'.

'They're all here for you,' Moby says. 'This is mad. You're their hero.'

'I don't like this one bit.' I blow into my new fringe, already damp from the heat. 'I don't want to be anyone's hero.'

I think about what the woman with the locs said to me, and the woman in the toilet just now. I didn't set out to catch the London Strangler. I was angry about Paul and Nikki, I lost my suitcase, I saw someone getting hurt. I didn't mean to do what I did.

My phone won't stop buzzing. I'm surprised it still has any battery left. Forty-seven per cent.

> **Save Em!** • @AbigailSPotter
> Maybe if more women went around stabbing abusers to death, then men would think twice about hurting us!
>
> **Pedro S** • @Pedro_Santiago
> Replying to @AbigailSPotter
> Yeah, great, let's encourage women to kill now, shall we?
>
> **Rivers** • @EllaSDLRios
> It's about time we stood up for ourselves.
>
> **#SaveThem Save Em** • @Marge72
> I wasn't going to go to the vigil, it was too depressing. But now there's hope. Let's #SaveEm

| **PR and Marketing Agency** • @SwanandSwallow
| We stand by Em #SaveEm

That last tweet is definitely from Kate. I wonder what Caroline will say about that on Monday morning.

With a heavy sigh I turn the 4G off my phone; I need to save the battery and stop the incessant buzzing. I put it back in my handbag, shaking my head at the thought of Kate writing that last tweet. I appreciate her trying, but we all know social media's a lot better at destroying people than it is at saving them.

A group of teenage girls exits the train station. They're wearing shorts and bra tops, holding placards reading 'KILL US – WE KILL YOU'. One is wearing a purple bra with fresh flowers woven into her hair like she's going to a Woodstock-themed party; another has #SaveEm written with black marker pen on her chest. They're laughing, passing a bottle of Prosecco from one to the other. Had they already planned a girls' night out in town and added a vigil for dead women at the last minute? Fun.

Two men in business attire step out of a black cab and head for the station. They slow down as the girls pass them. None of them have noticed Moby and me sitting against the wall. We remain invisible. But I'm watching them.

'This is getting out of hand,' one man says to the other, nodding at the girls. Then he turns his attention to them.

'What exactly do you think you're going to achieve by this charade?'

The teenagers fall silent. They can't be more than fifteen years old. Seventeen, tops.

'Do your parents know you're dressed like that?'

They look at one another as the men stand over them. Men that probably look like their fathers or teachers.

One of the girls steps forward, her jaw set in defiance. 'We just want to be heard.'

'And seen,' the second man says. 'It's a disgrace. We're all sad those poor women were murdered, but the killer is dead now. It's over. Let them all rest in peace. There's no need for this circus.'

The girls look away and try to walk around them, but the second man isn't having it. He blocks their path.

'That's it? You don't have anything to say for yourselves?'

I'm on my feet before I know it. Moby reaches for my hand, his fingers slippery against mine, but I'm not sitting back down.

'Leave it,' he hisses. 'It's not worth it.'

Except it is. I did nothing when Paul kissed me, I did nothing when those men stole Moby's water, or when all those men called me and Rose names, and I did nothing when Matt treated me like a piece of cheap meat. I didn't even speak up when I was sacked for the actions of someone else. I've spent my entire life doing nothing. Doing nothing was why I left Spain.

I shake Moby off. 'It's always worth it.'

'Great, here comes another one,' the first man says, rolling his eyes, his gaze settling a second too long on my cleavage.

The girls look at me, waiting for me to speak. But maybe I don't need words to say something.

I stare at the two men, and they crease their brows at me. Slowly, I raise my palms upwards, a hand either side of me, and begin to hum, my stare never leaving their faces.

One of the girls lets out a light giggle, but as soon as they see the men's eyes widen with fear and confusion the girls flank me, two on either side, copying me until our collective hum becomes deafening like a swarm of bees waiting to strike.

'What the hell are you . . .'

Each time the men try to talk, we hum louder, stand in their way, raise our palms to the heavens a little more. I stop humming and against the backdrop of the girls' chorus I mouth a string of silent words. The names of all who wronged me, who didn't listen, who failed to see me, who thought I was someone I've never been.

Their names become a silent prayer, an incantation, a spell.

The girls hum and we stare, and I say my words, until a crowd has formed around us. At first people watch, then a few of them join in. The men don't know what to do, where to turn, so they run. They actually run, all the way to the train station.

The humming slows down, and the girls fall silent. No one is laughing any more.

'What was that?' the girl with the hashtag on her chest says. 'What did we just do?'

I smile and place a hand on her shoulder.

'We did what many women have done before us. Bad guys don't listen when we scream, they chase us when we run, they don't ever want to see who we really are – but they will always be scared of witches.'

The girls give me a nervous smile and I walk away, joining Moby on the pavement.

'Is that your idea of keeping a low profile?' he says as I sit down beside him.

I grin. I can't stop smiling. Moby elbows me gently, leaning in close and lowering his voice.

'You might not *want* to be a hero,' he says. 'But I don't think you get a choice any more.'

31

The Guardian • @guardian

Dr Amanda Chambers speaks up about the guardian
angel who saved her life. 'I don't know who Em is, but
she's a hero. I'm alive because of her.'

'You're going to have to go at some point,' Moby says. 'I
mean, unless this is your life now. You're welcome to live
with me. This is my summer residence.' He waves around
the station. 'And in the winter, I plan to find a more urban
abode. Perhaps something with arched features and a river
view. Like under a bridge.'

He's joking, but I keep thinking back to the tweet I saw
earlier about homeless people dying because of the heatwave. What happens in the winter? Will he have somewhere
to go?

'Why don't you call your sister?' I say.

Moby sits up, shifting uncomfortably. 'She don't want
to hear from me.'

'How do you know?'

'Because families don't have to like you – they just have
to pretend to. She's probably relieved I'm out of her hair.'

He takes off his cap, scratches his head and pushes it back on again. 'What did your mum say when you told her you weren't coming back this weekend?'

Well played.

'I haven't called her yet.'

He makes an 'I told you' face, and I lean back against the wall with a sigh.

It's different, though. We're not the same, me and Moby.

'If I'd hit rock bottom like you – no offence – I'd call my mum,' I say.

Moby raises his eyebrows. 'Errr, Em, *no offence*, but you're homeless, moneyless, wanted for murder and don't even own a top. That's pretty rock bottom.'

He's right. I blow my fringe out of my eyes and we both stare at the groups of women forming at the gates to the station. Hardly any of them are wearing a top either; they're laughing and chatting like they're on their way to a party. Who knew murder could be so unifying and make people so happy?

'What's the last thing your sister said to you?' I ask Moby.

His eyes cloud over and he licks his sore lips again. 'Come back when you sort your fucking life out, you piece of shit.'

'Well, you've sorted your life out.'

'Excuse me?' He gestures at where we're sitting, people filing by but no one looking at us. Someone dropped a coin in his cup ten minutes ago, but it turned out to be an American quarter.

'You seem OK now, Moby Sam. What's stopping you?'

He raises his eyebrows again.

301

'Right. Listen,' I say. 'I'll call my mum if you speak to your sister.' I hand him my mobile phone. 'Take it, then!'

He bats my hand away. 'What year do you think this is? Nineteen ninety-seven? I don't know her telephone number off by heart.'

'What's her job?' I turn the 4G back on my phone and ignore all the notification buzzes.

'Hairdresser,' he mumbles.

'What's the name of where she works?'

'This is stupid. OK, fine. The Cut Hut.'

'Really?'

'It's her own business. I told her it was a crap name.'

I type it into Google and her Facebook page comes up straight away. Sally. Her and Moby look so alike they could be twins. Maybe they are. So Moby's from Bimingham. I should have guessed by his accent. I click on the blue telephone number link and it starts ringing.

'Here,' I say, holding out my phone.

He shuffles back like I'm waving a flaming torch at him. 'What are you doing?'

'Hello?' says a tinny voice on the other end.

I jab the phone at him.

'Hello?' the voice says again.

Moby takes my phone, gently like it's a wild animal, and places it to his ear.

'Hey,' he says. 'I sorted my life out.'

I can hear the high-pitched whine of someone crying. 'Oh my God!' the woman is screaming. 'Sam! Is that really you, Sam?'

Moby's chin trembles and he picks at his cracked lips.

'Yeah, I'm OK,' he says. 'I'm sorry.' His voice is thick, and I look away. I can't hear what his sister is saying, but out of the corner of my eye I see Moby nodding and rubbing his eyes with the back of his hand.

'Seriously, I'm fine. Yeah, I think so. No, not even booze. London. I'm going to try. I want to. Yeah, me too.'

He hangs up and passes the phone back to me. His nails are bitten down to the quick, knuckles black with pavement dirt. His hand is shaking, and I place mine over it until it stills.

I wait for him to say something, but he doesn't, he just stares into the distance, rubbing his eyes with his dirty knuckles. He really is young. Too young to have lived this life already.

After a few minutes he mutters something that I ask him to repeat.

'Your turn,' he says.

He means my family. I need to call my mother and my sister. I've waited long enough.

There are three missed calls from Marianna on my phone. I hold down the voicemail button and listen.

An hour after I was meant to have landed:
'What's going on?' My sister sounds so young. She is young. Even younger than Moby. *'Please get in touch. We're worried.'*

Two hours later:
'I've been calling you for hours, cabrona! I get married tomorrow and I don't need this stress. Why are you always doing this to us?'

Thirty minutes ago:
'Mama is ill. Please. We're so worried. Tell us what the hell is going on.'

I look over at Moby and shake my head slowly. They don't want to hear from me. They hate me.

'What am I meant to say to them?'

'I dunno. Tell them you're sorry. Tell them you love them.'

I love them, of course I do, but actions speak louder than words. After I left them to mourn my father alone and I never returned, my words will only be as hollow as my promises. I think of my mother, of how ill she is, and decide I can't talk to them. It hurts too much.

Moby turns his lips down at the edges, the smile of a sad clown. 'You miss them less when you tell yourself they don't love you, eh?'

I rub my face. My hands still smell of soap.

'Call them,' he says. 'You'll regret it more if you don't.'

'Says the guy who hasn't spoken to his own sister for nearly a year.'

His lips twitch upwards as he looks down and a sudden rush of emotion sweeps through me. He sees it and opens his arms, and I fall into his embrace. He's holding me, giving me the hug I didn't realise I'd been needing this whole time.

'Hey,' he says. 'It's going to be all right.'

We both know he's lying, but for a moment I allow myself to believe him, and it works. I sniff loudly in his ear and blink back tears. He's right. I have to call them.

There are four unread WhatsApp messages. The three from my sister are just like her voicemails, but the one from my mother is a screenshot. It's a fuzzy photo of me, one I haven't seen before, sitting on a park bench. You can see my face. I'm staring at something on my lap. My hands. Hands black with blood.

My mother has written just three words beneath the picture: 'Is this you?'

I can't speak. I'm choking. I'm dying.

Moby glances at my screen and lays a hand on my arm.

'Breathe,' he says quietly. 'It's OK.'

It's not OK. I look up at him. He's a shimmering mirage of a silhouette through my tears.

'Call her,' he mouths.

I can't. My family know the truth now. They have their answer.

I swipe the app away and look at Instagram instead. I deserve to hurt. I want to see the photo of that stranger kissing Nikki again – the only woman I have ever loved – and prove to myself that I did the right thing by keeping away from her. That I deserve this pain. I need to pick at the scabs that took so long to form, just so I can feel something sharper, deeper, real.

Nikki has posted a new photo. I swipe back, but the one

of her kissing the blonde girl has gone. In its place is a selfie of Nikki looking serious but still so beautiful.

The caption below starts off with a pink flower emoji.

Stay safe, Flower. I'm proud of you. I love you. You know where I'll be tonight. Right beside our king.

My hand shoots to my mouth, my fingers trembling against my lips. Flower. That's me. Nikki's referring to my surname, she's talking to *me*. I know exactly where she'll be waiting for me tonight. Does this mean she still loves me?

I place my handbag on my lap and drop my phone inside. Moby watches me silently as I get my purse out and pull out the money Rose gave me.

'Here,' I say to him.

He looks at it, incomprehension flooding his features. I know what he's thinking – *if she had hundreds of pounds in her bag all along, why the hell has she spent the last three hours sitting on a dirty floor with me?*

'What's this?' he says, not touching the banknotes I'm holding out to him.

'Your ticket home.'

'But . . . you need that. You need to get away.'

'I don't think I do, actually.' The sun is setting, dusty blue shadows creeping over golden paving slabs. 'There's something more important I need to do tonight.'

I drop the money in his lap. Then, holding his face between my hands, I plant a kiss on the top of his head and walk away.

32

The streets are packed with hordes of people heading in one direction. Trafalgar Square. I remember someone at work telling me what the last night of 1999 was like here when everyone flocked to the centre of the capital to celebrate the start of a new millennium. How it was so crowded their feet left the floor at one point and they were swept forward on a sea of bodies.

I imagine it was a lot like this. But instead of winter coats and paper hats with foiled '2000' on them, it's women wearing just their bras, holding up signs, clutching flowers and candles. Perhaps to them this is a new millennium. A new start.

For me, it feels like the beginning of something bad.

Trafalgar Square looks nothing like it did yesterday morning. The bases of the fountains are still empty and without water but now people are sitting on their rims and standing in the bases. The souvenir seller is no longer there; instead there's a mountain of flowers pressed up against the wall beside the steps leading up to the National Gallery. Among the flowers are cards, photos of the four dead women, and teddy bears. But there are also notes addressed to me. Notes to Em, thanking her. Me. Yet I'm right here. A real person. Walking among them.

Lining the street are vans, and it's not until I see a woman with a microphone that I realise they're TV crews. One woman, in a dark navy dress and heels, positions herself before the wall of flowers. I stand to the side and watch.

'Behind me is the start of tonight's "Save Them" vigil. What began as a remembrance gathering for Hanna Nilsson, the murdered daughter of Swedish ambassador Lars Nilsson, the movement has grown with each new discovery of victims of the London Strangler. Then, last night, the body of a man was found stabbed to death in east London. He was later identified as William Hennington, a civil servant with a violent past. A woman known only as Em is said to have intervened when she witnessed Mr Hennington attempt to murder his ex-girlfriend, Dr Amanda Chambers, stabbing him multiple times. "Em" has also recently exposed endemic sexual misconduct at the heart of leading PR agency Swan & Swallow, and all attention is now focused on discovering her real identity and how she managed to find the London Strangler before the police did. As you can see' – the woman steps to the side and the cameraman pans along the wall of flowers, then the crowded square to her right, where some women are singing, some drinking, but no one is praying quietly. I keep out of shot – 'from its origins as an intimate and peaceful vigil for the women who lost their lives to the London Strangler, the Save Them movement has quickly morphed into Save *Em*, a rowdy demonstration of girl power as thousands of women take to the streets of London in support of the vigilante's actions. Sinner or saviour, the mysterious Em has divided the nation. But who is she?'

I'm two metres away from this woman, but I find it hard to believe she's talking about me. Who *is* Em? I don't know.

The reporter is having to shout to be heard over the din of the protesters. People are chanting. It sounds like 'Stop them. Save Em.' Who are 'them'? Murderers? Men? The reporter turns to a woman beside her. I recognise her. She's a Tory minister. I've seen her on Twitter, getting angry about single mothers and woke millennials.

'Hillary Atkinson MP, you have concerns about this. Am I right?'

That's Matt's mother?

The two women look strange wearing smart knee-length shift dresses and heels while everyone around them is dressed in nothing but shorts and bras.

'I do,' says Hillary Atkinson. Her hair hangs limp, her glasses slipping off her shiny nose. The sun has set now, but the air is still heavy with heat and anticipation.

I look at my phone: it's just past nine o'clock.

'An unauthorised demonstration like this is hard to control,' the MP continues. 'We were aware of a peaceful vigil being planned, and adequate resources had been allocated for that, but a crowd this size without proper police presence is dangerous.'

'Why do we need police here?' a woman in the crowd shouts out.

I step further back into the sea of people as the camera swivels around to focus on the heckler.

'Because things can quickly get out of hand,' Hillary Atkinson says. 'This is nothing but a gathering of blood-thirsty women.'

Everyone around me rears up in anger.

'We're not here to cause trouble!' a young man shouts out. 'This is about protecting women.'

'If women are that worried about their safety,' shouts another man, 'why aren't they at home instead of walking around central London pissed and half naked?'

Hillary Atkinson looks at the reporter as if they are both exhausted mothers with out-of-control children.

'This is exactly what I mean,' she says. 'We can't have vigilantes killing those who do wrong, and we can't have the general public turning them into heroes. It's dangerous, it sets a precedent, and it's against the law. Not to mention divisive.'

The reporter looks back to the camera. 'Join us at ten o'clock, when we'll be talking to Pat Merrifield, Chief Commissioner of the Metropolitan Police and hearing his views on the hunt for Em.'

As if at some invisible cue, the camera crew bundles the reporter and the MP into a huddle and they all run like they're being chased, getting as much distance as they can from the spectators and locking themselves into one of the stationary white vans.

The thing about being part of history in the making is that it never feels like anything monumental is happening. It simply feels like survival. Change isn't the flick of a switch, the passing of a baton, it's messy and disruptive and people get hurt. Big things only happen after a long series of little violent things.

Those who report on it know that, yet those taking part are already in too deep to stop.

33

I shove my way through the gathering crowds and head for the steps of the National Gallery. There are clusters, mostly women, already sitting on the steps, with front row seats to all the action. I keep climbing until the huddles of people thin. As I reach the top of the steps I stare up at the gallery, majestic and floodlit, eight columns reaching up to a triangular roof topped with a dome like a small St Paul's. I keep going until I'm outside the gallery itself, standing between two of the columns. From here I can see the entire square swarming with people and banners and spots of light among the quickening dark.

Nelson's column is glowing white with light, reaching up to a clean, full-moon sky, four lions on each corner, an empty fountain on either side. Red buses and black cabs pass by in the distance and if I lean to the left I can even see Big Ben shining behind the buildings. London looks so much fun from up here. So clean. So safe.

Nikki is here, somewhere near the lions. Rose might also be here. It's like a page from *Where's Wally?* and for a second I tell myself if I try really hard I might be able to spot them. But it's too dark, too busy, too loud.

I sit down, hands on my lap, and rub my thumb over the tattoo on the inside of my wrist. A semicolon – the reminder that I could have stopped but I kept going. Instead of finishing something, I started something new. I came here.

My legs are dangling off the edge of the wall, the heel of my trainers banging steadily against the brickwork. It's not a long drop, maybe eight feet, but I'm instantly taken back to the day when I thought about jumping. When I couldn't choose between what I'd always had, what I wanted and complete and utter darkness.

It was a hot summer. But unlike the humidity and cloying heat of a London heatwave, summer in the south of Spain is dry. So much so that some days it feels like the hairs in your nostrils will singe with every inhalation and the slightest breeze is like a hairdryer to the face.

It was a day like this that changed everything.

I was living back at home at the grand old age of twenty-six, after my latest boyfriend had dumped me. I never did fit into the Marbella scene, and I didn't care enough to even try.

Each relationship after Juan had simply been a watered-down version of him. My first love and I had clung to one another for six long years, not wanting to waste all the time we'd invested in a future we could never agree on, but the more I pulled away from him, the harder he hung on, until he was nothing but a weight around my neck. We both hated him for that. The kindest thing I ever did was let him go.

Trips to Madrid and Barcelona saw me sleeping with interesting women and unavailable men, sometimes both at once, telling myself I was getting it out of my system. That my casual attitude to sex would change once I headed back down south and found a nice man who would help me become what I was meant to be. But not one of them ever filled that void, because none was as kind as Juan, and none really knew me.

After Marbella, my father convinced me to come back to Ronda and work for him, to manage the admin for his firm. My mother couldn't have been happier to have me under her roof again. It made sense to go back and save some money, let her fuss over me for a while, but after a few months it was clear my return had changed the dynamics.

Marianna was sullen about me being back home and didn't hide it. At nearly eighteen, she'd had the run of the house and all the attention. The way she acted, you'd think our family was normal and happy – that Sundays at home were spent going to church together then walking around town before enjoying a big lunch, like every other family. But our weekends were nothing like that. I wasn't ruining anything because there was nothing nice to ruin.

In my naivety, I thought, if I went back, maybe my dad would calm down a little. That he'd be outnumbered. Instead, it gave him more to push back against.

'Your father is out with his friends,' my mother said when I woke up that summer's morning. He had his routine every weekend. 'Better that way,' she continued, busying herself folding the clothes at the foot of my bed. She was out of breath. Looking back, she'd already started showing signs of being ill, but like everything else, I'd pushed it down. If I didn't talk about it, it wouldn't happen. Within three years she'd be given just months to live.

'He'll be home by two,' she said, gliding the diamond pendant of her necklace back and forth. A nervous habit. 'We can prepare lunch together, just me and my girls.'

My girls, she called Marianna and me. *My girls*.

'Don't you have to go to church?' I asked.

'We can go at five instead.'

I agreed. Not because I enjoyed cooking or cared about God, but because the idea of walking into church with both her girls brought a smile to my mother's face, and that wasn't something I saw very often.

We cooked seafood. She hummed as she pulled the pink shells off the prawns, snapping their heads with a twist and nodding encouragingly as Marianna talked about school. I cleaned the squid at the kitchen sink and thought about a girl I'd been talking to the night before at a bar. She was from Bilbao, a tourist passing through. She'd told me she was going travelling soon, to England, Ireland and Scotland. She made it sound easy, describing moss-covered castles and thatched cottages like she was about to step into a Tolkien novel. I'd offered to show her the sights of Ronda at night and taken her for a moonlit stroll around the surrounding countryside. We'd kissed in the vineyard, pressed up against the vines, enveloped by the scent of dry soil and ripe fruit. And I'd savoured every moment, secure in the knowledge that she was a stranger to all who knew me. That my secret would remain safe.

I knew exactly what my father would do if he ever discovered who I really was.

Dominoes was his game. Every Saturday, and some Sundays, he would meet the same five friends at the same bar and play dominoes. They didn't bet much, just a few euros per round. His friends would enjoy their coffees, sometimes a light beer, and if my father was winning, he would do the same. But sometimes he was losing, which meant whisky, which meant Sunday lunches could go in any direction.

Lunch was on the table, and it was nearly three o'clock. We were discussing whether to start eating without him when there was an almighty crash as the front door slammed against the wall.

'You couldn't even wait!' my father roared in English. He could speak Spanish, to a decent-enough level, but when he was angry it was English he shouted in.

My mother and Marianna instantly looked down at their empty plates and waited for him to finish his tirade. My father's moods were like a storm. If you battened down the hatches and stayed still and quiet, they blew over. Except I was fortified with my adventures the night before and the two glasses of wine I'd drunk waiting for him to favour us with his presence, so I made the mistake of speaking up.

'The squid has probably gone hard now,' I mumbled. 'You were meant to be back an hour ago.'

In the movies, when people get hit, they stay on their

feet and instantly hit back. Their faces don't even change colour from the impact. When my father backhanded me across the face, I flew, and the knock on my head against the cold marble floor was worse than the blow to my face. My teeth crashed together and my ears hummed, and it had all sounded so loud I was surprised to find the ceiling hadn't collapsed on us.

But no one had moved or made a sound. Nothing further happened.

My mother served the seafood, rice and salad, making sure my father got his first. He scraped his chair against the floor before sitting with a thud at the table, his head too heavy for his neck. I joined them. Marianna cut me a look that said, 'Now look what you've done,' and we ate in silence.

I pressed my empty glass against my cheek. My face throbbed and was hot to the touch, but I wouldn't give my father the satisfaction of seeing that his blow had hurt.

'Would you like some wine?' my mother asked him.

She always did that. He'd come home drunk, and she'd give him more. She told me it sped things up, that he'd pass out more quickly and be contrite and apologetic upon waking. It was her favourite part. Except, in the meantime, we had to hold on tight and survive the eye of the storm.

As I chewed the rubbery, tasteless squid I thought about England. I'd never been to London. Was it that easy to just go? I had a passport. I also had money in the bank. Not much, but the girl with the soft lips had said it was easy to find work in England if you spoke the language as fluently as I did. I dreamed about finding work as a designer. What if I could get into magazine design or work for a top ad agency?

My stomach twitched with excitement and I realised it was the first time since I'd graduated three years ago that I'd felt hopeful.

Going abroad meant I could reinvent myself. Or, more to the point, finally be the real me.

'I was thinking,' I said quietly. 'I might go to England.'

My mother's face immediately became cross-hatched with pain and worry.

'Just for a bit,' I reassured her, warming to the lie. 'Maybe a month.'

My father had been silent up to that point. I thought maybe he'd nodded off. He hadn't. In one swift motion he whipped the cloth off the table, sending our best plates and cut-glass goblets smashing to the ground. Splintered china scratched my arms as I covered my face.

'What is the fucking matter with you?' he hollered. 'Is our home not good enough for you? Always running. Always trying to chase a dream you will never succeed at.'

Marianna scurried to fetch a dustpan and brush, and my mother returned with a bin bag. Heads bowed low, mouths shut, they swept up the mess, salvaging what items they could.

This was never going to end. As long as I stayed here, lying to myself, this was going to be my life. For ever.

My chair fell with a clatter as I ran to the room I shared with my sister, locked the door and pulled out a lilac suitcase from under my bed. The handle was a little wobbly, but it would do. Why plan a trip when I could leave right now? This very moment. There was a bus to Málaga airport at six every evening, and no shortage of cheap flights to London, Manchester or Liverpool (not that I knew much about any of those cities other than the music they produced).

I didn't notice what I was packing, my vision blurred with tears, but I did it fast – ignoring my father's fists slamming against the door.

'Get out here, you ungrateful little bitch,' he was slurring.

I could hear my mother's gentle coos, like the soft call of a turtle dove, trying to calm him down. I don't know why she bothered; it never worked.

But there was no way to get out of the house without opening the bedroom door and facing him. Steeling myself, I zipped up the case and unlocked the door. My father swayed a little, stumbling towards me as I opened it fully. Marianna was behind him, eyes wide, warning me with short shakes of her head. My mother was still on the ground, cleaning, head down, keeping busy.

He saw my suitcase and wrenched it out of my hands.

'Sort your life out and stop running away,' he hissed, spit hitting my burning cheek. 'And you! Get up off the floor,' he shouted at my mother, pushing her over with the heel of his shoe. 'I'm surrounded by weak, pathetic women.'

My mother was on her knees, looking up at him. 'Would you like me to cook you anything else for lunch?'

Leaning on my luggage for support, he bent down, picked up a prawn from the floor and stuffed it into my mother's mouth.

'All you worry about is food, food, food, you gluttonous pig.'

She started to gag, but Marianna and I just stood there. Waiting. Waiting for what? How bad did it have to get until we acted?

'Go to church,' he spat at her, kicking at a broken plate and sending it skittering across the tiled floor. 'Pray to the only man you truly care about and ask him to make you a better wife.'

My mother didn't say a word as she used the suitcase to help her get up. She was fiddling with the zip of the front pocket. I didn't notice back then that she was no longer wearing her necklace, the one her own mother had given her on her wedding day. For luck.

My father snatched the case from under her, making her stumble, and threw it into the hall cupboard before turning and locking it with a small copper key which he then placed in his pocket. So many keys in this house.

'As for you . . .' he started, his droopy eyes fixed on mine.

But I didn't let him finish. I bolted to the front door and out into the dry heat of the afternoon. Then I did what I did best. I ran.

The streets of Ronda are ancient, and as I raced down them I thought of all the people who had run through these same streets over the centuries. Romans and farm-hands and dignitaries. Up winding lanes, banked by tall, dry grasses and crumbling buildings. I ran higher and higher, heading for the old wall, my favourite view. From Ronda you can see the mountains of Andalucía stretch out for miles, undulating waves of blues and lilacs fading into the misty horizon. I needed to think, and I knew exactly where to go so as not to be found. Even back then I was good at hiding.

I scrambled down a bank, through bushes and trees, until I came to an old stone wall. I climbed it, perched on its edge, sheltered from view, then looked down at the famous gorge with its tiny waterfall jutting out of the rocks and the giant viaduct to my left. If I squinted, I could just make out the tourists gathering at the viewing balconies, taking photos of the fields lit gold by the afternoon sun.

'Fuck,' I said out loud, my voice shaky as my fingers grasped the crumbling stones.

I couldn't even see the bottom of the gorge. I knew there were more vineyards down there, lots of countryside, a bubbling stream and orange rocks smoothed over time by wind and rain.

This is where I came to think, but sometimes I entertained darker notions. Like what would happen if I jumped, and how no one would find me for a long time. The thought of it sent a delicious, painful thrill through me, like poking at a wobbly tooth and hearing it creak as it pulls on the last remaining piece of gum.

I waved my legs back and forth as they dangled over the edge, imagining my own funeral. What would Marianna wear? Would she be happy for the excuse to ask for a new dress? To get her room back? What would my mother cook? Albondigas and tortilla. Her speciality. What would my father do? Would losing me heal him or give him more of an excuse to drink and ask for sympathy? Would my mother blame him, or herself, or pray for my soul?

Good Catholics don't kill themselves, but then I was already a bad Catholic. I was unholy. I was unclean. The kind and gentle man I'd told myself I'd loved all those years had never been enough because he wanted this life, this simple, stifling existence, and I knew there was so much more out there. Maybe even someone who made me feel complete. And, deep down, Juan knew something was missing. The truth.

Perhaps, had I been honest with him, our relationship might have worked out. Or maybe he would have been disgusted with me, cuckolded, hurt. It didn't matter anyway, because I kept that part of me hidden away, protected against my chest like a new-born kitten that hadn't opened its eyes yet.

Maybe that's what was missing between me and my sister too, the truth, along with an age gap so large it was a perpetual chasm of mistrust and misunderstanding. She was more pious than my mother. A mother who loved me so hard it was like trying to stay on my feet on a windy day. A mother who chose to stay with a man, a hurricane, who knocked down anyone who stood in his way.

Whatever I did and wherever I went, I always ended up back here, balanced on the edge of a mountain, looking out at a big, wide world I wasn't allowed to explore.

I had three choices: stay, run or jump.

To this day, I don't know if I was serious about ending it all, but I certainly thought about it. I couldn't decide what option was more terrifying, though, because all three felt like their own version of death.

The bells chimed their funereal call for Mass, and I took it as a sign. I knew there was no God, at least not one who cared about me, but I chose to believe that, somewhere, I was being called. My mother and sister would be at church, and my father would hopefully have drunk himself into a stupor. It didn't even matter that my suitcase was locked in the cupboard. I could still go home, quietly pack a smaller bag with whatever was left in my wardrobe without waking my father . . . and run.

Slowly, my head dizzy from the plunging view, I edged off the wall and focused on what I would do in London instead. I could have stopped, but I'd chosen to go on, and I would mark it in ink as soon as I was on British soil.

Yet when I got home I realised there *was* a God . . . and that sometimes He gave you exactly what you wanted.

34

Evening Standard • @standardnews

'The answer to violence against women is not more violence!' Prime Minister says.

It's dark now, but the crowds in Trafalgar Square have grown so large they're now spilling out on to the pavements and roads. There aren't many buses or cars, but the drivers are still honking at people holding up signs and banging on the side of their vehicles.

I glance at the time on my phone. It's nearly ten o'clock. Twitter notifications have intensified, with more photos of me being added by the minute. Some of those sharing news about me are people I vaguely know, brides whose weddings I help set up with Nikki or someone who happened to have me in the background of their selfie. But no one has said my real name yet, either because they're protecting me or because they don't know it. Very few people really know me.

Some photos posted under the #SaveEm hashtag aren't even me. Who the fuck posts a photo of a random woman they don't know, who happens to also have long black hair, and drags her into this mess? How can you accuse anyone of being a murderer without truly knowing?

I need a plan, but all I can think about is Nikki being somewhere in this mess. Thinking of me. Needing to know I'm OK. I deleted her number months ago, I don't have my own Instagram account, I have no way of telling her I'm right here. Luckily, I know exactly where she'll be – with our king. She won't have moved from that spot all night, hoping, wishing, I saw her message. Nikki was the one who watched all the romance movies. She believes in happy endings.

But I can't see her from here. I can't see anything but one homogeneous mass of people moving like a single entity. Bare flesh, trampled flowers, broken bottles.

> **Alice Shepherd** • @AliceTheNurse
>
> I can't believe men are on Twitter right now saying they're fearing for their lives. Seriously? #SaveEm

> **Sarah McFarlan** • @SMcFarlanPhd
>
> Just got back from a day out with my kids in London. Keep away from Trafalgar Square. It's not a vigil, it's a riot.

> **Guy** • @guy_D
>
> All these women claiming to be peace-loving, out there throwing bottles of wine at passing buses.

> **Mark Toulouse Foster** • @MTFoster
>
> I've never been scared to go out in town alone, but I am tonight.

> **Alice Shepherd** • @AliceTheNurse
>
> Replying to @MTFoster
>
> You do realise most women are scared to go out alone EVERY night?!
>
> **Mark Toulouse Foster** • @MTFoster
>
> Replying to @AliceTheNurse
>
> Is that the answer then? Because one crazy man kills women, you all want to go out there and kill me? Not all men are bad guys.
>
> **Alice Shepherd** • @AliceTheNurse
>
> Replying to @MTFoster
>
> The #NotAllMen gang has arrived!
>
> **Sarah McFarlan** • @SMcFarlanPhd
>
> Replying to @AliceTheNurse
>
> I'm a woman who supports women, but this isn't feminism. It's anarchy.

Large crowds of people are chanting, but not everyone is female; there are plenty of men too – although I'm not sure everyone's here for the same reason. I've seen this before, during anti-capitalist marches and BLM demonstrations. Nikki used to go to them all. She used to tell me that once the sun had set there would always be people joining any gathering for any cause, using it as an excuse to destroy things, to let out their anger and smash things up until everything was as broken as they were.

Three white vans pull up, and I wonder if they're more TV crew, but as the doors slide open dozens of police in riot gear spill out like cockroaches scuttling from a drain. Batons, shields, masks. Who are they here to fight?

A firework goes off, the air filling with white smoke and red light. People cheer. They're standing on the wall running around the square, some waving giant flags. I can't read what's on the flags, something written in big letters spray-painted red.

The police march in a line, but I don't know what they're trying to protect. The statues? The gallery? In their eyes, buildings and monuments are probably worth more than people, but no one has broken any laws. Have they?

An empty bottle of beer is hurled through the air and lands on a police shield. It's started. The people are giving the police exactly what they came here for. I haven't even descended the steps to the square yet, but now that everyone is running towards the police vans there are thousands of people between me and the lions. I need to get to Nikki. She's my only plan. If I can get to her, hold her, tell her I love her too, maybe I will survive this.

Someone is screaming. A policeman has a woman on the floor, her hands behind her back, one breast hanging out of her lacy bra. She's pinned down, and I see it all over again, the man on top of that woman, his hands around her throat, Paul's fingers, Sunday dinner. The woman's mouth is gaping, searching for air, a landed fish, her skin slippery with the heat. Her head is thrown back, her hair tangled under his black boots. I can't see his face behind his helmet, but I can see his eyes. He wants to hurt her.

More people surge forward, and the shields push them back.

This is no longer about dead women, the man who murdered them, or the woman who stopped a serial killer. It's about them and us. And the 'them' keeps changing.

I push my way towards the top of the National Gallery stairs. There's a good view from here and I can see that the crowds have formed into factions, each one with police at its centre. Some people are running like starbursts in all directions towards the Tube and main road, but just as many are running towards the melee. Shirtless men and women in bras, slick flesh rubbing against other sweaty bodies, chants of '*Save Em, Save Em*' ringing through the crowds. Are they fighting the police for me? Do they think they're protecting me?

The noise is getting louder as cars start beeping in unison, whether in support or at the people running into the street. Someone is sitting atop a statue of a man on a horse. I know it well, it's right opposite Pret, where I get my sandwiches in the morning. I've never thought to check who he is, though. So many statues of so many important men that people forgot to admire a long time ago.

Something is glowing in the distance. Fire. Pret is on fire.

Sirens wail as more people are pinned to the ground, hands behind their backs, cheeks grazing the paving slabs.

I inch my way down the steps, my gaze set on the lions.

A line of police, five of them, stand shoulder to shoulder, guarding the base of the stairs and stopping anyone else from nearing the gallery. I shuffle against their backs, squeezing past them and the shrine of flowers behind me, as their eyes stay trained on the wall of women screaming and pointing at them.

One girl steps forward. I recognise her purple bra and the flowers in her hair, long dead and leaving sticky petals in her curls. People are taking photos, pointing their phones at her and recording as she walks right up to the line of police. I keep out of view and watch as she turns both palms up to the ink-black sky and starts to hum.

Her friends join her and do the same. Four teenage girls, eyes fixed forward, humming to the heavens. The idea quickly catches on, and suddenly the crowd turns up their palms as one and becomes a nest of hornets, gradually reaching a fever-pitch drone. My head aches with the vibrations and I can see the switch forming behind the eyes of the police. These women, these girls, who are not saying anything – not being violent – are making sure they're being heard. They're in their face, challenging them without words, without using their bodies. It's too much.

With a sickening crack, one of the policemen lashes out with his baton and knocks the girl to the ground. I take a photo. I capture his snarl and her young face, and her friends surrounding her, wearing shorts as tight as knickers and flimsy A-cup bras, trying to pull her up from the ground as she shields her face with her hands.

And finally, that piece of elastic inside of me that's been stretching and stretching since I found myself on a park bench covered in a stranger's blood, it snaps. If these people are here for a saviour, then that's what I'm going to give them.

I take out my phone and I type.

Words Will Never Hurt Me • @Em_Dash_93
He killed. We mourned. They came. We fight!
#SaveEm

I add the photo I just took – a girl on the ground, a policeman's fist raised, Nelson's column glowing white and rising like a beacon behind them both – and I post it with my comment on Twitter. I have nearly a hundred thousand followers now. Rose was right, people really do love a good murder story.

The reaction is instant, like lighting a match on a mound of dry kindling. One hundred retweets in one minute, five hundred, two thousand. Within five minutes the hashtags #SaveEm and #WeFight are trending.

Daisy Copper • @DaisyCopper4538
#SaveEm #WeFight
She's here! Em is in Trafalgar Square OMG
KaiaLomina • @kalomiFSW
WE LOVE YOU @Em_Dash_93!!!! #SaveEm #WeFight

The reporters parked around the square are back out of their vans, pointing cameras in people's faces, asking them where Em is.

Yet nobody looks at me as I push my way through the

throngs towards the four lions. All I care about now is Nikki. I can feel her. She's close.

Silhouettes of raised fists stand out against a backdrop of orange light from the fire across the road, fire engines blocking traffic as crowds surge along the pavements, smashing more windows, chanting *'Fuck them, Save Em.'* The air is white with smoke, red fireworks shooting overhead, police grappling and losing against yet more people surging towards the square.

London has snapped, and I did this. All of this.

When I killed William Hennington, all I was thinking about was the woman pinned beneath his knees, her eyes blank, her mouth gasping for air. All I wanted was to stop him. I didn't want *this*.

But now I do. Now I want the entire city to feel my rage.

'What are you doing here?'

I feel a tug on my arm, a slippery grip against my own clammy skin. My first instinct is to hit out, to run. I've been found. Instead, I look up.

It's her.

35

'Rose?'

She wipes her gleaming brow with the back of her hand, her eyes smarting from the smoke in the air. She peers at me more closely, checking it's really me beneath the choppy new hair.

'Are you fucking demented? What the fuck you doing here, Em?'

Her fingers bruise my skin as she grasps the top of my arm and pulls me towards the corner of the fountain wall. We climb over its low edge and into the centre, where there are fewer people. I think she's trying to keep me hidden, even though I've been in full sight since I said goodbye to her nearly six hours ago.

'Why aren't you on a plane to the fucking Canary Islands by now?' she hisses in my ear.

'I didn't leave,' I say.

She runs her hands through her hair. 'No shit. For God's sake, Em. You know the whole world is looking for you, right? Your face is everywhere. You would have got away if you'd got on a plane when I told you to, but fuck knows what you're going to do now.'

I know all of this.

'Why are *you* here?' I answer.

She shrugs. 'I did some window shopping, had a Wagamama's, then decided to pay my respects before going home. I didn't expect it to kick off like this, though. Fucking police. I was trying to get through the square and head to the station when I saw you.'

'You still have your top on,' I say.

She shakes her head. 'And you don't. Why are you half naked, like the rest of these fools?'

'I took my shirt off at Matt's and he walked in on me like this, so I had to run.'

'Right. And you've somehow started a topless riot too. Jesus. I saw that cunt, Matthew, on the news, by the way. I can't believe you fucked the son of a Tory MP, and you know I'm not all that fussy about who I sleep with. I like your new hair do, by the way. Very *Pulp Fiction*.'

I blow my fringe out of my eyes and slump to the floor. She joins me. We aren't the only two women huddled low or in a corner, keeping out of the way and dodging flying missiles.

Some people came here tonight planning to hold a candle and say a prayer. I doubt half of them here now even know the names of the four women who died.

'You know they smashed up your work offices?' Rose says, jerking her thumb in the direction of the Strand. I can't see it from here through the crowds of people and smoke lit in shades of red and blue from the police vehicles. 'A big mob broke in and set it on fire. It's all over the news. I guess people really like you.'

I groan, rubbing my face and thinking of the people I used to work with. The ones I actually liked. 'Everything's a mess.'

'You killed a serial killer and called out a sexual predator all on the same day,' Rose whispers. 'What did you think would happen? Wait. Why's your head bleeding?'

I dab at my sticky forehead. Every inch of me hurts, so I hadn't noticed it stinging. 'I lost my temper with a bathroom cabinet at Matt's flat.'

'Should have been him you beat up.'

I breathe out a light laugh. 'Also, I don't have your money any more. Sorry.'

She shrugs. 'I don't care about the money.'

'I gave it to a homeless man . . .'

'What the fuck.'

'He's my friend. He just wanted to go home.'

Her face softens and she bumps her shoulder against mine. 'You're a good person, Em. So what's your plan now, considering you completely ignored my great advice?'

'I don't have one. But my ex, Nikki, is here.'

Rose sits up and looks around, as if she has the power to spot my ex-girlfriend in a crowd of thousands when she's only ever seen a couple of photos of her.

'How do you know?' she asks.

'Instagram. A coded message.'

'But isn't she with—'

'She says she still loves me. I need to find her.'

Rose gets to her feet. 'I'm coming with you.' I screw up my face, and she sighs. 'You think I'm going to miss your big, dramatic reunion after the shit you put me through the last two days? Call me a soppy romantic, but I'd like today to end on a high note.'

But we both know this isn't how it ends. This isn't a movie where I find the girl of my dreams and we're surrounded by people cheering us on and we kiss against a backdrop of fireworks and Big Ben. Maybe I *will* find her, maybe I'll even get to kiss her, but it won't be the end. This story still has a long way to go, and I can't see any happy in it anywhere.

I reach for my mother's necklace, clutching at the diamond one last time.

'Here,' I say, my fingers fumbling at the clasp. 'It's worth more than three hundred quid.'

Rose pushes my hand away. 'Give your family heirloom to someone who matters.'

I clutch the diamond again, biting my lips together at the thought that Marianna won't ever get to wear our mother's necklace now. Will she still get married tomorrow? Or have I ruined that too?

I give Rose a weak smile. 'I just wanted to give you something to remember me by.'

She laughs her dry cackle. 'You think I'm ever going to forget *you* in a hurry? Fuck me. Come on.'

'Wait.' I pull back. 'I need to know something.'

She tips her head to one side, her large hooped earrings grazing her shoulder. I think back to the first time I saw her and how much she scared me.

'What were you doing on that fire escape the first time we met?'

She screws up her forehead, as if she has no recollection of watching me urinate in public.

'I was hot, Em. And really fucking hung over. I just wanted to sit in the shade for a bit and have a fag.'

That was it? Just a woman, far from home, wanting to be alone and quiet and out of sight for a few minutes. Perhaps it's not people we fear but the unknown, the things we don't understand. All the things we can't predict.

There's just one more thing I need to know, so I can complete my picture of Rose. So I can feel like I really know the woman who saved my life more than once.

'Rose? What's your job?'

'For real? You're asking me that *now*?'

I shrug.

'I'm a cloud application architect.'

'I don't know what that means.'

'Exactly. Which is why it was a stupid question. Now shut up and let's go and find this girl of yours.'

The crowds are thinning in some places but knotted in others. Police are making arrests; more vans have pulled up since my tweet and a different kind of crowd is here now. More men, younger women, people ready to fight. Even from here I can see the memorial wall is growing, even though the flowers have been trampled and the wall has been written all over.

We edge our way past a group of women huddled in a group. One of them is holding her head while blood gushes through her fingers. Her eyes are black with smudged mascara, a limp home-made flag hanging by her side bearing the words 'Save Em' written in lipstick.

Her friends are trying to comfort her as she sobs something about how she didn't expect it to be like this.

I turn around and head towards her. I have to explain.

Rose yanks me back. 'Where the fuck do you think you're going?' she hisses. 'They'll recognise you. Just keep going.'

'It's gone too far. This isn't what I asked for.'

'That's where you're wrong,' Rose hisses, her face inches from mine. 'I saw your tweet, Em. You sent out a fucking call to arms.' She jabs me in the chest with her long nail. 'This is *exactly* what you asked for.'

People are standing at the base of Nelson's Column, different heights dotted around the steps beneath the statue. One of them is shouting into a megaphone. 'We mourned! They came! We fight!' she's shouting.

Those are my words. She's shouting about me, and she's quoting my words.

Rose is right. *I did this*. I started this, and somehow I have to end it.

'Show me what Nikki looks like again,' Rose says, the fight leaving her face.

I get my phone out of my bag. Nikki's added another photo of herself, she's standing beside one of the lions, her hair a halo of orange as the fire burns behind her. I was right, she's waiting for me beside our king.

This time the caption is neither long nor in code, it simply reads '#WeFight'.

Another woman staggers past us, her broken bra strap

hanging off one grazed shoulder. She doesn't look like a goddess or a warrior, she looks like a victim of war. A war I started because I finally did something. I refused to stay quiet, and look what happened.

'Is that her?' Rose shouts out to me.

She's pointing at one of the lions. The woman with the megaphone is still hollering my words into the smoky night. People are surrounding her with banners, including one woman who's completely topless, her pert breasts painted red like two giant drops of blood. And standing one step below her is Nikki. Nikki, with her serious face, her serious, beautiful, kind, strong face, scanning the crowd, searching for something.

For me.

Everyone is looking for me, but she's the only one who has seen me. Nikki has always seen me. Her face lights up as our eyes lock on one another, and my chest contracts.

'Go on,' Rose says, shoving me gently. 'Tell her everything.'

I squeeze Rose's hand one last time and she winks at me before I run into the crowd.

36

Nikki hasn't even made it to the base of the column before I'm standing in front of her. As I was pushing my way through the crowd, I had images of her throwing her arms out wide and our mouths colliding; bruised lips, teeth crashing together. But as I near her, I slow down until we're inches apart.

Nikki, my Nikki, the woman I've always had trouble describing but who, no matter how hard I tried, I couldn't forget.

She's wearing denim dungaree shorts over a white tank top. No bra statement for her. She has cowboy boots on and five necklaces around her neck, and her hair is longer than I remember it.

'I'm sorry,' I say.

I'm not sure if she can hear me over the sound of the sirens or the shouting of the woman with the megaphone behind her. But I keep saying it, over and over again, my words tripping over one another.

I'm sorry. For acting like she never existed while we were together. For being someone she never thought I could be. For being a murderer.

'I'm so sorry for keeping you – *us* – a secret. It was wrong. You are the best thing that ever happened to me.'

She stays silent and I can't read the expression on her still face. Her gaze falls on every part of me – my eyes, my lips, my hair, my blood-splattered bra. Like there's too much to take in at once. All those parts of me that she once told me mattered.

'I thought you were dead,' she finally says.

Five words. She's looking at my wrist now, my tattoo, the first thing we had in common.

'I said we were over, but I didn't expect you to disappear, for ever. I was hoping we could talk about it. I've been so worried about you. Then I saw you on the news.'

I look down at the ground, at her hands, at her own tattoo. Her fingers are covered in rings. All of them. The one on the third finger of her left hand is a diamond. *My* diamond. She's been wearing the engagement ring she bought me.

I go to say something, to apologise again, but Nikki has already thrown herself at me. Her chest slams into mine, her arms circling my neck. When she used to hold me, her words would fall into my long hair, but now my neck is exposed and when she talks her words land like whispered kisses on my collarbone.

'I've missed you so much,' she says. 'I didn't know if you'd see my message. I didn't know if you would come. Part of me didn't want you to, I wanted you to get as far away as possible, but at the same time . . .'

I know.

Our bodies shake as we cover one another in tears and unspoken words – all the things we should have said, but didn't, falling around us like snow. Something wet lands on my shoulder. Not snow, not tears, rain. It's raining. The first drop of rain in over a month.

Nikki looks up and laughs, tiny specks of water collecting on her eyelashes.

'What is this? A fucking romcom?' I say.

She laughs even louder, because she knows I hate rom-coms, but I always watched them with her because they made her happy. She loved the kissing in the rain scenes best.

Her face is inches from mine, her hands climbing up the back of my neck, her fingers threading into my new messy bob. She pulls me towards her, and I close my eyes because I don't want to see thousands of angry faces any more. I don't want to see police pushing women to the ground, or posters with my name on. I want to pretend this is a movie and that I get a happy ending with my girl in the rain.

I breathe in her warm breath, her lips grazing mine, and I pull her closer. But nothing will ever be close enough. Her kiss is like finally coming up for air. She smells of soap, that clean, fresh scent she wears like sun-dried linen and wind in your hair. Our kiss deepens, hungry for one another, tears mixing with the rain and mouths filling with water.

I swallow and pull away. My throat is thick with regret, and I don't know what to say next. I've fucked up so badly. Nothing has gone right since I left her. Nothing.

The weight of it is too big and too heavy. I can't see a

way out of this. We can't get around it, we can only push through it.

She takes my hand as we climb the steps, walking around the back of people until we reach another lion statue. Her Mufasa. She pulls me up and, in an instant, we're hidden in the beast's shadow. It's darker here, and although it's not any quieter, we're being sheltered by our king.

'I saw your photos,' I say. 'On Instagram.'

'I don't love her.'

'It doesn't matter.'

'It does. I saw your tweets,' she replies. 'Once I realised that was you, I read all your posts. Why did you never tell me how you felt?'

How can I explain that the only way I'd stayed safe all these years was by saying nothing and doing nothing? Bad things happen when you speak out and fight back.

'I would have been there for you,' she says.

'You always were.'

She presses her hand against my wet cheek. 'I never stopped loving you.'

'Don't say that.'

The rain is falling faster now. The crowd is getting soaked and my bra has grown transparent. People are cheering, dancing in the rain, while others are still being thrown to the ground. But I don't care about them, I don't care about anything but the woman beside me right now.

I rub my face. 'It's too late, Nikki. You look happy with your new girlfriend. You need to stay happy.'

She's shaking her head, as if I'm not making any sense.

'Beth is lovely, but . . .' She has my face cradled in her hands. 'She's not you. No one is you. I thought I'd lost you once. I can't lose you again.'

'You already have,' I say softly. 'This isn't going to end well. Look!' I gesture at the mayhem around us. Instead of driving the demonstrators away, the rain has given them more energy to shout louder and push harder.

'We can leave now,' Nikki says, letting go of my face and taking my hand. I'd forgotten how it felt in mine; her rough palms from working with water and thorns, all her rings clicking together, the way our wrist tattoos touch as if they are kissing.

I hold her hand tighter. 'I have nowhere to go.'

'Stay with me. We'll do this together. I can drive you out of London, get a taxi or ferry up north. Do you still have your passport on you? You can go anywhere. I have money. I can help.'

The woman standing behind us is holding a metre-high photo of my face. Nikki looks over to where I'm looking and her lips settle into a grim line. I think back to the police taking boxes out of Matt's house. My face is everywhere, and my name will be soon too.

'If any border control sees my name, or recognises my face, I'll be arrested,' I say quietly. 'Everyone knows what I look like now, and what I did.' I take a shaky breath, the rain making tendrils of my hair stick to my mouth. 'I killed a man, Nikki. I didn't mean to, and he was a bad man, but that doesn't make me a hero. It makes me a murderer.'

She's shaking her head in tiny motions. She reminds me

of Marianna when our dad got angry with us. *Be quiet, don't say anything. It will all be OK as long as you don't say what you're thinking.*

But it won't be OK. All of this happened because I didn't say enough, soon enough.

Someone with a large black umbrella is standing in front of our lion. It's the camera crew from before. The same woman, with her sensible shift dress and clip-on pearl earrings, trying to stop her hair from getting wet as she finds the perfect backdrop.

And this is it – the lions, the woman with the megaphone, a giant photo of my face held by women whose breasts are showing through wet bras, the mounting fire still raging behind us and everything shimmering that much brighter in the rain.

Nikki's hand is still in mine as, from the shadow of the statue, we watch the woman position herself, smooth down her dress, and nod at the cameraman.

'Live from Trafalgar Square, we're witnessing history in the making. As the heavens open for the first time in thirty-four days and reports come in of Save Em riots erupting across the nation, we're all asking, "Is *anyone* safe on our streets tonight?"'

And just like that, I know what I have to do.

I get to my feet, emerging from behind the woman.

'What are you doing?' Nikki hisses, standing up and gripping my hand tightly.

'Here,' I say, pulling away from her hold and unclasping my mother's necklace. She shakes her head. She knows what the necklace means to me and what I'm saying. 'Please,' I say, stepping behind her and wrapping my arms around her neck. I breathe in the scent of her for the very last time, my lips brushing her earlobes as I whisper, 'Give this to my sister. My mother would have loved you; my whole family would have. Tell them our story, and that I'm sorry.'

Nikki brings a hand to her chest where the diamond glows amber from the light of the flames behind us. She's shaking her head, her mouth opening and closing as her lips try to form the words she doesn't want to say.

Soundlessly, she mouths the word 'no' over and over again as she tries to pull me down out of view, but there's only one way to go now.

I tap the leg of the woman above us who's still shouting into the megaphone. She kicks out, thinking I want her to stop, but I shake her leg harder until she looks at me. It takes a while for her to realise who I am. She stops shouting, her forehead creasing into three crooked lines as she jumps down off the step.

'It's me,' I say, pointing at the giant poster of my face the woman above us is holding up. 'I need to say something.'

She nods dumbly, passing me the megaphone, but Nikki is pulling my arm back again.

'No!' she's screaming over the cries of the crowds surrounding us. 'Please, no! You can get away. I'll help you.'

I kiss her lightly on the lips. Our last kiss, though she doesn't know it yet. 'Stay happy,' I say. 'It's better this way.'

Then I climb as high as I can to the top step of Nelson's Column and I start to speak.

'My name is Emygdia Garcia Flores, but most of you know me as Em.'

The news reporter in front of me whips around so fast she knocks the umbrella out of her assistant's hand. But she no longer cares that she's getting wet, because people have heard me and are slowing down, grinding to a halt; everyone has stopped shouting. The individual clusters of protesters are merging together, forming one mass, all facing in the same direction. The camera points up at me as the police talk into their walkie-talkies.

London holds its breath. And I say it again.

'My name is Emygdia Garcia Flores, but most of you know me as Em. Last night I killed a man. But he wasn't the first.'

37

'A good friend once said to me, "It's not the big things that send you over the edge, it's the little things. The stuff that sneaks up on you, while you're busy holding on to the things that matter."'

I look out over the crowd that's swelling and shifting at the base of the column. People are holding up their phones, tiny dots of light punctuating a sea of faces. I think of footage I've seen of concerts from the point of view of the singer. Is this fame? Or is it infamy?

A blue cap floats on the wave of shadows and I think I can see Moby smiling up at me. I think I can see Rose too, and Kate and Dante holding hands. I don't know. Maybe not. But Nikki is here, right beside me, her eyes brimming with fear.

'Last night I killed a man because my suitcase broke . . . and then I broke.' I try to steady my breathing. 'Twelve hours earlier, I kept calm when I lost my job, even though it was taken from me because I was on the verge of telling someone about the sexual abuse I'd been subjected to. I didn't make a fuss, though. Neither did I get angry when the Tube closed and I had to walk ten miles to the airport, the whole time being told by our government the best way to avoid being murdered by a serial killer. But I didn't complain, I just kept going, because I had to get back home to Spain, to my dying mother and my sister's wedding.'

My voice shakes and I sniff, swallowing down snot and tears and the lump forming in my throat.

'I didn't say anything when I was told how to dress by women in the street, and I still didn't make a scene when man after man after random man insisted on talking to me, remarking on my appearance, touching me, insulting me, telling me to *fucking smile*. And even when I found out my flight had been cancelled and there was no room at the inn, I still didn't shout at anyone. I was a good girl. I stayed quiet.

'In fact, I didn't do much at all until I was faced with the prospect of nowhere to go, close to midnight, alone, in a part of town I was unfamiliar with. And even then, I just curled up in a ball and cried, because I didn't want to be a bother to anyone.'

No one is saying a word. A line of police has formed around the perimeter of the crowd, but they too need to listen. I'm live on television, I'm making a confession. While I remain on this step, megaphone in hand, I'm safe. What happens when I finally stop . . . I don't want to think about that.

'But then my suitcase broke,' I say again. 'As I pulled up the handle, my suitcase tumbled down a slope into a park, leaving me with a jagged metal stick in my hand. And when I entered that park, alone, in the dark, to look for my bag, that's when I saw a man, sitting astride Dr Amanda Chambers. He had his hands around her neck, a stripy tie on the ground beside her.'

There's a collective gasp. I imagine the cameraman zooming in for that line. I imagine how many people are live-streaming this – the millions of people around the world watching me stand here in a torn skirt, transparent bra, rain streaming down my face. I push my hair back and square my shoulders.

'I didn't know what I was looking at. All I knew was that he was hurting that woman, and . . .' Tears are streaming down my face. Can they see them? Or does it look like rain? I squeeze my eyes shut and sniff. 'She looked dead, and he was so busy putting all his weight against her throat he hadn't even seen me. Can you imagine the audacity of this man? To be killing someone in plain sight and be so fucking sure of yourself that you don't even notice a woman is watching you?

'But it was the little thing, the suitcase breaking, that sent me over the edge. And that rage, thirty years of rage, it finally came out. I didn't look at what I was doing, all I saw was the lifeless face of Dr Amanda Chambers, and I had to stop him. Because this wasn't the first man I'd come across in my life who took pleasure from watching a woman suffer. But he ended up paying for the wrongs of all the others.'

The megaphone is heavy and my grip is getting slippery. I swap hands, catching sight of the tattoo on my wrist.

Everyone is waiting for my second confession, the one

that no one has ever heard before. The reason why I never returned to Spain.

'You see, I could have been Hanna Nilsson, Jennifer Buchanan, Farah Mitri, Zhao Li, Dr Amanda Chambers. Any one of us could have been them. Through no fault of our own, pure bad luck, we could have been a name scribbled on a wall.' I point at the pile of flowers and teddies behind the crowd. 'I know what it's like to be pinned down, unable to breathe. My father was a bully, a violent drunk, and my mother was the woman who taught me how to survive by doing nothing. But it was me doing nothing that killed him.'

I'm back in Ronda, my legs scratched from scrambling off the stone wall, my feet aching from running back home. I'd told myself I'd sneak into the house quietly, that my mother and sister would be at church and my father would be asleep. But he wasn't. He was on the floor, crawling, his arms stretched out to me as I let myself in. He was clutching his chest, his lips mouthing silent pleas. He was asking for my help.

'My father had a heart attack, the day I chose to come to England. And I did nothing. I could have saved his life, but I didn't – I just stood there and watched him suffer. This big, strong man crawling around on the floor like a baby learning to stand. So weak. So powerless. He needed my help, but I did what I was told worked best when a woman needs to survive. I kept quiet. I did nothing.'

He'd been attempting to cross the room to reach the door. When he realised I wasn't going to help him he tried to pull himself up by our ugly wicker bookshelf, light brown and flimsy and full of books nobody read. I watched as he leaned on it and the shelves and all the books collapsed on top of him, pinning him down. One book, the biggest and heaviest, landed on the side of his head so hard I heard his teeth crack together. Its sharp corners left a gash on his head, blood tinging its white spine.

The family Bible.

I don't know how long he lay there, but I stayed rooted to the spot, waiting for him to finally stop moving. When I was sure he was no longer breathing, I searched through his pockets, found the key to the hall cupboard and got my suitcase out. I smiled as I picked up the blood-splattered family Bible and added it to my bag. It was over. His life, and my own life as I once knew it, were over for good.

'I killed one monster by doing nothing, and another by doing everything I had ever wanted to do to those who'd wronged me. So I'm not your hero. I'm just a woman who's spent her life scared. I was scared in Spain, I was scared moving to London, I was scared going to work every morning, I was even scared yesterday, walking alone from one side of the city to the other. And . . .' I take another shaky breath. 'I'm scared right now. Really scared.'

I can't see everyone's faces, but I can see that some are crying. Are they scared too? Even some of the police have lowered their shields. Were they scared tonight?

'I came here, to the vigil, because four women died at the hands of a man who chose to do what he did instead of seeking help and talking to someone about his fears. I killed that man because he was hurting someone, but also because of my own hidden rage, because I kept silent for too long. I never spoke out about my father; I didn't tell my family that I was in love with a woman who saw in me the person I only ever dreamed of being.' I feel Nikki's hand on my arm, and I keep going. 'I kept quiet when Paul Wilkes abused me at work, I didn't tell my flatmate to go fuck himself, and I didn't ever tell anyone who cared about me what I was feeling. That silence is what allows so many awful things to happen. When we lock up the secrets of others, when we protect those who do wrong because we're scared, we're ashamed, we don't want the attention to be on us. All we're doing is helping them.

'But it's not our fault. The things that have been done to us, and the way we have managed our pain, that's not our fault. But tonight, we all have the power to speak out and break that silence.' I place four fingers on my chest. 'Hanna, Jennifer, Zhao, Farah!' I shout, then raise my clenched fist in the air. 'Never again.'

Everyone in the crowd does the same, hands on their chests, then raising their fists in the air.

'Speak out!' I shout. 'If you know someone who hurts people, report them. If you've suffered at the hands of someone, tell others. If you're struggling, if you have dark thoughts of your own, get help. I don't care if you're male, or female, we are *all* hurting. But nobody – *nobody* – should ever have to die because of the things left unsaid.'

I look down at Nikki, her eyes searching mine. She's begging me not to do what I'm about to do next.

'I may have saved countless lives by killing a murderer, but I still took a life. I don't want you to save me, I need you to save yourselves.' I look over at the police, who are inching closer, pushing against the crowd, who have linked arms to keep them back. Nelson's Column is surrounded by protesters, all stopping the police from reaching me.

'Let them through!' I shout. 'I'm done.'

38

Everything happens in a blur.

Nikki is beside me, but instead of kissing or hugging me, she's pushing me down the steps. People are screaming, there are shouts of 'Run!' and 'Leave her alone!' as the police try to break through the crowd. Fireworks go off overhead, or maybe it's gunshots. The air is so thick with smoke I can hardly see.

Suddenly I'm surrounded by people, arms and legs, my head being pushed down, my feet hardly touching the ground as I'm carried through waves of hands and bodies passing me back and forth like a plastic bottle on a stormy ocean.

Then my feet are back on the ground and I'm on the other side of the road. People are screaming at me to run. Police sirens sound, but the streets are heaving with people in bras, some of them holding banners, all of them with fists clenched in the air.

'Run, Em!' they scream at me. They part like I'm Moses, then close back around me as police chase me on foot and police bikes screech to a halt. Once again, I'm running. I'm running like I've always done, but I don't know where I'm going. All I see are wet bodies and angry faces and fists rising out of the smoky air. My feet pound against the pavement in time to my heart beating in my ears and my handbag thudding against my hip as I run down the Strand.

The station is on my right, The Savoy hotel , where last night's awards took place, is around the corner, the offices of Swan & Swallow are further along, and right in front of me is the Coal Hole pub. None of this would have happened if I hadn't gone for that drink and let Paul walk me to the station. Or maybe it would have. Maybe I was always destined to be a murderer.

A tiny alleyway runs along the side of the building and I take a sharp right, practically falling down the stairs. I keep running, past the back of office buildings and the side entrance to the hotel, until the street opens up and I'm in Embankment Gardens. Exactly where I was yesterday morning.

I slow down to catch my breath. The air rings with the sound of distant chanting, the night sky tinged red from the fireworks. I can't see people, but I can hear their cries of 'Save Em, Save Em.'

Why didn't they listen? I told them I wasn't their hero – that I didn't need saving.

Breaking into a jog, I continue racing through the park, running on grass, just like I did this time last night. I'm wearing the same skirt, the same trainers, the same bra. And like last night, this park is also empty, although the floor is slippery from the rain, which has now slowed to a drizzle.

The flowers could have done with all this water weeks

ago. Everything is dead now. Even the one single white rose that I stroked yesterday is lying like a fallen angel in the mud.

But I don't stop to touch it this time, I just keep going. I'd never been alone in a park this late at night until I killed a man. Maybe I'm the one people fear in the dark now?

The shouting is getting nearer. I keep running until I break out on to the main road, the river shining like a strip of tar to my left and Embankment station to my right. Straight ahead are the stairs to Hungerford Bridge.

I tell myself that while I keep moving, I have a chance of getting away. But what am I really escaping? Because this weight that I'm dragging behind me, heavier than any suitcase, isn't going to get lighter. It's going to weigh me down for eternity.

I climb the steps of the bridge and stop.

It's empty. The rain has driven away the late-night tourists and the riot has scared away everyone else. It's just me, and the night, and the whole of London spread out before me.

In the distance, St Paul's shines like a beacon; Farah Mitri's tomb. The water of the Thames rushes below me, the same water that carried Jennifer Buchanan's body to Westminster Pier. To my left, beyond the plumes of smoke, lies St James's Square, where Hanna Nilsson was found. And straight ahead, beyond the tower blocks of Canary Wharf where the river curves, is east London, where Zhao Li was murdered and where Dr Amanda Chambers nearly became the London Strangler's fifth victim.

This city, the place I ran to all those years ago, was meant to save me. But hidden among its bright lights and ancient buildings lie secrets and darkness. I was never safe here. No one is.

I stumble forward, then realise I'm not alone after all. Blue and red lights flash on the South Bank, the wail of a siren getting nearer, a dark mass congregating on the other side of the bridge. I'm trapped. I can't go forward, and I can't go back.

I take off my trainers and socks and, using my numb toes and broken fingernails, I pull myself up over the edge of the railings. The shouting is getting closer, yells and chanting.

As I position myself carefully on the edge, my handbag lands on my lap. The bag that's been with me since I left the house yesterday morning, permanently looped over my shoulder. It's buzzing and ringing.

I don't believe in signs, Ronda's church bell wasn't a sign, yet . . . maybe it was. Maybe someone can save me.

Keeping my balance on the cold metal barrier, I take out my phone and glance at the flashing screen. My throat constricts. It's my mother. She never calls me. Sometimes she texts, most of the time she leaves voice messages, but she never calls.

I have 6 per cent left on my phone and it's just passed midnight. I answer.

'Emygdia,' she says in one exhale, like she's been holding her breath.

I close my eyes at the sound of my name, wishing I could keep them closed for ever and stay right here, listening to her voice as a cool summer breeze strokes my hair.

'Happy birthday.'

I bite my lips together and look up at the starry sky. Of course, I turned thirty years old two minutes ago.

'I saw you on TV,' she says. She's talking lightly, her voice strained, like I'm a street cat she's trying to lure out from beneath a car. 'Is it true?'

My mouth's dry, my tongue coated with something bitter. I don't want to talk; I just want to stay in this stillness. This hollowed-out moment, where it's just me and London and the night.

'Which part?' I croak. 'Was which part true?'

'That you loved someone but were afraid to tell us.'

I really did love Nikki. I always will.

'I thought you wouldn't approve.'

'*Hija.*' Her voice is thin and wavering. 'You think *I* know anything about love? You found happiness, and that isn't something many of us can say.'

I reach for my necklace, my mother's diamond, then remember I gave it to Nikki. Will she find my family? Will she tell them our story? My mother likes a good love story.

Shadows are forming at the end of the bridge, feet thundering against metal steps.

'I'm sorry,' I say to her.

'Whatever for? You saved the lives of many women.'

'I'm talking about Papa. What I did.'

'So am I.' My mother takes a shaky breath. 'You saved my life, *hija*, and your sister's, and your own. What you did that day, and the things you said tonight, you're braver than I've ever been.'

And, in that moment, I realise that the times when I thought of her as weak and pathetic were the times when she was loving me the hardest. That even when she was on the ground, cowering beneath my father's boot, she was always thinking of me and praying that I'd escape. That's why she left her most treasured possession in my suitcase for me to find. She gave me the luck that she should have kept for herself. She pushed her own dreams aside and stayed, fearing the unknown more than the pain she was already familiar with.

She should have run; she would have enjoyed the wind in her face.

A single tear rolls down my cheek as I imagine never feeling her arms around me again. Never hearing her say my name again, calling me her *hija*.

My girls.

'Tell Marianna I'm sorry I missed the wedding.'

'I'm here,' my sister says. 'I can hear you.'

'Marianna! I'm so sorry I let you down.'

'Never.' My sister's voice is cracking, but it's stronger than I've ever heard it before. She's doing that for me. 'You've always been my hero, Emygdia. I've missed you.'

It hurts to swallow, my tears blurring London into streaks of colour.

'I love you both so much. I'm so sorry, Mama.'

My phone beeps; my battery is flashing red.

'Come home, *hija*.'

The shadows are nearing, the shouts growing louder, police radios crackling into action. They've found me. What if I just run? It's dark. Maybe I can make it to the other side and hide among the labyrinthine passageways of the Barbican and the skating park. I want to go home. I have a life worth living after all. I matter.

Carefully, I turn, attempting to manoeuvre myself off the edge, and that's when I see the BBC breaking news post pop up on my screen.

BBC Breaking News • @BBCBreaking

'Murdered Essex man William Hennington is not the London Strangler,' Pat Merrifield, Commissioner of the Metropolitan Police, confirms. The body of Naomi Gelb, found strangled in Greenwich Park in the early hours of this morning, has been identified as the London Strangler's fifth victim. 'We are doing all we can to find the killer,' Merrifield says.

I stare at my screen, trying to make sense of the words.

'This is the police!' a man shouts through a megaphone. 'Get down off the ledge and put your hands up.'

I can't stop staring at my phone. The light is dimming, the battery at 4 per cent.

So it was all for nothing? I killed a violent man, but it made no difference, because the one everyone wants is still at large. There will always be more. Women aren't safe. Children aren't safe. Even men aren't safe. No amount of hashtags will stop that.

Who did I think I was, imagining I could make a difference?

Noises are coming from both sides of the bridge now.

Police to my right, boots stomping, black shapes swarming. A crowd to my left, chanting, white boards raised, fists in the air. Footsteps thunder across the bridge as a dark mob of people, so many people, get nearer and the noise grows louder.

'Get down and put your hands up!' the policeman shouts.

'Save Em!' the crowd chants.

London twinkles on both sides of a river that divides the city like a bleeding wound, the moon so heavy I imagine it dipping into the inky water and disappearing for ever.

I can hear my mother's tinny voice calling my name. My finger hovers over the blue Twitter button and I contemplate writing one last post. A call to arms. A thank you. A final goodbye. Instead, I twist my torso and let go of my phone, dropping it to the floor of the bridge behind me. The screen shatters and the light goes out.

It doesn't matter if I'm in London, in Ronda, or staring into an unknown future, because no matter where you go, there are only ever three options. You stay, you run, or . . .

Clasping my handbag to my chest, I jump.

39

The Guardian • @TheGuardian

Six weeks after London reached boiling point with the Save Em riots, the search for William Hennington's murderer, Emygdia Garcia Flores, is called off.

'We believe she did not survive her jump into the Thames. It's over,' Pat Merrifield, Commissioner of the Metropolitan Police, confirmed. 'Em is dead.'

> **Linda M** • @LindaCraftMagic
>
> This is nonsense! I won't believe #Em is dead until they find her body.

> **Chris T Rennolds** • @CTR_85
>
> There's no proof that the woman people saw jump off the bridge was even her. They found her phone, but nothing else.

> **Holly #SaveEm** • @HollyHenderson92
>
> Now maybe the police can look for the #LondonStrangler.

> **Chris T Rennolds** • @CTR_85
>
> Replying to @HollyHenderson92
>
> Those murders stopped as soon as Em disappeared.

Makes you wonder if maybe she was behind them all.

Holly #SaveEm • @HollyHenderson92

Replying to @CTR_85

That doesn't even make sense. She had nothing to do with the women who were killed, if anything she saved lives. The London Strangler will come back, just watch!

Meredith Stonewell • @StonewellM

Did you see that buffoon, Matthew Atkinson Carter, on morning television? Piece of shit milking this tragedy for all it's worth.

We Fight! • @EmStanAccount

Replying to @StonewellM

I bet he ends up with a book deal or on some celebrity TV show. He's loving it, slimy bastard!

Meredith Stonewell • @StonewellM

Replying to @EmStanAccount

I'm so glad @RebeccaMcGuire dumped his ass.

Rebecca (not Becca) • @RebeccaMcGuire

Replying to @StonewellM @EmStanAccount

Can't believe I ever considered marrying that scumbag. #Em saved my life. I wish I'd been able to save hers.

Caroline Taylor • @Carol_T

People need to let all this Em stuff go! It's all anyone's been talking about for weeks. What about the victims? What about finding the actual serial killer?

We Fight! • @BooksAndBiscuits

Anyone know what happened to that bastard who abused Em? She should have finished him off too!

Meredith Stonewell • @StonewellM

Replying to @BooksAndBiscuits

I heard he got sacked and his wife left him. I hope he never finds work again. He should be arrested for what he did.

Stan the man • @Stanley0701

I saw #Em. I swear I saw her in Tesco yesterday. Same hair.

Chris S • @ChrisMCFC

Replying @Stanley0701

You're tripping. Sure you didn't see Elvis too?

Stan the man • @Stanley0701

Replying to @ChrisMCFC

Straight up. She wasn't even hiding her face.

Michael The Wolf • @wolfmanmickie

Disgusting how women have started wearing bras as tops and getting their hair cut like that murderer. That Em woman was messed up in the head, not an icon. Hennington wasn't the London Strangler!

Jackie Silver • @JackieBSilver

Replying to @wolfmanmickie

He was still trying to kill a woman ffs!! #Em will go down in history as a hero.

Fuck Em • @MichPFCFL

She's a man-hating killer. I won't feel safe until she's found!

Laura Peterson • @LauraBPeterson1
I feel safer imagining her out there tbh.
Kamaria Brown • @MojitoMama
#Em just posted something. WTF?????

I refuse to die • @Em_Dash_93
Good girls don't keep quiet. They scream.
#TheFightsNotOverYet

Author's Note

I had the idea for this book in 2021 while driving through France after a long summer in Spain. I was thinking about the murder of Sarah Everard and the demonstrations that followed; how helpless women always feel after such tragic events, knowing there's nothing we can do to stop it happening again . . . or from happening to us.

The following week I was watching the 1993 movie *Falling Down*, with Michael Douglas as William Foster – a man down on his luck who, during a hot LA summer, finally reaches the end of his tether – and I wondered what that would look like if it were a woman. In London. When the streets were even less safe than normal. What would it take for a young woman to finally snap? And how far would she go?

Good Girls Die Last came to me fully formed and I knew from the very first word this book would be loud. Writing it felt charged. Electric. Dangerous. I needed it to be raw and from the heart because it was about me, and about my friends, and women I'd never met, and the women my daughters would one day grow up to be. I didn't want to be subtle nor careful, yet neither was my intention to write a didactic, man-hating book. I simply wanted a story that contained the tension, fear and frustration every woman carries with her on a daily basis.

Having lived in London most of my life I find it hard to set my books anywhere else. The city holds a very special energy with its ancient newness and mix of famous sites and unknown corners, a tourist mecca with a filthy underbelly. To some extent London is the main character in this book, and I hope I did her justice.

As for Em – she's a character we can all relate to. She's not me, and I don't share her background (other than being half-Spanish and an immigrant), yet we've all been that woman who said nothing, the one who bit her tongue, because we have all been in situations where it's safer to be more like Em than Rose.

I'm always on Twitter (@NJSimmondsBooks), I know the power it has, and I wanted to explore that. In a world where social media dictates what we think, and what others think of us, it was important for me to show the collision between the digital world we often hide in and the real world we wish to hide from. They are symbiotic and we must never forget that.

I got angry writing *Good Girls Die Last*; nearly every encounter Em experiences has happened to me at some point in my life. I cried, writing about Nikki's wonderful father and the sacrifices Em's mother made for her, because without family many of us would struggle to remain strong. But most of all I sweated. Writing this book in the autumn of 2021 was fine, but editing it in the heat of 2022 was tough going. It was also somewhat surreal to invent a heatwave that reached over 40°C in London and included wildfires, something that was unimaginable the year before, then watch it all come true (thankfully without a serial killer).

Although I write fiction, and my aim is always to entertain first, I do hope this book has helped my readers feel seen.

Whether you are a woman who has been abused in any way, someone who has struggled to be heard, or (like me) an immigrant that has never felt they truly belong anywhere – I hope you know you matter.

All of you matters. Even the broken parts.

Acknowledgements

Being an author is a funny old game. Much like a roller coaster it can involve a lot of waiting, a lot of climbing and false starts, and eventually – if you are fortunate enough – it can suddenly send you on a crazy ride that leaves your head spinning and heart thumping.

This book has been nothing but a thrilling journey from the very beginning.

Firstly, a massive thank you to Amanda Preston, my literary agent. Amanda – not only are you totally kick-ass, but your passion and excitement for this book blew me away from the very beginning. I couldn't ask for a better person by my side and I can't wait for us to bring more books out into the world together. Another big thanks to my film agent, Emily Hayward Whitlock at The Artists Partnership, for making my wildest author fantasies a reality. Lots of exciting things to come!

A huge thank you to Toby Jones, UK editor extraordinaire. Every email from you is an absolute treat and has me laughing out loud, there are no men in my book as nice as you. Here's to more Soho lunches! Thank you also to the fantastic team at Headline who have made all my book dreams come true. A big thank you, Isabel Martin and Sarah Day, for all your hard work and the most eagle-eyed of edits, Jill Cole for your excellent proofreading, and Alara Delfosse for all your help with publicity and events.

Another big thank you to my TV and Film agent, the wonderful Emily Hayward Whitlock from The Artists Partnership. Thanks to you STV Studios will be developing Em's story for TV and I couldn't be happier. I couldn't ask for a better creative team to work with than Sarah Brown (Creative Director of Drama) and Claire Armspach (Head of Drama Development) whose vision for this book was everything I could ever dream of. I can't wait to see Em, Rose and the rest of the characters come to life!

A big thank you, as always, to my readers, my social media followers, bloggers and booksellers for enjoying my stories and helping to get them into the hands of readers.

This book would never have got this far were it not for two very special Ems in my life, both fabulous writers and my first beta readers.

Emma Cooper – without you this book wouldn't exist. I will never be able to thank you enough for all your help and support. How very ironic that it was a simple tweet that launched this book in the right direction.

And Emma-Claire Wilson – I would have certainly given up at the plotting stage had you not sat me down and forced me to get those bastard Post-It notes out and plan this bloody book.

And thank you to my other first readers, who also happen

to be fab authors; Anna Day (God, I love writing with you), Alexandra Christo (cocktails and critiques all the way) and Sarah Norris (sorry I had you sticking your head out of the window at 3 a.m.).

A big shout out to all the others who have travelled alongside me on my writing journey over the years, all wonderful friends and amazing writers: Jacqueline Silvester (my Caedis Knight co-writer, mother of my godson, my ride-or-die bestie), Isabella May (always), Teuta Metra, Meera Shah, A. J. West, Laura Lam, all the writers in the Debut 2023 gang (especially Meera Shah for setting it up), all the fabulous authors who blurbed this book, and every other author I know who I've moaned to, laughed with and leaned on. Thank you!

And finally, a big hug to my friends and family – sorry for being an obsessive asshole who is always glued to her laptop.

My mum Christine, my biggest champion, my amazing sister Jemma, and all my fabulous aunts, uncles, cousins and friends who are always happy to hear my story ideas. A very specific thanks to Ana and Mike Brand for all your enthusiasm in November 2021 and insisting I watch *Summer of Sam* after hearing the premise of this book. I'm not sure I would have pitched it so well had I not watched that movie!

This book is full of terrible men, but the three who have shaped my life are amazing and I wouldn't have got anywhere without them.

My dad Desi, who showed me the importance of creativity

and the joy of storytelling. My stepdad Bob, who has taught me that there's no point doing anything in life if you don't do it with all your heart. And my husband Peter – my rock, my everything, the man who I have shared the best moments of my life with and with whom I can't wait to have many more adventures.

And finally, a big hug to my daughters, Isabelle and Olivia. Thank you for your patience, for giving me the space and time and ideas for my stories, for your enthusiasm and for making me the proudest mum in the world. Of all the things I have created in life, you two are the most perfect.

The world can be a scary place at times, but it's also full of wonderful people. Many women have enriched my life over the years – from friends and family to complete strangers. So, to all the women who have ever helped me, listened, cheered me on, looked after me, inspired me, confided in me, and for all those who have fought, survived, been terrified but done it anyway . . . this book is for you.